The

SHOEBOX

A Novel

Tracy Ploch

tracyplochauthor@gmail.com
Published in the United States of America
Printed by CreateSpace, an Amazon.com Company
First printing, 2015
First Edition
ISBN 978-0-9965283-1-3
www.tracyploch.com

Chapter illustrations:
Designed by Sarah Bracken
Copyright © 2015 Tracy Ploch
Author photograph by Cassie Mahar

To anyone who has ever felt like
they didn't have a passion...
you do.

"Once the feet are put right,
all the rest of him will follow."

– C.S. Lewis, The Lion, the Witch, and the Wardrobe

ONE
July 2014

"This would be perfect for an 80s rock-n-roll themed party. I'll keep it... at *least* until Halloween."

That's what I told myself as I was packing for my move to Ireland two years prior and the sheer, leopard print blouse with leather cuffs and collar was on the chopping block. It was one of the classic lies I'd tell myself – right up there with "I'll keep this for when I lose 10 pounds."

I had bought the safari-meets-biker blouse to wear at the office just like the model on the poster at Banana Republic – the model who had never stepped foot in corporate America. Whenever I had gone to wear it, I felt more like an attention-starved intern than the executive-bound businesswoman I was going for. I had always swapped it out for a basic tee and casual blazer before running out the door, telling myself "next time". I knew full well I'd never wear it.

Flash forward two years...

It was July 2014 and I was packing up my life in Dublin for another big move. After years and years of taking up space, it was time to let go of the unworn leopard print blouse. I tossed it in the 'Donate' pile. That pile was mostly tank tops and graphic tees I had held onto because I kept telling myself I could wear them under a cool jacket. None of my 20+ jackets and blazers must have been cool enough because I sure as hell never wore any of the shirts (in public). I wore some of them to bed or to go buy milk – great reasons to hold onto them.

I didn't have as much of a problem letting go of things and I told myself less of those lies. I was throwing shit into the 'Throw away' and 'Donate' piles without hesitation. My tiny flat was littered with clothes, shoes and random belongings I had accumulated over my two years in Ireland. I had mentally labeled the piles: 'Keep', 'Throw away', 'Donate' and 'Undecided', but there wasn't much in the 'Undecided' one. If I had learned one thing, it was that an 'Undecided' pile might as well be a 'Throw away' one – either you want it or you don't. The quicker you figure it out and get rid of what you don't want, the more space you'll have for the things, and people, you do. That was one of the many lessons that Dublin and the burgundy boots had taught me.

There were still three weeks before our flight, but I had to FedEx some boxes beforehand. My fella didn't have a problem with the three suitcases per person limit, but I certainly did.

I noticed during the packing that I had a lot of clothes and a lot of shoes, yet I wore the same ten things all the time. By no stretch of the imagination would I consider myself a fashionista – I don't know labels, and the nicest place I shop is Zara. I buy all my shoes from discount department stores, with the exception of my running shoes and, when I found THE ultimate riding boots. I try to keep up with trends, but I hate the act of shopping. That is why, fashion-wise, I was always comfortable in Dublin. The people wear whatever they want, from super trendy to super grungy – anything goes. I'll never be a fashionista, and Dublin will probably never be a fashion capital… 'Dubs' and I have a lot in common like that.

That's why it's funny that my time in Dublin was when I learned many important life lessons… through *shoes*.

The most significant soul-to-sole lesson was with the burgundy boots. I had been in search of THE ultimate riding boots – ones that met all my criteria and that I could wear with anything, any day of the year. It was the same with dating, really. Dating is essentially a search for The One – someone who meets your criteria, someone you want to be with through everything, every day of the year. During my quests for both the right boots and the right guy, I had accumulated a lot of boots I no longer wore… and a lot of men I no longer dated.

During both those searches, I'd find myself thinking back to a great pair of shoes I gave away and a great love I gave away. The shoes were Converse, the same brand half the Western world owns. But mine were special. The canvas was a caramel color and the leather trim on the toe was brown instead of white. They were so comfortable and fit me like a glove, but I nonchalantly gave them away to a friend. She wanted them despite their wear and I figured they'd be easy to replace – after all, they were *just* Converse.

Well, it turned out they were a limited edition and that style was no longer sold, not even online. Likewise, throughout my adventures in dating, I'd often think about Brad. He was special. He was my best friend and first love. After five years together, we became too comfortable and we took each other for granted. When we found ourselves in a rut, I thought he'd be easy to replace too. Well, it turned out... it wasn't. I could never ask my friend for the Converse back and Brad had gotten serious with someone else. Both of my limited editions were gone – I had thrown both away.

Luckily, while in Dublin, I found the burgundy boots. It was right around the time I met Aidan. Both were exactly what I had been looking for and more.

That day I was packing was a miserable one, even by Irish standards. The wind was beating the branches against the kitchen window – a sound I hadn't heard the entire two years I lived there. I drew the kitchen curtains and took mental pictures of my neighbors' Georgian doors: one yellow, one red, and two blue were in sight. Everyone had a colored Georgian door on my street, but I was in a small concrete block with a generic door in the back of the building that didn't shut properly. I had wanted a red door when I moved to Dublin but quickly realized that brightly colored doors come with a brightly colored price tag. Next to go from my apartment hunting checklist were hardwood floors, a dishwasher, a full-sized refrigerator and a mattress I could sit on without feeling the box springs. It's those quirks I would remember and miss the most. My time in Dublin was a journey taken in many different shoes, but it was time to go… time for *us* to go and start a new adventure somewhere else.

I sprinkled a big scoop of crunchy peanut butter with Himalayan sea salt, licking the spoon while staring at my belongings scattered around. I savored every detail – the musty smell of my flat when the windows were closed (they had to be closed when it rained as there was no screening) and the living room wall where the paint was lighter than the rest. I had run out and refused to spend €30 on another liter. The wire case still hung from the ceiling – every month when my landlord came to collect the rent, he'd promise that he'd have someone come 'sort it out' the following week. The concrete walls, the faux carpet I never walked on barefoot… I loved it all. I especially loved the memories that were made there – first on my own and then with Aidan.

I didn't usually drink alone, but being locked inside all day sorting through my memories surely warranted a bottle or two. I chose the bottle of wine with the fanciest-looking label and nodded in satisfaction, as if there'd be a chance I wouldn't like it.

Sitting atop a box was a framed picture of Lindsay and me with two huge suitcases on either side of us. It was taken in our apartment the day I moved to Dublin. Lindsay left shortly after because she couldn't handle going to the airport with my parents to see her best friend move so far away. My hair was longer and blonder in the picture, with natural tousled waves like a true beach baby.

My parents were my rock in the weeks leading up to the move. They helped me sell my furniture and stored a bunch of stuff, including my Jeep, so I wouldn't have to pay for storage. I had my first and (knock on wood) only panic attack after the movers came. That's when everything suddenly became real: I was moving to a country I had never been to before and I was going alone. That was the scariest part because not only had I never lived on my own, but I really had never done *anything* on my own. I was always in a relationship, always surrounded by friends and family. Technically, I was moving for my career – a chance to be 'distinctive' as my boss called it – a 'distinctive opportunity' that would position me nicely for the promotion to our Chicago headquarters that I so desperately wanted. That was the reason that I told everyone, but the real reason I volunteered was because I was in a rut. I wanted to do something different, something big… something on my own. I was fresh out of yet another four-month relationship when the opportunity came up, so the timing was perfect. I was going to get my first stamp on my passport, live alone, make all sorts of new friends in Dublin and kick ass at work… on my own.

When the movers left my Tampa apartment, my doubt and fear boiled over. I broke down crying on the floor of my empty living room and called my mom. I couldn't muster up a complete sentence to save my life, but she eventually calmed me down. She reassured me that the move would be the adventure of a lifetime and the best decision I'd ever make. As always, she was right.

At the Tampa airport security, just before I went through the scanner, another panic attack started to come on. I turned and frantically searched for my parents, assuming they had already left. But they hadn't. They were jumping and waving their arms over the crowd. I could hear them yelling, "Jessie! Jessie, we love you! You'll do great!"

while they blew kisses. As I waved back, a calming confidence washed over me. I walked through the scanner with a smile, knowing everything would be alright.

In my apartment, I tripped over a pair of leopard ballet flats Lindsay had given me for my 25th birthday. I had only worn them a handful of times in Florida, but after the two years in Dublin, the soles had become thin and scuff marks revealed their overuse. I'd wear them every day to walk to work – well, when it wasn't raining. I'd wear my rain boots (or 'wellies' as the Irish call them) when it rained.

Placed on the top of my oversized plastic box of shoes was a pair of blue suede heels. I bought them for a charity fundraiser where the theme had something to do with the color blue. I thought I was clever to wear blue shoes and blue accessories against a white dress, but half the women attending had the same 'clever' idea. I remembered those heels never hurt my feet in the slightest – even as we danced into the wee hours at the Buck Whaley's after party. Why hadn't I worn them after that night? Why had I chosen more painful or more boring shoes to go out in when those were so fantastic? Maybe the heel height was right on the cusp of where I'd feel too tall? I tossed them into the 'Keep' pile with a note to self: start wearing these!

A half a bottle of wine in, I went through my collection of boots. There were my go-to pointy-toed, black ones I got on clearance six years prior. I had worn them a million times – they were classic and looked great with any (nighttime) look, but they had seen their last days. The soles were virtually non-existent and each time I wore them, I'd pray the heel didn't break. But they pulled in compliments from time to time and made me feel sexy. Nothing to think about there… into the 'Keep' pile they went.

It was ludicrous how many pairs of boots I owned, especially being a born and raised Florida girl where a cold front was 70 degrees Fahrenheit (I never converted to Celsius). Boots in Florida look as unnatural as a deep tan in Ireland, yet I had tons. I liked all of them but didn't love a single pair.

Several pairs were kept behind the sofa to save on space in my tiny Euro flat. I pulled out a pair of Steve Maddens with wedged heels. I liked everything about them except the mid-calf height – particularly since my calves are unusually thick compared to my otherwise thin frame. I'd tell myself the years of cross country running had given me muscular calves, but there's no denying I have cankles. Why I bought them in black when I didn't love the brown ones I already had was a mystery to me. Into the 'Donate' pile both pairs went.

All the boots I bought had met most of my criteria, but I knew I would have been better off if I had been more selective. All the discounted boots were cumulatively much more expensive than if I had waited… waited to buy the one expensive pair I was crazy about. Plus, they had taken up space in my already cluttered apartment.

I moved away from the boots and picked through the plastic shoebox, coming to some casual ones. I usually wore my navy Vans in place of the Converse I gave away. They had evolved from my 'concert shoes' to my 'Aidan shoes' because they were the shoes I wore the weekend we started dating. The wine and shoes distracted me from calling him, but I needed to talk to him about the farewell drinks planned at Café en Seine that night.

The rain was still falling hard, but the wind had died. I tripped over one of my wellies that had fallen over. I kept them propped up against my washer/dryer combo (which I would *not* miss! I had to run the 90-minute cycle three times to dry a tiny load – energy saver my ass!). I set the fallen wellie upright.

Another important shoe correlation I noticed was between my parents and my wellies. Neither are the coolest or the most fashionable, but they're the only ones that I could depend on to protect me from the elements – life and the weather, respectively. My first few months in Dublin were horrible. I had no friends, no car, no clue and it rained *all* the time. It wasn't until I started wearing my wellies, at the advice of my dad, when things started to get better. Eventually, things were great. Every journey is easier with the right shoes.

With a decent wine buzz, I stared out the window and drifted back to the day when, for me, the journey in Dublin began. It began with a change.

A change of *shoe…*

TWO
September 2012

"Are you kidding me?!" I yelled at the blue Peugeot that sped through a puddle at the corner of Leeson Street and the canal. The splash left the bottom half of my pants completely soaked. I was already 20 minutes late for work, so I couldn't go back to change. I read the 'LOOK RIGHT' painted on the road before crossing; I relied on it as I wasn't used to cars driving on the left side of the road. It was my fourth day in the new office and I was determined to make it a better one than the previous three.

I had spent the first few workdays jumping through the hoops of Irish bureaucracy involved with opening a bank account. It was the most complicated and inefficient process I had ever experienced. The bank insisted the letter from my company that confirmed my employment and my temporary address had to be on company letterhead to be dubbed 'official'. I found that humorous, but the humor soon turned into annoyance when the second letter was also rejected. Apparently, it wasn't addressed to a specific Bank of Ireland branch, which was another one of their pointless requirements. The third attempt was almost another failure because it wasn't signed in *black* ink. The lady helping me knew I was about to lose my shit so she waived it as an act of good faith. It took all my remaining energy to appear grateful and not roll my eyes. It was a full week before they finally opened the account and cashed my relocation check. The bankcard arrived in the mail *another* week later. In the meantime, I had paid a small fortune on foreign currency fees and commissions to get euros out of my US account.

I kept telling myself it was all part of the process and once I moved out of temporary housing, I'd establish a routine and everything would be fine. I finally found a flat I could afford, but it was a dump. It needed a deep cleaning, numerous trips to Ikea and a few coats of paint before I could think about calling it home sweet home. Nonetheless, it was a step towards normalcy and, at the very least, a permanent address for the bank to send my debit card to.

I felt the clammy wetness of my feet squishing in my Sperrys with every step. I hadn't seen any Dubliners wearing Sperrys, which I should have expected. The preppy loafers were more ideal for my lifelong coastal existence. Whenever I'd arrive at the office wearing them (before changing into work appropriate shoes), I'd get an awkward compliment on them typically followed by, "You're SO American!"

My Irish work colleagues were nice, but I couldn't wait to move past the standard questions and comments about why I had left the sunshine to come to such 'shite' weather. It was easier to smile and laugh as if it were my first time hearing such a hilarious observation than to rattle off my reasons for wanting a change. I considered telling people I was from some random city in the Midwest – one that didn't sound as sexy as Tampa, Florida. That way, I could avoid the mindless weather chats.

I wasn't expecting to make a ton of friends immediately, but I was bummed that the only social invite I had received was from Orla, a Galway girl with an accent as thick as her foundation. There wasn't much about Orla that wasn't bold and that was apparent the moment I met her…

I was making a cup of tea when a booming, "Hiya! How ye gettin' on?" caused me to jump. The loud voice belonged to a fair-skinned head of wild curls dressed in layers of statement pieces. A flower patterned blouse peeked through her green tweed jacket that she paired with a navy A-line skirt. Gray tights, black ankle boots and a chunky necklace completed the busy outfit.

"Uh… I'm good, thank you for asking." I extended my hand. "I'm Jessica; it's really nice to meet you!"

"Oh, sweetest God! You are actually SO American!" She laughed loudly, shaking my hand with a light grip.

"Yep, guilty as charged. What gave it away?" I said, playfully.

"Ah sure, come here. The Irish would never be that enthusiastic on a Monday morning." I laughed half-heartedly, confused why she said 'come here' when I was standing next to her. "I knew we were expecting you, just wasn't sure when, but the blonde hair and the tan give you away." She looked me up and down. "So how ya finding it?

Where ya living?" Orla spoke a mile a minute and I tried to keep up while also keeping an eye on the microwave.

"I really like it here so far. It's only been three weeks in Dublin, but everyone has been so nice and welcoming. I just moved in to my apartment last Saturday – it's in Ranelagh." I didn't feel it appropriate to mention my frustrations, homesickness or how my apartment was a massive downgrade in every way except for the increase in rent.

"Ooh, Ranelagh is lovely! Some *gorgeous* restaurants and the pubs there are good craic. Who ya living with?" The microwave dinged.

"I'm living on my own," I answered, pulling the cup of water from the microwave.

"Ah, fair play to ya! See now, that wouldn't be common here." She pressed a button on the steel jug that I assumed held coffee. "Ermm… is the kettle broken?" she asked.

"Oh, I don't know; I didn't try to use that thing. What's it for?"

"You don't know what a kettle is?!" She was completely shocked.

"Oh, it's an electric kettle! Sorry, I've only ever seen the stove top ones. In America, we use our microwave for everything – we're all about that instant gratification," I said, trying to make fun of myself. One of those kettles came in my furnished apartment. I put it in the storage closet not knowing what the hell it was.

Orla must have sensed my embarrassment. "Well, I'd say hot tea wouldn't be big in America, but in Ireland we are mad for it! Here, I'll show you." She dumped my microwaved water in the sink and filled the kettle. I took note as she placed it on the base, pushed the button and

17

retrieved a miniature container of milk from the fridge. "Right so, come here... a proper cuppa must be made with *boiling* water and Barry's brand tea bags." She held the red box, showing me the label. "Barry's is much better than Lyons. The Dubs prefer Lyons, but it's absolute shite, so it is." I took more mental notes: use 'Dubs' instead of 'Dubliners' going forward.

It was nice to have a conversation with someone other than the bartenders at Searsons or Smyths, where I'd had dinner almost every night. As nervous as I was about eating alone at a pub, it was better than eating alone in my apartment. It wasn't that bad talking to the bartenders and after a couple of weeks, I became a regular.

Orla was easy to talk to and her kindness was genuine. She asked if I 'fancied' going for lunch that day, which of course I did. What I really 'fancied' was a friend.

We went to KC Peaches in the City Centre. I continued making mental notes: practice eating with my fork *upside down* and in my *left* hand like everyone else did. Orla gave me the lowdown on everything Dublin, from taking the Luas (the light rail) to Dundrum for shopping, to where I could get the best scones and sausage rolls. She gave me an 'Irish Sports for Dummies' crash course, explaining to me hurling, Irish rugby and the lads' obsession with the Premier League. D4 and some of D6 (including the area I lived in) were 'posh' Dublin and I'd see a lot of rugby players out and about. My favorite tip was that I wouldn't be a true Dubliner until I had a night out at Coppers – she didn't elaborate further on that one.

She vented about how Irish men are absolute 'shite' when it came to dating. Apparently, they lacked confidence and would text for ages before asking a girl out. Basically, I should lower my expectations and prepare to wait a while before a proper date. After her rant, I was shocked to hear she had a boyfriend, Gearoid, who lived back home in Galway. I was even more surprised to hear they'd been together for five years and weren't living together – hell, they weren't even trying to live in the same city! Apparently, that was normal in Ireland too. In America, they would have already been married a couple of years and planning their unborn child's gender reveal party by that point.

I doubt the lunch date that day was anything special for Orla, but to me it was the first glimmer of hope in making a friend abroad. I called my mom later that night to tell her I'd had lunch with someone – you would've thought I'd won the lottery from our excitement.

* * * * *

The following week I made it to the office, again with wet feet and soaked pants. I had planned on arriving early to take care of some more administrative burdens involved with the international relocation. I was bombarded on both sides of the pond. My old apartment in Florida was charging bogus fees, my US bank had frozen my account (the only account I had the first few weeks) due to 'unusual activity' reports, the IRS needed information regarding my tax status, my home office had a million forms to complete... the list went on and on. Meanwhile, the international phone calls were expensive and, of course, there was the five-hour time difference to make things even more inconvenient. My mom, bless her heart, called American Express pretending to be me but got caught when she didn't know one of the security questions. Nothing was easy. As soon as I'd resolve one issue, three more would surface. I couldn't catch a break. My new boss had been more than generous with giving me time to settle in, but the grace period had run out.

I felt like an idiot again (after the electric kettle incident) when I didn't know who the Irish Prime Minister was. My co-workers probably thought I had made a pathetic attempt to learn about the country I moved to. Meanwhile, they were all so interested and informed about the 2012 US presidential campaign. 'Learn basics of the Irish political system' was added to my ever-growing mental list of things I needed to do or learn in order to settle in.

The Dublin office did things so differently than my home office. The roles and responsibilities were more hierarchical, so I wasn't sure what was actually expected of me. They used an older system for analyzing the media sales data, which was even more inefficient than the bank account set-up process. The few work meetings I had attended didn't seem to boost the team's energy or get the creative juices flowing like they did at home. I hoped it was just semantics and that I'd get used to the differences quickly.

I left work that day at 'half six' which I quickly learned meant 6:30 and not 3:00. I went straight to Dunnes Home Store to pick up some necessities for the new apartment. I had received a picture from my friend, Maggie, back at home. My heart stung when I saw the picture text of our entire group at the beach in swimsuits with Miller Lite cans in hand. The message read:

Maggie: Happy Labor Day Jess! Bet you're celebrating on a beach in Spain with your cool new friends, but we all wish you were HERE! :(We miss you! xxx

I hadn't realized it was Labor Day. I thought of all the other American holidays that weren't holidays in Ireland. I wished I hadn't been reminded of the good times I was missing out on while I walked, alone, in the cold gloom of a strange new city.

At Dunnes, I bought an over-priced set of sheets and duvet so I wouldn't have to sleep another night using the blanket that came with my apartment. I also bought four bath towels so I didn't have to use sweatpants to dry off with.

At Stephen's Green, I hopped on the Luas to go home to Ranelagh. Wanting to avoid the Labor Day posts on Facebook, I instead checked my email. I had a notice about an outstanding charge on my Corporate Amex. It was another thing to take care of – awesome.

"Ranelagh," the recorded voice on the Luas said, first in English and then in Gaelic. The Gaelic pronunciation sounded like the English version but while hocking up a loogie. I grabbed my bags, but one of the handles broke, so I shoved it under my arm. My Chapstick fell out of my purse, but I left it as my hands were full and I didn't want to miss my stop. I stood in front of the door, waiting for it to open. It didn't open... weird. I stepped closer to the door, assuming I needed to trigger some motion detector, but still, no luck.

It felt like I had missed a flight when the Luas started moving again and I watched my stop pass by. I didn't have the energy to get mad or to move.

A deep Irish accent behind me said, "Awk love, ye have to push the button." My eyes watered when I saw the button – bright green lights flashed around it for fuck's sake! How could I have missed it? The few times I had used the Luas previously, there were other people getting on or off so *they* would have pushed the button. I had just assumed all the doors opened automatically at every stop.

"I think you dropped this, love." I turned to see the grey-bearded accent holding my Chapstick. "Erm… I'm just gonna stick it in your wee bag here, so I am."

It was all I could do to raise the corners of my lips and mutter a meek "thank you".

Seeing my watery eyes and flushed face, he offered, "Ye can get off at the next stop and get on the next one to go back the other way. They run every five or six minutes, or sure, ye could walk it just the same. It's hardly 10 minutes on foot."

"Oh? I didn't realize. Thanks for letting me know," I mumbled.

"It's no bother; good luck to ya!" His 'bother' sounded like 'bodder'.

I got off at the next stop where the display board showed a seven-minute wait time. If I waited and caught it back to the Ranelagh stop, I'd still have to walk ten minutes to my apartment. I considered calling a taxi but felt silly as I was in my neighborhood and it'd take longer for it to arrive than to walk. I pulled up Google Maps to see where I was and which direction I needed to walk toward. I had a purse, a laptop bag and two stuffed shopping bags – one of which was busted. A headache had developed, which could have been from the stress of the crap day or the lack of quality sleep. I'd been without a pillow since I left temporary housing. I couldn't wait for my shipment to arrive – my memory foam pillows were in it.

All of a sudden it started… uh… what's the phrase the Irish use? *Pissing rain.* Yep, it was absolutely pissing rain and I didn't have an umbrella or a free hand. I picked up the pace, keeping my head down. My Sperrys were absolutely ruined.

I managed to put the cherry on top of the shitty Monday sundae by walking into a pole, which caused me to lose my grip on the broken bag. I tried to catch it, but it was so wet, and being a stupid eco-friendly paper bag, it completely busted. My new turquoise bath towels were scattered on the road, getting drenched.

I wanted to laugh, but my optimism had completely run out. I raised the white flag and let the tears fall along with the other shopping bag, my purse and laptop bag. I sat on the edge of the pavement, head in my hands and had a good cry.

The black mascara on my hands was proof I looked as bad as I felt. I wanted nothing more than to be home – my real home. Home… with my friends, celebrating Labor Day in the sunshine. Home… where I didn't have to worry about public transportation and ripped shopping bags because I'd have my gasoline guzzling Jeep to put them in! Why the hell had I left? It was not the 'experience' I signed up for. I wiped the screen of my phone with my undershirt and called my dad, not expecting it to go through.

"Hi, sweetie!" he answered, overly enthusiastic and crystal clear. As soon as I heard the familiar voice, I smiled and closed my eyes tightly. I was trying not to let him hear straight away that I had completely lost my shit.

"Jess? Jessica? Honey, are you alright?" That was it... the waterworks came pouring.

"I want to come home, Dad. I don't know what I'm doing here. I can't do this, I just want to come home," I sputtered between the gasping sounds that come out during those ugly cries.

"Where the hell are you?! Jessica, tell me right now where you are!" he shouted.

I was mad at myself for calling him like that and worrying him over something so stupid.

"I'm fine. I'm okay, really. I just... I just... want to come home," I repeated, trying to regain some level of composure but failing miserably.

"Are you in your apartment?! Dammit Jessica Elizabeth, tell me where you are!" He used my middle name; he was definitely worried. We had watched the movie *Taken* together so, imagining Dad as Liam Neeson, I knew I needed to clarify the situation.

"I'm sitting on the sidewalk outside, not far from my apartment, but I got lost and it started raining and my bags broke and now my shit is all over the ground and I didn't sleep last night. I hate my new office and I'm just so... alone. I want to come home; I can't do this." I spewed out the complete nonsense while sucking back snot and wiping away tears. I couldn't care less what the couple walking by, hand in hand, were thinking.

"Alright, Jessie, pull yourself together. You are being too hard on yourself – it hasn't even been a month. It's going to take time," he said in a calm, stern, fatherly voice.

"I'm trying, Dad, but I don't belong here. Everything is such an ordeal. I can't get anywhere without some sort of fuck up or getting rained on!" I shouted, still crying hysterically.

"Hey, hey! Watch your mouth, young lady!" he teased. I laughed, realizing I usually turned off my sailor mouth when speaking to my parents. "Jess, honey, look… it won't always be like this. If anyone can move to a new country and make it work, my money's on you. Just give it time. But right now, you need to get yourself home – your current home. Please do that for me. I don't care if you have to take a taxi a few blocks, don't hang up this phone until you get inside." I should have just called a taxi in the first place – what would another ten euro have been at that point?

"I'm sorry for calling you like this. I'm just having a bad day. I'll start walking home." I was a horrible, selfish daughter. I shoved one of the towels in my purse, draped two over my laptop bag and the fourth one around my neck. I headed home while my dad continued his pep talk.

"You belong there, Jess. But you have to adapt to the new surroundings – they say it takes at least six months," he said.

"Who're *they*?" I asked.

"I've been reading online all about the struggles that expats face. In almost every instance they end up loving their new country and find it hard to return home." Imagining my burly dad (who has zero patience for surfing the Internet) sitting at the computer reading blogs from expats warmed my heart. "Listen, Jessie, if you give it your best shot and you feel the same way at the end of this year, *then* you come home – no harm done. At least then you'll know you gave it a chance." I turned onto Charleston Road – my apartment was just a few blocks away.

I was almost 'home' when the creepy black cat I had seen lurking around crossed in front of me. If there was ever a time for a black cat to cross my path, it would be that day – I could not have been any more unlucky.

"Okay, I'll give it another shot. I just want to get inside and take off my shoes. My feet are soaking wet and covered in blisters," I whined.

"Jessica?"

"Yes…"

"You live in Ireland now. It rains. You don't have a car, so you're going to be walking a lot. So why then, are you wearing shoes that don't keep your feet dry?" he asked.

"What? Like rain boots? Dad, the girls here don't wear them. They're so bulky," I said, not wanting to hear the obvious.

"Okay, suit yourself. I'm just saying you might want to think about it. You can't expect the same things that worked at home to also work for you in Dublin."

"You're right. I'll figure it out. Thanks for listening, Dad. I'm home now."

"Okay, good. Just relax and get some sleep tonight, and remember what the old wise man said… this too shall pass. Give it time, little grasshopper, give it time." I had known one of his token motivational quotes was coming.

"Yeah, yeah, yeah. Bye, Dad. Love you."

"Love you too, baby."

It was only 8:30 pm when I got ready for bed that night. I tore open the duvet from its package, shoved a wadded-up sweater inside an old t-shirt for a homemade pillow, and headed to the kitchen to wash my face in warm water. That was my solution to the bathroom having separate hot and cold faucets – both of which were extreme temperatures. I crawled onto the flimsy mattress and checked my phone. I received a picture text from Dad. It was Clive, the famous micro pig, standing inside four bright red rain boots. I laughed out loud and set it as my phone background. Before going to bed, I read what Wikipedia had to say about Enda Kenny, the current *Taoiseach,* or Prime Minister of Ireland. It was one small thing to cross off my list.

I did as my dad suggested and wore my rain boots the following day… and I pushed the hell out of the green button on the Luas.

THREE
December 2012

Through the chilly autumn months and into the holiday season, I wore my wellies every time it rained and always kept an umbrella on me regardless of what the forecast called for. I actually preferred the Dublin drizzle to the one-hour torrential downpours every day at 4:00 pm in Tampa.

I bought a bike with a cool basket and quickly learned my way around the city. Every time I went for a run, I'd explore a new area. I had made friends and really took a liking to the pub culture. I had also been on a lot of first dates, but no seconds. I was keeping busy and certainly wasn't sitting around wishing I was back home in Florida.

I turned off my alarm and read the text message from my best friend, Lindsay:

Lindsay: *Miss you Jessie!! Skype date tonight please??*

It had been a couple of weeks since our last Skype date. She had a huge catering event she was planning and stressing over, so we hadn't been sending our usual daily texts. I responded that I had a date that night but would be home before she got off work – thanks to the five-hour time difference.

I moseyed to the kitchen to wash my face in the single-faucet sink while the electric kettle boiled next to me. I'd get to hear the latest update between Lindsay and her boyfriend, Jason. I really liked Jason. He was funny, charming and he absolutely adored Lindsay. The fact that he was a gorgeous doctor who frequently made the local news for his pro bono work didn't hurt either. That's how they met – his practice had hired Lindsay to plan a charity fundraiser at the Hilton Downtown.

At the time of my leaving Florida party, they had been dating for a few months. He carried her from bar to bar so she didn't have to walk in her sky high stilettos. I could see him carrying her out of a church in a poufy wedding dress. Jason could, and wanted to, give her a beautiful life – one with a big, perfect house and family. He'd be the type to suggest sending cheesy family Christmas cards (with a picture of them in matching sweaters) every year. They'd go on annual trips to Disney World and Myrtle Beach and their kids would go to Ivy League universities. Lindsay had wanted a prince charming for so long and she finally got one; Jason couldn't be any more of a gentleman.

Only problem was, Lindsay did not want children – full stop. But Jason came as a packaged deal with his four-year-old son, Cody. Jason had been married before and had already ridden the rides at Disney World a time or two.

Lindsay would be the first to admit she didn't want to give up her glamorous lifestyle for motherhood. Her taste in high-end labels wouldn't leave much discretionary income for labels like OshKosh B'gosh. We had always joked that she didn't have the mom gene and I didn't have the bride gene. Well, there's truth to every joke...

For me, the thought alone of planning a one-day wedding for a year brought on anxiety. Never mind the politics of choosing a bridal party and guest list, no thank you! It's not that I was against marriage, but my 'dream wedding' would be quiet, understated and non-traditional. Lindsay, on the other hand, had been planning her wedding since before she had her first tea party. When Brad, my first love, even first *mentioned* marriage, Lindsay started sending me venue options, wanting to plan a wedding that was never going to happen.

I sipped my cup of tea, leaning against the oven, peering out the kitchen window – my favorite spot in the apartment. I drifted back to the year after college graduation...

> Brad and I had been living together for a year after we graduated. It had become obvious that we had been living in a bubble the previous four years of our relationship. Once we started our real jobs and paying real bills, small problems quickly turned into big ones. I began to emotionally disconnect. I didn't know how to fix it because I didn't know what *it* was.

I became increasingly annoyed with everything – from the way he wrote his texts, to how he ate his food, to how he drove with one hand on the steering wheel. After years of a healthy physical connection, I no longer wanted to even kiss him. The worst part was that he seemed to be okay with the rut we were in. I was waiting for that night when he came home with blood-shot eyes and a story that didn't quite add up. It was my excuse to burst the bubble and not have to take the blame or deal with having to talk about what was really going on – pretty fucked up looking back. I had to get out of there, but I didn't have enough money to get my own place. Lindsay insisted I stay with her, so I did... for three years. She eventually confessed that she had gone with Brad to help him pick out an engagement ring the month before I threw us away. The upcoming 'work trip' he had in Orlando was really a trip to West Palm to ask my dad for my hand in marriage.

I showered and got ready for work. I knew I shouldn't have been thinking about Brad, especially when I had a date that night.

The date was with a guy named Gareth whom I had met while out one night with my co-workers. Gareth was sexy and oozed the trendy European vibe. I couldn't decide which was sexier – his scruffy beard or his Northern Ireland accent (which was hands down my favorite of all the different Irish accents). He approached me in his tight, maroon skinny jeans and commented on my bright orange heels – said they looked *class*. I got them at the discount Irish department store called Penneys (not at all associated with the American department store JC Penney). I was stocking up on pajamas and socks when I saw the wild pumps in my favorite color. They were only a 'tenner' (about 13 dollars back then), so I would have been crazy not to buy them. It was a way to try something outside my fashion comfort zone with no risk… or so I thought. They were fun and flirty the whole night just like Gareth and I were, but I caught the heel on the uneven pavement while hailing a taxi and went down like a sack of Irish potatoes. The heel had completely snapped off. Thank God no one saw and the only thing hurt was my pride.

Gareth was a lot like those orange Penneys heels. We had a blast at the pub – absolutely exhausted ourselves from being witty all night. By 1:00 am, we were drunk and making out at the bar like snakes eating mice. I was excited to see him again, but the next day, my interest deteriorated with each text message I received. It would have been easier deciphering Morse code than trying to figure out all the abbreviations, slang, blatant misspellings and complete disregard for grammar in his texts. I remember lying in bed hung over with the busted orange heel on the floor and equally busted text messages in my hand:

Gareth: hey gurl. good 2 meet u last nite
Gareth: soz 4 keepin u out late. how r u?
Gareth: Im drivin home 4 d wknd

I knew he had an iPhone so, with autocorrect and all, it actually took effort to text on that level of stupid. I told myself not to write him off over something so trivial – after all, he spoke intelligently. I figured it was only that bad because he was driving.

I had to choose an outfit that would be acceptable both in the office and for the date so I didn't have to go home to change. A long sleeve, plum sweater dress and black tights did the trick. Plus, it'd match the black ankle boots I kept stashed at the office. It looked nice outside, so I wore ballet flats instead of my wellies but grabbed an umbrella… just in case.

At my desk, the moment I turned on my computer, I received an instant message:

Simon: The hot guy with the geek chic glasses sitting along the file cabinet outside the boardroom… gay or straight?

I laughed out loud. Only Simon could get away with such inappropriateness as a standard 'good morning' greeting. Simon was from our London office. He was brought over to Dublin just after me to revamp the Marketing Relations team. They were the schmoozers responsible for obtaining new clients and keeping them happy. I was part of the group that designed and managed the social media packages to suit their advertising needs. It's not quite the designing of billboards and making pitches for TV commercials I had in mind when I graduated with a degree in marketing and advertising, but I liked my job and most importantly, it was a stepping-stone for the position I wanted in Chicago.

I changed into the ankle boots and responded via text to keep the sexuality assessment off the company's network:

Me: *Straight as an arrow!*

He ignored the hint to take the conversation offline and replied again through our work instant messaging system:

Simon: *Ugh, I think you're right.*

In true Simon fashion, he was over the topic:

Simon: *Wanna come with me to this gig at Whelan's tomorrow night?*

Me: *What kind of music?*

My response was irrelevant – I'd go no matter what kind of music it was. I had no other plans that night and Whelan's usually has good artists.

Simon: *Synthesizers. If there's a heaven, there will be synths upon my arrival to greet me.*

I laughed and shook my head as I typed:

Me: *Amen to that. OK sounds good, I'll wear my dancing shoes ;)*

The workday flew by, as they tended to once I had gotten used to the new office. I nailed a big presentation and got great feedback from my boss. It was a good day... and then I saw the text from Gareth:

Gareth: *how's u? still ok 2 meet @ 6 @ d mkt bar?*
Gareth: *c u there?*

I was suddenly more excited for the sangria and tapas at the Market Bar than I was for the company.

*　*　*　*　*

I no sooner walked in the door, back from the date, when I heard the Skype ringtone from my laptop in the living room. After a few flashes, Lindsay's face came in clear. A purple martini glass was on the table next to her – it was from the set I got her for Christmas a few years prior. Lindsay has a soft, ultra feminine beauty that could have landed her on a runway if she were a few (or ten) inches taller. Her bright green eyes pierced through her long, lightly painted lashes. In the nine years I'd known her, I'd never seen a blemish or her porcelain skin.

"Is that a martini I see?" I teased.

"Yep! Just finished that big event at the Don Caesar, so I may even have two. Question is... Why don't *you* have a martini?"

During the three years that Lindsay and I lived together, we'd have a 'martini night' at least once a week and catch up. We'd infuse Ketel One vodka with fresh jalapeno and use garlic stuffed olives. It was our signature dirty martini. Even when I was in Dublin, we tried to keep the tradition alive through Skype.

"I'm out of olives and you know I like 'em dirty." The dirty martini innuendos would never get old.

"That's why we get along." There isn't a scandalous bone in Lindsay's body. "Speaking of... how was your date?"

"Eh... *cauliflower,*" I replied, making a face.

"Ugh, lame." She knew exactly what that meant. *Cauliflower* was our code word meaning there was no need to discuss any further. The inside joke began a few years prior, when I had started dating again after my breakup with Brad...

> It was a year after the breakup and I had agreed to go out with Tommy. We met at the gym, but I never saw him as dating material – probably because he was too nice (i.e. too boring). I was caught off guard when he asked me out while I was in between reps at the chest press machine. I didn't know how to say 'no' without hurting his feelings or

making it awkward, so I agreed to dinner the upcoming Friday. When Friday arrived, I was all worked up about having to go on a date I didn't want to go on. I called Lindsay a few hours before the date, flustered and rambling: "Lindz! What do I do?! I really don't want to go out with him... Should I just go to be nice? But then I'm a bitch for leading him on. Should I make up an excuse? Ugh, no because then he'll just reschedule, but at least it would buy me time. Should I just tell him the truth? No, NO! I can't tell him the truth because the truth is that I'd rather stay in tonight and try out this new cauliflower soup recipe my mom gave me!"

From that day on, anytime one of us would prefer to stay in on a Friday night boiling vegetables over going on a date... the poor guy is *cauliflower*.

"Yeah, lame. Anyways, how are *you*? How's Jason?" I asked changing the subject.

"Good, he's picking up Cody tonight. He's excited to have him through Monday since he was with *her* family for

Thanksgiving." Lindsay had only ever referred to Cody's mom as *her* or *she*. Lindsay wasn't jealous in the present tense, but she was always jealous of her boyfriends' pasts. For her, acknowledging that Jason loved another woman before her was a harder pill to swallow than being a step-mom. "Which by the way, it was so weird not having you here for Thanksgiving and Black Friday shopping – and you'll be missing Christmas! You're not allowed to miss them ever again."

I smiled. "Deal. I'll be home for all of the holidays next year," I assured her. "Are you doing anything with Jason and Cody this weekend?" I asked in an 'it's okay to say no' tone.

"Yeah, he's gonna bring Cody to the dog park to play with Tucker and we might go see *The Lorax*." The tone in her voice screamed *cauliflower*.

We continued catching up, covering everything from the Pilates class I started taking to the big holiday sale at Neiman Marcus she had planned to check out that weekend.

"I just want to see if they have Louboutins on sale," she said. Lindsay had wanted a pair of Louboutins for years and years but hadn't pulled the trigger. She knew it'd be a splurge, so she wanted to make sure it was the right pair.

"What's a sale on Louboutins? 500 dollars?"

"Or…. 1,000." She scrunched her face, aware of how crazy it was to spend that kind of cash on something wedged between the floor and a foot.

"Jesus, Lindz!" I blurted out. I knew most of her shoes were in the 200-dollar range, but four digits is another level. It explained why she had gone years without buying them – it was quite an investment.

"I know it's ridiculously expensive but, Jess, I can't stop thinking about this one pair – the Laurence lace-ups," she confessed. "I don't just *want* these shoes, I *need* them! It's not even about the label – I love everything about them. I try them on every time I'm in the mall and I just know I need to have them. I swear, when I get them, I won't buy another pair of black heels ever again… they'd be it for me!"

"Hey, you don't need to convince me, sister! At least you know the pair you want – I buy so many boots I never end up wearing. I just didn't realize Louboutins were *that* expensive, but seriously Lindz… if you're that sure, you need to get them. You deserve it; and if anyone can rock a hot pair of heels, it's you," I said truthfully.

"Thanks Jess – and *if* I were ever to let someone borrow them, it'd be you," she said, taking the last sip of her martini.

Lindsay talking about the Louboutins she wanted reminded me of my search for the perfect riding boots, only… she already had her exact pair picked out. Just like she had already found the perfect man and I was still in search of mine. For her, the search was over. To get the heels and man of her dreams, she just had to be willing to part with some cash… and accept the fact she'd need to be a stepmom. For me, it seemed I'd never find whatever it was I was looking for.

FOUR
April 2013

The months flew by. I survived my first Irish winter. The trick was to wear thick, knee-high socks and the wellies. It turns out they not only block out the rain and mud but the cold too. Orla's impression of dating Irish men proved to be a lot harsher than reality. Although there weren't any formal dates, I had casually gone out (i.e. meeting at the pub on week nights) with a lot of different personalities. The most amusing were the hipsters who were fixated on trying to appear 'different' but in *exactly* the same way. The ones I went out with all listened to the same music, wore the same clothes and hung out at the same places where they talked about the same topics – sort of like a cult. Then there were the professionals who were pretty much the same as the American businessmen but didn't seem to take their careers as serious. The most fun were the guys who played sports and were so into English Premier League football and rugby that our 'dates' consisted of hanging out at a pub, screaming at the TV. The rugby was the closest thing to watching

American football at Hooters. Instead of chicken wings and Miller Lite, it was cocktail sausages and Guinness.

I still had my eyes open for THE ultimate riding boots. I'd often ask random women on the Luas or walking in town where they got their boots from. The responses were usually that they got them in some boutique… in Italy… five years ago. It was like getting a glimpse of Mr. Right just before finding out he had a girlfriend… or was gay.

* * * * *

"We should probably call it a night, Simon. If I have another whiskey, I won't be able to run tomorrow." Simon and I were out fake-celebrating his birthday for the tenth time – such a birthday whore.

"Come on, one more, it's my birthday week!" he begged.

"Nice try, but your birthday was two weeks ago… I'm over it. Plus, we have that charity race tomorrow morning."

"Ah, bloody hell! Why'd I agree to that?!"

"Because you love me," I said, batting my eyelashes.

"I must. It takes either love or the lust of a sweaty Latino named Juan to derail my Sunday routine. I had planned to lie in bed all day – wake up around noon, ignore the piles of laundry and dirty dishes, finish Season Four of *Buffy* and order Zaytoon. Now I have to… exercise?"

"You can lay around in squalor after the race. It's for a good cause."

"Ugh, so what do I need to wear to this thing?" He sucked the last bit of whiskey from the glass of ice.

"Claire had neon shirts made for us, so just wear crazy accessories – the brighter, more outrageous, the better."

"How about a neon speedo with gold body paint and glitter? I've got loads of that. I could even get my hands on a set of wings."

I rolled my eyes and laughed.

"As much as I'd love to see Declan's face when he sees the office golden boy split-leaping around Phoenix Park, sprinkling glitter around, let's save it for a night out at The George."

"Do you think Declan would be all weird if I came out of the closet at work?" he asked.

"I think he's old school traditional – he met his wife when they were eight years old, for Christ's sake. So he wouldn't *mean* to be weird, but... yeah, he would be," I explained.

"Yeah, that's what I thought too," he said, pondering.

"You'll tell him when the time is right."

"Yeah. Well, if we're not gonna get pissed and dance on stage while people in fairy costumes shoot Jäger in our mouths with squirt guns, then... let's go." He grabbed my coat from the back of my chair and helped me into it. I wanted to walk home, but Simon hailed a taxi and insisted I take it. Even when he was hammered after crazy nights out, he'd never let me walk home.

"See you tomorrow, dahling!" he said, kissing me on both cheeks. He opened my taxi door and walked off in the opposite direction.

* * * * *

The next morning, I received strange looks on the Luas to Phoenix Park. I might have gone overboard with the purple tights under my neon blue running shorts and yellow knee-high socks. It was all topped off with the hot pink boa I brought over from Florida. Just like with the leopard print blouse, I had told myself I might need it for an 80s themed party or for a festival, and I should keep it… at *least* until Halloween. Good thing I did!

The oversized sunglasses with thick, white, star-shaped frames were just the right touch. Dressing up for the race made me feel better about missing Gasparilla back home. It was only the greatest day of the year for anyone living within a 100-mile radius of Tampa. Everyone gets dressed up in pirate ensemble and spends the day drinking and waiting for the pirate ships to come invade the city with a parade.

I hadn't realized how big Phoenix Park was. Once inside, it took 20 minutes just to walk to where the race began. I found my co-workers who weren't decked out at all – except for Orla. She had on sparkly tights and face paint with brightly colored pieces. Claire had on one of those headbands with bobbing clovers, surely out of her Paddy's weekend box. Everyone else was clearly relying on the shirts that were made. As the newest associate, Claire was chosen (or forced) to organize a social event each month. She was stuck when coming up with the April activity, so I recommended the charity race to support the Maternity Hospital. I had helped her come up with questions for a table quiz in January and she had asked me for advice each month since. There wasn't a strong enough connection for Claire and me to form a friendship outside the office, but I enjoyed our frequent coffee breaks where she always shared the office gossip.

Our group stood together stretching our legs while Orla talked a mile a minute about the knobhead her sister had started dating. She was telling us how he was a complete gob-shite when Simon finally strolled up.

"Dahling! You made it!" I said, extending my arms so the boa made a diagonal line. I threw my head back into an exaggerated Hollywood pose.

I felt someone looking at me.

"Ah, dahling, you're brilliant! But tell me, does one bloody park really need to be so bloody big?" he asked in between three alternating kisses on my cheeks.

Simon was telling me about the granny who literally pushed him out of the way as she 'Dublin walked' along Georges street. I half-heartedly listened as I looked at the tall guy with long, wavy dark hair staring… no, *judging* me. My giant sunglasses allowed me to observe him without being too obvious.

"So, I got a hot dog from that stand across from Whelan's after you left. Hot dogs are so fucking good," Simon blurted.

"They're good at baseball games with crackerjacks and watered down American beer," I said, still observing.

"Well, this one was good enough that I went back for a second."

"Simon, that's gross. You weren't even drunk."

We huddled up at the start line while the announcer thanked everyone for coming out and supporting the cause. It was the perfect running weather and I couldn't be any more in my element – apart from the boa and whatnot.

I ran well and didn't see the guy with the staring problem again. Donal, a guy from the IT department, and I were first to finish from our team. Simon finished last and after complaining about his shins, was the first to leave. The rest of us exchanged pleasantries before going about our separate ways. I planned to head into town and check out the big boot sales at Aldo and Clarks. While looking through my race bag – a Lucozade (i.e. Irish Gatorade), a magnet, a bunch of flyers and a banana – I heard, "Jess! Hey Jess, wait up!" It was Claire. I pulled out my headphones as she ran toward me. I figured I had left something behind.

"I was gonna go get something to eat, wanna join?" she asked. No, I didn't. I wanted to shower and go shopping... alone.

"Oh sure, that sounds great!" I fibbed. She was trying to extend a friendship and although I had made friends, it wasn't like I had a ton. I figured what the heck, we'd get a toastie together.

"Great! Let me grab my bag," she said. "My best friend's brother ran in the race with his law firm – I was gonna ask him if he wants to join too, if you don't mind? I haven't seen him in ages!"

"Okay, cool!" Ugh, why hadn't I walked away faster?! She disappeared into the makeshift tent to fetch her belongings.

"Alright, all ready to go," she said minutes later from behind me. I turned around to see *him*... the guy with the staring problem at the starting line.

"Jessica, this is Aidan." First thing I noticed was the intensity of his dark eyes analyzing me. I felt uneasy and… nervous?

"Hiya. Love the get up," he said, raising his thick, dark eyebrows. When he extended his hand, I noticed how short his shorts were. Holy hell! I tried not to look at his crotch area, but it was just… there! Stop it, Jessie, look up… look up while you shake his hand, I coached myself.

Had he asked Claire to invite me? Oh God, was he interested? He looked too grungy to be my type and those shorts were just too much.

"What were you listening to?" he asked me. The headphones were hanging from my hand. Dear Lord, please don't let my playlist have switched to a Taylor Swift song. I hit the power button, relieved to still see Brendan Urie smoking a cigarette on the cover of the Panic! At the Disco album.

"Far Too Young to Die," I responded, showing him the screen.

"How melodramatic of you," he smirked, revealing a crooked smile.

I was right about him – presumptuous asshole.

"Excuse me?" I said, with a sour face. "It's a running mix and the song has a good beat. Is it not up to your musical standards or something?"

"Apologies, Jessica, but I think you've misunderstood my joke. I wasn't being facetious; I found it humorous that you're decked out like a Hollywood starlet and the song has such a dramatic title. I guess it was too cryptic, forgive me."

Good one, Jessie. Way to put your foot in your mouth.

"Ah, I see." I tried to laugh it off. "So what's on *your* running mix?" I asked, trying to make nice.

"I prefer to run without music – clears the mind and allows you to take in your surroundings. You really should try it sometime."

Nope, I *was* right – presumptuous asshole.

"Thanks for the tip," I said, raising an eyebrow.

I turned to Claire. "Shall we go eat?"

FIVE

That day was the beginning of the warmest and driest season Ireland had experienced in the past decade. Outside Phoenix Park was littered with people drinking pints of Bulmers on ice. We got takeaway sandwiches from Junos and found a spot on the grass to eat them just inside the park's entrance. There was something about Aidan I couldn't put my finger on. He flirted with the line between confidence and cockiness and I couldn't tell if it was attractive or a turn off. I didn't find him particularly attractive at first, but his tall, confident presence made him someone I couldn't take my eyes off of. The only thing putting a kibosh on his swagger was his super short shorts.

He and Claire were discussing the last time they'd been home, which I found amusing considering their parents only lived about 10 kilometers from their apartments. Aidan hadn't been home for Sunday dinner in over a month, which he said his mum was going to disown him for.

"Ah, I've been in Dublin long enough to know she's bluffing. A son can do no wrong in an Irish mum's eyes," I said, getting comfortable on the lawn.

"Ah, not Babs! She's not your stereotypical Irish mum. She wanted both her sons out of the house after secondary school and can you believe she never ironed our underwear?! The biggest embarrassment she bestows on the Irish mum's reputation is that she can only cook a potato three ways – everyone knows a proper Irish mum has mastered at least eight," he nodded matter-of-factly.

Claire chimed in, agreeing that his mum didn't fit the stereotype. When she asked Aidan who he was living with these days, I remember being very interested to hear his response.

"I'm still living with Killian. The first year went well, so we just renewed our lease for another."

"Is he the guy you met in Japan?" Claire asked before biting into her sandwich.

"Yip! Two solo travelers brought together at the Mt. Fuji summit, 10,000 kilometers away from home," he answered.

I had gotten used to how common travel was from Dublin compared to America. Dubliners take a month to go traveling like it's nothing; meanwhile, most Americans don't even have passports. Places like Paris and Rome were places I always thought were reserved for extravagant honeymoons, but in Ireland it was a little weekend getaway. Even so, I hadn't heard of anyone going to Japan on 'holiday' and certainly not alone.

He told us the story of how their group climbed all day and night so they were at the summit for sunrise. He and Killian hit it off and stayed with each other the remainder of their trip. When they returned to Dublin, they moved in together. Talk about a small world!

Aidan told all sorts of stories about their Japanese adventure. From the monkeys that stole his camera (and gave it back an hour later), to the bloopers that came from using public transportation when he couldn't read the signs.

He also told stories from other trips. He had gone to Cambodia the year before he went to Japan. He didn't mention who he went with, but *they* went to Siem Reap to see the ancient temples where *Tomb Raider* was filmed. The beer was cheaper than water and they got three-dollar massages every day for two weeks! I hung on to every word. It was all so interesting and inspiring – I suddenly wanted to go to Japan and Cambodia instead of Spain. He told the stories so effortlessly, as if he had told them a hundred times before. He wasn't at all the pompous prick I had pegged him to be before the lunch. I wanted to hear more of his stories; I wanted to know more about him. What I really wanted to know was if he had a girlfriend.

I no longer cared about the boot sales. I didn't want the lunch to end.

I was bummed when after almost two hours, Claire said, "Right, I better get going. I need to do some bits and bobs around the place. It was lovely to see you, Aidan. See you tomorrow, Jess. And thanks a mil for helping me put this together."

She gathered her stuff from the grass and left.

It was just Aidan and I, which was slightly awkward. I wondered if we should have left too. When he started to move, I figured he was going to stand up to leave – but no. He pulled his legs around to lie on his side. The sunlight hit his face, brightening his steel gray eyes and accentuating his facial stubble. He was casually propped up on his elbow like a Greek statue (well, a pale Irish statue). I remained upright, hands in my lap, nervous and excited to be with him one-on-one.

"Alright, Jessica – tell me three things you love about Dublin," he blurted. The bluntness caught me off guard. No one had ever asked me to list why I loved something, especially in Dublin. It was usually: "Why would you want to leave Florida to come to Dublin?!"

There were a lot of things I loved and appreciated about Dublin, but I was struggling to articulate a response that didn't sound stupid. I scolded myself; come on, think, Jessie! You don't want him to think it's such a struggle to come up with something!

"Hmm. Well, love is a *tricky* word," I sighed. "But I do love how everything here has character," I nodded, satisfied with my response. "Each building, each shop or cafe, every house – whether I'm in town or my own neighborhood… it's all very one of a kind. People must think I'm crazy walking around staring at the architecture – the doors, the structure, the shape, the color and the uniqueness of everything. I love how the pubs have pots of fresh flowers hanging from the outside." My cheeks were pushing against my eyes as I spoke. "It's just so different from what I'm used to – cookie-cutter neighborhoods and massive apartment complexes. The buildings at home are so modern, so calculated, so deprived of charm." I noticed I was rambling.

"Awk yeah, America is still a new country – hasn't had time to develop that character. I bet those apartment blocks are going up left and right." Still on his elbow, he adjusted himself, moving closer to me. "Okay, what else you got?"

"Oh, the pressure!" I laughed. "Hmm…" I gazed up, tapping my finger on my chin.

"You clearly don't like rocket," he said, referring to the pile of green leaves I had picked off my sandwich. "What do you think of the food in Dublin?" he asked.

"I actually love it. There are so many great restaurants and everything is so fresh. I never knew that bread and yogurt weren't supposed to keep for weeks, or that apples are so small when they're not on steroids. At restaurants, I love how the servers don't rush you out as soon as you've taken your last bite."

He laughed.

"Ooh, ooh… I have another one!" His eyes widened, telling me to continue. "I love the attention that Dublin gives to drinks."

"Drinks?! Come on Jessica, we're not *all* drunks!" he joked.

"Nooo, that's not what I meant!" I laughed and pushed his shoulder like we were kids. "Every – and I mean *every* – drink is always served in a glass here. Beer? Always in a pint glass. Whiskey and coke? I get a shot in a glass alongside a tiny glass bottle of coke. Soda at a restaurant? Glass bottle. In America, soda always comes from a fountain and most bars serve beer in plastic cups."

"Interesting… I never noticed that. But yeah, there's been a big push for recycling the past decade, so that probably explains all the glass," he suggested.

"Also, tea and coffee here are always on a saucer." I didn't bring up that I didn't know what an electric kettle was when I first moved to Dublin.

"You don't use saucers in America?" he looked surprised.

"I mean, we have them but usually only at weddings or at fancy restaurants. You wouldn't see them often. Our coffee shops and normal restaurants wouldn't typically use them," I clarified.

"Well, that's a good observation. I like this game, tell me more," he said excitedly.

"You're really putting me in the hot seat, huh?" I was less nervous knowing he was interested in what I had to say. "Alright, so I didn't like this at first, but now... I love having minimal options in the grocery store. I mean, in America we have an entire aisle, top to bottom, dedicated to peanut butter – which I'm obsessed with, but it's completely unnecessary! It's just ground up peanuts for crying out loud!" My hands waved wildly as I spoke.

"Ha! Ah, well, Americans *are* known for excess in everything. It's cool that you now appreciate the simplicity." He laughed.

"So you've been to America, I take it?"

"Just once. I did a three-month exchange program where I lived with a family outside of Atlantic City, Jersey in an area called Egg Harbor. I was only 12, so I don't remember anything except going to the Golden Corral for the all-you-can-eat buffet every Friday night; it was horrific!"

"You were a foreign exchange student?! Oh my God, that's awesome!" I said, with way too much enthusiasm.

"You are SO American!" He had a great smile. Only the left corner of his lips rose, but the crookedness was attractive.

"Whatever! I've become SO Irish!" I joked back.

"Ah sure, look, it's *awesome,*" he exaggerated the word.

We talked about our favorite restaurants, how to change a tire and our shared fear of clowns. We carried on for hours. The conversation flowed with ease and it wasn't the standard introductory topics, which was nice. The temperature dropped when the clouds rolled in. My boa was the only layer I had over my shirt.

"It's getting late; I really should get going," I said, brushing the grass from my hands and putting my Hollywood sunglasses back on. We walked together till just past the park entrance where he told me he'd be going in the opposite direction.

"Right, so. It was great chatting with ye, so it was. Sure I'll see you around sometime." I took note of the Irishism overload. I didn't know what to do for the goodbye – should I give him a hug? Shake his hand? Flash the peace sign? What I decided on was probably the worst possible option.

I stood awkwardly. With one hand on my hip and the other waving like Forrest Gump did to Lieutenant Dan, I said, "Well, have a nice day!"

His head fell as he laughed and said, "You are SO American!"

I was SO embarrassed, that's what I was! I couldn't come up with a witty comeback and I could feel the heat rising to my face, so I just shrugged my shoulders and walked away.

During the commute home, I replayed everything I knew about Aidan. I was both disappointed and somewhat intrigued that he didn't ask for my number. I was sure that he'd leverage our connection with Claire to get in touch with me the next day.

SIX

April 2013 - One week later

"Jessie Boo Boo!" Lindsay screeched when I hit the button on the computer to answer the Skype call. I despise all forms of baby talk, but for some reason, it doesn't bother me coming from Lindsay.

I raised my martini glass to the laptop screen. "Cheers!"

"So... any word from that guy?" It was very Lindsay to cut to the chase.

"Negative." I pulled my lips to one side, making a face. It had been eight days since the lunch in the park with Aidan.

"Ugh, he totally has a girlfriend. Why else wouldn't he ask your friend for your number?" she said, reaching for her martini glass.

"Ah, I didn't get the girlfriend vibe; I think he's just not interested. Oh well... NEXT!" I sipped my martini – the telltale sign that I was feeling uncomfortable. I changed the subject, asking her how Jason was.

"Hold that thought... one minute." She held her finger up and ran away, her dark auburn hair swaying as she ran out of sight from the screen.

When she returned, the screen bounced around as she adjusted it downward and slammed her foot onto the chair. Covering her foot were intricately laced, black leather straps. Her manicured toes peeked through the front opening. When she turned her foot, I saw the signature red sole – she had gotten her Christian Louboutin Laurence lace-ups.

"Eeeeeek! They're gorgeous!" I shrieked. I was happy, knowing how much she wanted them and how long she had waited to buy them. They really were beautiful – trendy yet classic.

"I hardly ever go into Saks, but they were having their annual sale – 20% off everything, so I checked it out and... BAM! These little gems were an additional 25% off. No way could I pass them up at almost half off, especially when they only had two pairs left – equivalent to a US size 6.5 and a 9."

"That's always the case! Aren't you a US 7.5 though?" I knew because I've borrowed some of her shoes before and I'm a US size 8 so some of them were just a tad too tight for comfort.

"Yeah, I usually need a 7.5 in heels, especially peep toe because I'm not down for the toes hanging over the front look; it reminds me of a trashy *Jerry Springer Show*." I love when my sweet Lindsay turns into bitch Lindsay without warning. "But, the 6.5 actually fits fine. I guess Louboutins run big... you never know with French designers, especially with the whole size conversion thing. They're a little tight, but the leather straps will stretch out; I just need to wear them a few times and they'll be perfect."

After looking closer, I could see that even without putting any weight on the shoe, her toes *were* hanging over the front – the very thing she wanted to avoid. Unless the base of the shoe was going to grow a half an inch in length, she was completely lying to herself. Maybe that's why they're so expensive – they're made with magical leather that will mold to its owner's foot?

"Well, as long as they fit and they're comfortable, then the size is just a number. I'm glad you got them Lindz; you deserve it!" I was such an enabler.

"Thanks! I can't wait to wear them on mine and Jason's next date night." She still had her foot up on the chair as she untied the strappy contraption. She wanted them so badly that she couldn't turn down the sale, even if it meant wearing shoes that were going to be painfully uncomfortable.

"Jason is good… he's too good, Jess! He's actually perfect and he makes me feel special every day. I think he's The One." She pulled her foot from the jungle of straps. On the laptop screen, I could see the red marks all over her foot where the straps had been – they had a lot of stretching to do. "He was telling me about some pro bono work he did in Kenya for three months… and another project in Peru. He's saved so many lives, Jess. All I've ever saved was Tucker, from the pound."

"Don't forget about that abandoned bunny you nurtured back to health in college! Seriously, Lindz, don't put yourself down."

"I'm not. I just worry he'll get bored with me. I've had the same job since I graduated, I've never traveled, I don't know half the things he knows." She sighed.

"You're six years younger than him – of course he's going to have a lot more experiences under his belt; it'd be weird if he didn't. You can always travel to new places together."

"I know, you're right. Speaking of travel, I need to get my passport so I can come visit you!"

"Yes! Yes!" I clapped my hands like a little kid. "Hurry up because my time here is up in five months." She told me that she was going to get it in the next month and that she wanted to do a trip to Rome or Paris as well.

I asked her about Cody – if they had done anything recently or if there were any plans coming up. I wanted to make sure she didn't get off the hook and avoid the subject like she had the past few Skype dates. She sipped her martini and sighed.

"Jason is planning a party at Chuck E. Cheese for his fourth birthday. Jess, I'm freaking out! I'm not ready to meet other parents and the thought of being there with all those kids made me break out in hives the other day."

"Well, Chuck E. Cheese can make anyone break out in hives. It's a band of scary, singing forest animals and a pool of germ-infested plastic balls." I was being an enabler again – making her feel better but ignoring the issue at hand. "But Lindz, it's been a year… you can't keep thinking something is going to magically change between you and Cody. If it's ever going to really work out between you and Jason, you're going to have to dive into that pool of plastic balls sooner or later."

"I choose later," she said without hesitation.

"I meant sooner *rather than* later, you goof. You're running out of options except for: accept both of them or neither of them."

"Cody is great… I know he'll grow on me; I just need time," she said, nodding her head with her eyes fixed on her lap.

I realized Cody and Laurence, the size US 6.5 designer heel, had a lot in common. She wanted things with Jason to work out so badly, she'd do anything… even if it also meant being in a relationship with Cody which was painfully uncomfortable. Lindsay was hoping Cody would 'grow on her' and that Laurence would 'stretch out.' My best friend was lying to herself all around.

Despite our decade long friendship and how brutally honest we could always be with each other, I couldn't bring myself to state the obvious: don't buy size 6.5 shoes when you *know* you're a 7.5… and don't date a man with a son when you *know* you're missing the mom gene.

SEVEN

The next day at work, I couldn't stop thinking about Aidan. I went back and forth on whether or not to ask Claire about him. I kept going back to the conclusion that he had a girlfriend and so I took the cowardly route and decided to never bring him up. I was creeping through social media, trying to find him, when I was interrupted by a message from Simon:

Simon: *I made out with a Brazilian last night; pretty sure I had beer goggles on.*

Me: *Ah those foreigners will get you every time! Low key Thursday night huh?*

Simon: *I was just having a beer at Front Lounge and this guy messaged me on one of my dick apps. His picture was just his abs — Goddamn, you could grate cheese on those abs!*

Me: What's a d**k app? Simon, you're not getting into any risky business are you?

I imagined him drugged up at some strobe lit orgy festival.

Simon: God, I fucking love you.
Simon: It's basically gay Tinder.
Simon: He was only the second guy I've met up with from a dick app and both were PG-13 so stop worrying. But let's just say my experience last night made me sign up on Match.com.

Simon had only ever mentioned one long term ex before and even then, he wasn't keen to talk about it. I had always seen him as the type that enjoyed the casual dating scene and had little interest in ever wanting a serious relationship. I felt like a jerk for not knowing where he stood or what he wanted relationship-wise, especially when we had become so close.

Me: I think that's a great idea! I've been to a couple of Match weddings – I totally believe in the system.
Me: Keep me updated on all the sexy men you virtually meet.

Simon: For sure, I'll need your help psycho analyzing all my matches.

Before I could respond, I received an email alert, so I toggled to my inbox to see the header in bold:

Aidan McGovern   Awesome American   19/04/2013 11:26

I felt anxious when I saw the name. The excitement was quickly followed by disappointment when I clicked into the message:

From: Aidan.McGovern@ESKlaw.com
To: J.Dunhour@mediatech.com
Date: 19 April 2013 – 11:26
Subject: Awesome American

http://www.bbcamerica.com/mind-the-gap/2012/08/09/10-things-americans-say-and-what-they-really-mean/

Please see #1
Aidan

That was it?

I clicked on the link. The BBC America page loaded slowly until I eventually saw the heading, *10 Things Americans Say… and What They Really Mean*. I laughed out loud as I read through them – agreeing whole-heartedly with most of them. Number one, the one he had referred to, was about how when an American shop assistant says, "Have a nice day," what they actually mean is, "Honestly, I don't care what kind of day you have, but please tell my manager I was friendly so I get extra commission." My favorite was number nine – how an American saying they need to use the 'restroom' actually means they need to use the loo and not that they need to find a room to have a quiet lie down.

He must have gotten my email from Claire. Did he have to wait over a week though?! I couldn't send a generic response back, so I did a quick internet search and found the Irish equivalent article.

My reply back was nothing but a link to a page on http://irishmammies.ie and below it, my own words: Stereotypes come from somewhere…

The article was about how Irish mammies think their sons are the greatest men in the world. How no woman will ever be good enough and how they get angry when their sons don't come home on the weekends to be fed and have their laundry done… even in their thirties.

I went for lunch with Orla and Simon, which kept me from hawking my inbox. When we returned, I continued stalling on checking my email. I figured the longer I waited to check for a response, the more my odds of having one were increased. I went to the restroom – erm, toilet – made a cuppa tea in the break room and stopped to chat with Claire. She told me that Aidan asked his sister, Emma, to ask her for my email address a few days prior.

It had been almost two hours since I sent my message, so it was plenty of time for him to have responded. I was right:

From: Aidan.McGovern@ESKlaw.com
To: J.Dunhour@mediatech.com
Date: 19 April 2013 – 14:05
Subject: Re: Re: Awesome American

Well played, Miss America, well played. But I told you, my mum is not the standard Irish mum. She doesn't iron my boxers and she actually wants me to get married. She'd much prefer to talk to you about shoes and fashion than to talk about me. It's true, she's a different species…. almost American if you ask me ;)

So, what does an American living in Dublin do
at the weekend? Any plans?

Aidan

She'd much prefer to talk to *you?* Clearly he could have
written "She'd much prefer to talk about...," but he wrote,
"She'd much prefer to talk to YOU!" Not only was he single
but also he totally wanted me to meet his mom! Jessica
McGovern… it sounded so authoritative!

Was he asking about my weekend plans to be polite, or
was he going to ask me to do something? I drafted a
response but waited a few hours to send it so I didn't appear
too available.

From: J.Dunhour@mediatech.com
To: Aidan.McGovern@ESKlaw.com
Date: 19 April 2013 – 17:01
Subject: Re: Re: Re: Awesome American

Unless your mum resorts to one of the
following at least twice a week for dinner:
Hamburger Helper, Kraft mac-n-cheese, Stove
Top or Marie Callenders frozen lasagna – then
it's safe to say she's not an American mom. We
like everything instant, especially our stuffing.

I'm meeting friends at Slatts tonight. Tomorrow
I'm going to a concert at the Olympia.

What does an authentic Irish lad do on a
weekend in Dublin?

Jess

As I was changing out of my work pumps and into my ballet flats, ready to leave for the day, I received another response. It was only 15 minutes from when I sent my previous message.

From: Aidan.McGovern@ESKlaw.com
To: J.Dunhour@mediatech.com
Date: 19 April 2013 – 17:16
Subject: Re: Re: Re: Re: Awesome American

And I was afraid you were going to say you hang out in Temple Bar! The Olympia Theatre is a brilliant venue, enjoy the tunes. This weekend my housemate, Killian, and I are heading over to Kerry to golf. Maybe a bit of hiking if the weather holds out.

Ok, I'm signing off, enjoy your weekend!

P.S. What the hell is Stove Top?

Aidan

After reading his response and then re-reading the entire chain, I thought to myself: I have a last name, I know he's a lawyer (well, either a solicitor or barrister, which are the two types of lawyers in Ireland), he likes to golf and he obviously wants me to meet his mom. I was intrigued. I was giddy.

I turned off my computer and headed to Slattery's. I felt like a little girl with her first crush as I rode on my bike with a big grin on my face.

EIGHT
May 2013

The witty emails between Aidan and I continued for weeks. They progressively got more and more flirty but it wasn't till after a few weeks of emails that he finally asked for my phone number. He said he wanted to send me a picture. It was a cake someone had made for a colleague at his firm who was going on maternity leave. The cake was in the shape of a baby... one that had an uncanny resemblance to the Chucky doll. The picture he sent to me was of the Chucky look-a-like cake with one missing leg and his side hacked into. They really didn't think that one through.

Having each other's digits meant that our communication continued on outside of the Monday through Friday, 9am to 5pm window that we started with. What it *didn't* mean was that we were any closer to going on a proper date. At first, I enjoyed the innocent flirting and getting to know each other. But after weeks, he still had only texted – hadn't called, hadn't asked me out. His behavior was more in line with what Orla had explained of Irish men. Assuming Aidan taking his time was somewhat of the Irish standard norm, I held out patiently. We had accumulated a lot of inside jokes and silly puns during those weeks of texting. One of them was sending links to songs to go along with whatever we were doing or talking about. Like when I checked my phone in the middle of lunch and started blushing... Claire said, "Wow, that boy has really got a hold on you!" When I texted him to tell him about Claire's comment, he replied with a link to the Smokey Robinson classic: "You've Really Got a Hold on Me".

Although I told him about that comment from Claire, I never told him about the others such as, "I figured Aidan would fancy you... he's such a lady's man." Claire was the gossip queen, but I knew her sibling-like comments were because of their long history and not that he really was a womanizer.

The weeks turned into a month and our flirty messages continued. It was six weeks from when we had met at the charity race. We still hadn't met a second time and I had given up hope that we ever would. Those antics might be typical of Irish men, but I'm not Irish and I was done being a pen pal. I told myself it was better that way since I was moving back to America in three months – at best it could only have been a summer romance.

The concert was on a Saturday at the end of May. The Iveagh Gardens venue was perfect for the dry, warm weather. I was with Simon, Orla and her boyfriend, Gearoid, who was over from Galway that weekend. We started the day as you would start any concert... day drinking. We slammed back pints at Bruxells, downstairs where it's less touristy. Orla and Gearoid were trying to teach us Gaelic words and phrases. We made friends with a group of Irish rocker dudes and they all got a laugh out of us butchering the language. I was having a great time, but when I looked at my phone with disappointment, Simon could tell something was on my mind.

"My dahling J. D. – what's the matter?" he asked, slamming his pint glass and putting a hand on my shoulder.

"Oh, it's nothing," I replied, putting my phone back in my purse.

"Bullshit! Don't you bullshit me; we're better than bullshit," he slurred, struggling to keep his eyes open. "Plus, you can't bullshit a bullshitter. But… I'm not a bullshitter. I love you J. D.," he rambled before finishing his beer. I laughed.

"That made no sense, Simon, but I love you too." I toasted his empty glass and took a sip. I was tipsy but not as much as he was – probably because he had two more pints than me. Plus, he was three or four inches shorter than me… it's just physics that my little bullshitter would love me at that point. "I'm just over this texting thing with Aidan. He's sending me really mixed signals. I can't deal with it anymore. My mom said to stop texting him, so I pretty much did. I only respond to his messages with really short, generic responses, but don't initiate new conversation – nothing like what we used to."

"Is he still texting you?" he asked. "Or did he get the point and give up?"

I toggled my head side to side like a confused puppy dog. "Both. He definitely notices. There were a couple days this week where we didn't talk, but he'd always come back with just enough to keep me interested."

"Ugh, piss. That is annoying. Sounds like my life in dick app world. What's the last you heard from him?"

"Yesterday. He sent a message about it being Friday with a link to "Friday I'm In Love" by The Cure. I only sent a smiley face back."

"A link to a song? A fucking great song, yes, but J. D. you're so much better than this," he said, shaking his head.

"Nah, it was cool. It's kind of a thing we do – erm, used to do – or what am I talking about? It was never anything. This is stupid – if he liked me, he'd ask me out and he hasn't. End of story; let's drink. I'll get the next round." I made a beeline to the bar without giving Simon a chance to respond.

When it was time to leave the pub and head to the gig, Simon and I had the genius idea to buy a bottle of Jameson and I'd sneak it into the concert inside my handbag. Some of the bottle had spilled in my bag, causing it to reek when I opened it for security. They didn't say anything and I concluded Irish security wasn't very strict, or they were simply in support of a good time.

During the opening act, we all danced and drank from the coke bottle I had mixed with the whiskey. Seeing Orla outside of the office, dancing and drinking, made me like her more than I already did. As the opener finished up, so did my bootlegged bottle of coke. During the intermission, I went to the port-a-potty before buying a burger, chips and a new bottle of coke. I got back to our designated spot, claimed by the bedsheet Orla had remembered to bring. In the smack dab middle of the sheet was Simon, passed out and snoring. I sat next to him to eat my food, deciding to let him sleep. After I devoured my messy dinner, I went to mix a new drink. I opened the coke bottle and took a sip to make space for the whiskey. When I brought it back in front of me, I read the marketing message: Share a Coke with *Aidan*. I laughed at the serendipitous message and really wanted to send Aidan a picture of it. In my drunken state, I decided to break the deal I had made with myself... the one to cease cyber communication with him. I held the bottle in my left hand and snapped a picture. In the background was nothing but the grass covered with plastic beer cups and rubbish and my navy Vans – my Aidan shoes. I added the picture to the message box and stared at it, debating whether or not I should send it. I didn't want to play the game anymore and knew sending it would encourage it to continue. Oh well, I sent it. No text message, just the picture: Share a coke with Aidan. Within minutes he responded:

Aidan: *Haha! As always, well played!*

Followed immediately by a second message:

Aidan: *I trust that there isn't just coke in there.*

Then a third:

Aidan: *Hey, are you at Iveagh Gardens?*

Oh shit. That meant he was there too! First time he meets me, I'm wearing a pink boa. Second time, I'd be drunk, looking like a hot mess in mismatched, hippy concert attire with Simon passed out at my side. I looked at Simon – his shirt had a huge picture of a cat smoking a cigarette with the phrase: *Cool Cat*. The shirt wasn't as bad as the ridiculous Union Jack sunglasses. Ugh, why did I send that stupid picture?! There was a fourth message:

Aidan: *My roommate, Killian is there. I'm not.*

OH THANK GOD! I sighed in relief. Trying to appear casual, I sent:

Me: *Yep, I'm here*

I put my phone back in my bag in an effort not to send anything else. It worked… mainly because the battery died.

NINE

May 2013 – The next day

What?!

I was shocked to see the name on the screen of my ringing phone: **Aidan McGovern**. He had never called before that day. My mom was right about backing off.

My heart raced as I cleared my throat and practiced my best, "Well, hello there," to make sure my voice wouldn't have any weird cracks when I answered. Ugh, it sounded sarcastic. I tried again, "Hey you!" Oh my God, no! I might as well say, "Hey there, buddy!" I wanted to stay out of the friend zone. Come on, Jessica, make up your mind before he hangs up or worse... hears your lame voicemail you never updated. Another note to self: make a better voicemail message.

"Heeeyyy," I answered, dragging the word out. Good one, Jessica... the best you could come up with was a slutty sounding "Hey?!"

He laughed. "Sorry, wasn't expecting such a loud, cheerful greeting. How ya doing today? You in bits after the concert?" he joked.

"Ah, I had a headache this morning, but nothing a coffee and some brunch couldn't sort out," I replied, proud of the smooth delivery and effortless use of 'sort out', which is a major Irishism.

"Good stuff. So what are the plans today?" he asked.

Oh shit, what should I say?! I had planned to go food shopping, buy a replacement light bulb for my kitchen, go for a run and get take away. I couldn't tell him all that because it'd come off like I was too busy (being lame) to meet up with him if he wanted to. But on the same note, I didn't want him to think I had no plans and was sitting around twiddling my thumbs. Ughh... THINK, JESSIE!

"No major plans, just running a few errands," I said in my best attempt to sound cavalier. Meanwhile, I couldn't stop pacing back and forth and sweating from my palms.

"I remember you saying you try to Skype your mum and dad on Sundays – what time is that at?"

I had been texting with my mom the past few hours. I knew she'd be fully supportive of me ditching our Skype date to go out with Aidan.

"Very thoughtful of you to remember, Mr. McGovern. I was actually just gonna call my mom here in a minute."

"You're very good. Sure look, I was ringing you there to see if you fancied meeting in town tonight – posh pizza and craft beers?"

Oh my God, oh my God! I repeated in my head, thankful he couldn't see me jumping and making a silent shriek through the phone.

"Hmmm, that depends... will you be in your short shorts?" I teased.

"How about you wear your pink boa and Hollywood sunglasses and I'll put Daisy Duke to shame," he said.

"Sold. When and where?" I wanted to get off the phone so I could scream, report to my mom and start getting ready.

"Skinflint at 8:00? Does that suit?"

"It suits just fine." That gave me plenty of time to get ready… picking out the perfect 'casual' look takes me longer than getting ready for a ball.

"Do you know where it is?"

"Nope, but I'll find it."

"Are you sure? It's kind of hidden down a little alley. I can meet you at Trinity and we'll walk over together?"

"That's nice of you, but I got this." I didn't want him to think I couldn't figure out simple logistics on my own.

"Ah, apologies – I forgot about the American confidence."

"It's alright, just don't let it happen again." Had I really used Dad's famous line for anytime someone said they were sorry? His little phrases had certainly rubbed off. "Alright, I'll see you at eight – I'll be looking for the short shorts."

"I'll have them on with a single stemmed rose between my teeth."

"Ah, so cliché! See you soon."

"Looking forward to it," he said sincerely and oh, so sexy.

EEEEEEEK!! I finally let out a squeal when we hung up. I immediately called Mom to tell her the update. I knew she'd be the only person who would find it as exciting as I did.

Where is this friggin' place? I thought to myself.

Google Maps showed it on Crane Lane, which I knew I had turned onto (after passing it twice). I looked closely on both sides of the alleyway for a Skinflint sign, but I couldn't see one. I had come to the end of Crane Lane, so I turned around and tried again. Still nothing. I decided to call the damn place, but I saw I had a text from Aidan:

Aidan: It's on the right side when you turn from Dame Street. Big glass windows, no sign. See you soon.

Ah ha! It was right in front of me.

I was relieved to see how casual it was when I walked inside. Six or seven tables filled the cozy space. Aidan emerged from my left with a huge grin. I could tell he was excited to see me. I could feel my face getting hot. Thank God for the dim lighting of the Edison bulbs that dangled above each table by a wire pendant. He wrapped his arms around my shoulders and pulled me in; he smelled so good! The mix of laundry detergent and musky cologne was light enough that I had to be in his embrace to smell it.

"You look great," he said, pulling away. "Although, I'm disappointed you're sans boa." God, that smile! "Come sit, I ordered you a beer – Pilsner okay?"

"Perfect. Just not a fan of pale ales," I said, taking off my jacket and placing it on one of the empty stools. The tabletop was made of a distressed wooden door panel. Exposed industrial pipes complimented the funky and eclectic décor.

"So, I have to admit – it was quite entertaining watching you walk back and forth just there, and were you... talking to yourself?" he joked, pouring me a glass of water from the green Martini and Rossi bottle. It was stripped of its label, but after all of mine and Lindsay's martini nights, I could recognize that bottle a mile away.

Ah shit.

"No! I was singing!" I said, unconvincingly.

"It's okay; I've been on dates with crazier. Right so, I think Tess and Maria look absolutely delicious," he blurted as I nearly choked on my swig of beer.

"Oh yeah? Wanna tell me about them?" I said, assuming there was a nuance implied.

"Well, Tess is thick and meaty with pulled pork and braised fennel, whereas Maria is more delicate with potato, truffle oil and mushroom." He pointed to the menu. "What do ye reckon?"

I kept a straight face and scanned the menu quickly.

"Hmmm... I don't know, Vonie is lookin' mighty fine to me. Harissa, hens egg, serrano ham and mozzarella – she sounds like cheesy, meaty, spicy deliciousness," I said just before our skinny, hipster server approached. Aidan ordered us the Vonie and Maria.

"So, are you a foodie?" he asked. I totally am a foodie, but it felt like an odd question. I pictured myself drizzling my Lambda olive oil over a bowl of Haagen Dazs dark chocolate ice cream and topping it with pink Himalayan rock salt – the only way to eat ice cream. But it seemed like a presumptuous thing to confess, especially on a first date. Not to mention, I didn't want to create the wrong impression because Lord knows some nights I have cereal for dinner.

"Umm, I appreciate good food but a foodie? Nah… not me."

"My sister's taking classes at the Ballymaloe Cookery School. It's grand because she'll go to Mum and Dad's and try new recipes because they buy all the ingredients *and* clean up – I just eat. She's really good."

"That's awesome," I said, taking another sip of beer, trying to calm my nerves. "And this is Emma?"

"Nope, Kate. Kate is the baby. She's 23. She's really quiet – keeps to herself, reads all day and night. Then there's Emma, who's 25 – she's the complete opposite. She's a bit of a wild child."

"A wee Irish family of three, huh?"

"Nope. There's Philip, who's 29; he lives in Australia with his girlfriend – and then I'm oldest at 32."

He switched the conversation back to me. Next thing I knew, I was telling him about the indoor forts my brother and I used to build during big storms. We'd use every cushion, pillow and blanket in the house. I told him about our vacations to St. Louis every summer and Dad taking my brother, sister and I camping at Silver Springs. Mom would never go because she's deathly afraid of snakes. He wanted to know it all – he even managed to uncover my social awkwardness at age four. My mom had to take me out of preschool because I cried all day, every day – the teachers told her preschool wasn't for everyone. Aidan, on the other hand, had no problem leaving his mum when she dropped him off at the crèche and the only time he cried was when they took him out of the sandbox.

"I was mesmerized by the sand; the wet sand was the best!" His face lit up when he talked about the damn sand. I laughed hysterically at his theatrical interpretation of a child playing in a sandbox.

He looked completely different from the day of the race. It wasn't just because of the tight, dark brown jeans and leather jacket, or the fact he was cleaned up for the date – it was more than that. He made me feel like there was nowhere else he'd rather be than at that table, talking to me about nothing and everything.

It wasn't until an hour later that we touched on anything that reminded me I was an expat.

"So how have you made friends here if you didn't know anyone?" Our second round of beers arrived and the empty plates were cleared.

"It just sort of happens, slowly but surely. In the beginning, I'd tag along on any invite, usually from co-workers. I hit it off with some more than others, so I'd go out with them. I'd meet their friends and maybe hit it off with some of them and so on. All of a sudden, my contact list filled up and now I have a good group of friends." He leaned in over the table and looked me in the eye.

"I'm intrigued, Jessica Dunhour. I want to know so much more about you." He flashed his crooked grin.

"Thank you. Compliment accepted." I could feel myself blushing as I finished off the last of my third beer. We were there for three hours when our server informed us it was closing time.

"I know it's Sunday and we have to work tomorrow, but I don't want the night to end. Do you like cocktails?" he said, lifting an eyebrow.

"Umm, yeah!" I said, enthusiastically. I had a meeting at 8:00 am the next morning, but it wouldn't have made a difference if it were at 6:00 am. I'd gladly take a hangover at work to spend more time with him.

"Alright, missus, forgive me, but we're going somewhere pretty touristy." I liked that he called me missus – I wondered if that was just an Irish thing or if he was already giving me a nickname.

"But the place has a nice terrace and they stay open late. What kind of shoes do you have on?" Damn it. I was wearing my navy Vans – the ones in the background of the picture I sent him the day before at the concert.

"Oh, they're super casual… are they not going to let me in?" I asked, sticking out a foot.

"Are you kidding? This is Dublin, not Manhattan. I asked because the cobblestone down the alleyways is uneven. Wanted to make sure you'd be okay if you had heels on."

"Aw, thanks dad," I teased as we walked out into the night.

When we stepped off the pavement onto the cobblestone, he grabbed my hand.

"Just in case," he winked.

We went to Fitzsimons and ended up staying for three cocktails. I was tipsy but not sloppy. It was warm and dry, had been for the past couple of weeks. The view from the terrace wasn't incredible, but still Dublin had never looked so good. We talked about... well, I don't remember exactly what all we talked about thanks to said drinks, but there was a lot of laughing on both ends. I couldn't believe how goofy he was compared to my first impression at the starting line when I thought he was judging everything about me.

I do remember sharing embarrassing stories about our friends. He told a story about when his friend Dane filled his tank at the petrol station and got distracted by a pretty girl, causing him to leave the pump in the tank and his coffee on the roof. When he drove off, the coffee spilled down the windshield before he heard the loud noise of the petrol hose breaking from the station. He walked past the pretty girl with his head down and the broken hose in his hand.

I can't believe I told him the story about when my friend Maggie fell asleep at our college library while studying. She had her head on the desk and legs crisscrossed in her chair. When she realized she was late for class, she quickly got up and ran toward the door, oblivious that her legs had fallen asleep. After a few steps, she collapsed and her books flew all over the floor while she lay there paralyzed and unable to get up. A good looking guy came to help her, but apparently she had lost feeling in her whole lower body and started farting uncontrollably. Thanks to the booze, I acted out the story as I told it. We were both laughing so hard, I'm impressed I didn't fart in the midst of telling it.

It was 2:00 am, and we had closed down another place. We walked through Temple Bar and before we wandered onto the Ha'Penny Bridge, he grabbed my hand. Despite the liquid courage, I was nervous. I needed to break the silence, so I awkwardly asked, "So, how did the Ha'Penny Bridge get its name?"

He pulled hard at my hand, forcing me to turn into him. He grabbed my other hand and backed me up against the ledge of the bridge.

"I don't care about this bridge except for that I'm going to kiss you on it." He put one hand on my face and the other slowly followed. He held a deep stare and I tried to keep my breath slow, unlike my racing heart. At the perfect moment – just before it felt uncomfortable – he pulled my face to his. We were the only people in all of Dublin, there on the Ha'Penny Bridge, kissing. I had to remember to breathe.

We walked around the quiet city streets for another hour, stopping often to make out like teenagers. We were laughing and holding hands the entire time. Everything was funny, everything was right. He hailed a taxi for me and kept it waiting for a while as he told me what a great time he'd had. After another make out session, I was in the back seat, mentally recapping the night. Just as I was wondering if he felt the same way, I received a text from him asking if I was free the next night.

Oh yeah, he felt the same way.

TEN
June 2013

The weeks after our first date flew by. Aidan and I were inseparable. Everything seemed to be better; the sun didn't set before 9:00 pm and everyday was warm and dry. We'd meet after work at Merrion Square, Stephen's Green or the lawn at Trinity and talk for hours. He'd tell me the history of Ireland – the Celtic invasion, the potato famine, the fight for independence from the Brits and 'The Troubles' in the north. I felt guilty for never having known any of it. I figured my school curriculum focused mainly on American history and his focused on Irish and European history – made sense. He told me what it was like in Dublin during the economic boom of the Celtic Tiger era. Back then, his dad had opened his own business; he and his friends had spent money like it was water. Everyone he knew was buying a house and things were good. With the recession that followed (and that the country was still recovering from), his dad lost the business, the friends went underwater with their homes and that's when Aidan went to school to become a barrister. I loved listening to his stories.

We'd wander the city and people watch. We had a game where we'd scope out someone and make up a background story for them – couples having an awkward first date were the best victims. He took me to new restaurants, pubs and hangouts – most of which even my Irish friends hadn't heard of. Other than with Brad, I was never really comfortable with P.D.A., but Aidan and I didn't walk anywhere without our hands interlocked, frequently stopping to kiss. He'd sit on the same side of the table as me which was more to embarrass me after I told him I thought it was odd when couples did that. He was silly like that, I loved it.

One time when we were walking on College Green, we saw someone had put soap in the fountain, causing mounds and mounds of bubbles to overflow so it looked like the statues in and around it were causing mayhem. He couldn't resist covering my face with an armful of the suds. When I tried to get him back, a foam war broke out between us in the heart of the city. It ended with us passionately kissing as the passengers of the open top Viking Splash Tour bus oohed and ahhed as it drove by.

Those first few weekends, Aidan would plan all of our dates – none of which involved sleepovers. Although he couldn't keep his hands off me, he didn't seem like he was in a rush to get me to bed – an uncommon trait in American men. I decided it was either very respectful or just an Irish thing, but either way it was nice to take it slow in that area.

We went to an exhibition at the Ambassador Theatre, an Irish craft beer festival, and a couple of music gigs at quirky venues like The Twisted Pepper and the basement of an art gallery. I was seeing the city beyond the lively pub scene.

I don't know if during that first month I fell in love with *Aidan*, but I'm certain that's when I fell in love with *Dublin*. It was the beginning of my love affair with *both*.

It was a Friday night – two days shy of one month since our first date (Who keeps track of that? I do.). I was catching up with Simon and Orla over pints at The Bernard Shaw. I hadn't been out with either of them since Aidan came into the picture, and I was especially anxious to hear how Simon's online dating was going. He was telling us all about Merrick, the guy he had been messaging with on his dating website. Orla and I were super impressed with the pictures. He was pretty much a European Abercrombie model with dark features and the biggest, brightest smile. The pictures of him shirtless on a beach were pure eye candy. Simon lit up telling us everything he'd found out about the gorgeous man's life story. Merrick was half Portuguese, half British and grew up in Leeds, so they had the UK connection. He'd been living in Dublin for a couple of years. He was an entrepreneur – some tech start-up thing. In between the whiskeys, Simon read some of their messages from the previous weeks.

"See? He's smart and interesting – not just a pretty face. Oh and he's 6'2"; I've never dated someone that tall!" he said with wide eyes. Orla quickly reminded Simon that most guys would be tall compared to him as he's *maybe* 5'4"… and that's with styling wax in his hair and dress shoes on.

"When are you guys going to meet in person?" I asked. "You don't want a pen pal, certainly not one that lives in the same small city." He explained that Merrick was in Portugal for work for the next two weeks, but they would meet up for a date when he was back in Dublin.

"Well, definitely keep us posted!" I said. Orla concurred before butterflying over to a group of people she knew, leaving Simon and me to talk about Aidan. I hadn't mentioned to Orla I was seeing him; I wanted to keep it hush-hush mainly to avoid a daily round of questioning at work.

"I was looking for a reason not to like Aidan when I met him the other night, but I couldn't find one. I mean, he's no Ryan Reynolds, but when he said he loves Hot Chip, I totally wanted to jump his bones." He said it so casually, as if he were stating that he liked the color blue and not that that he wanted to molest my boyfriend. "It's bloody disgusting how adorable you two are together, but I have my eye on him... you're my girl, J. D."

"Don't worry, you'll always be my 'one-life stand'," I said, making the cheesy reference to a Hot Chip song. "But yeah, he's a keeper." I smiled.

"And what is Prince Charming up to tonight?"

"He's out with the guys; it's one of their birthdays. He asked me to come out and meet all of them, but I don't want to be that girl who crashes a guys' night."

"Oh, please! Your skinny ass would out-drink them and they'd fall in love with you too," he said, squeezing my knee.

"Knock it off! I see what you did there with that use of *too*!" I pushed him back.

* * * * *

The next day, Aidan was coming to pick me up at 4:00 pm. We were going to see a movie at the Lighthouse Cinema, just next to his apartment building and then he was going to make dinner for me. I could get there on my own – the red line stopped at Smithfield, just outside of his complex, but he insisted on coming to get me. We had been texting about the logistics:

Me: *Either chivalry is not dead or it's a plan for a sleepover... ;)*

Aidan: *You caught me. There will be a lot of wine involved so I can't drive you home and you're not taking the red line at night...*

I smiled and blushed. He followed with:

Aidan: *But I'll call you a taxi if that's what you choose...*

I knew I was not going to take a cab home. I wanted to stay the night; I just didn't want to rush things by sleeping with him. I'd tackle that bridge when I got there. I responded with only a link to the Dean Martin and Helen O'Connell song: "How D'Ya Like Your Eggs in the Morning?" To which he promptly responded:

Aidan: *You never cease to amaze me missus. I can't wait to see you.*

I went for a run before getting ready. I purposely didn't shave my legs – figured that would help enforce my decision not to put out if I found myself in a moment of weakness.

I tried calling Mom – no response. Tried Dad – nothing. Weird. I hadn't spoken to either of them in over a week and when I looked at our text history, I had only received a short response from Mom three days prior. There was a time, in college, when I'd be annoyed talking to my parents once a week, but as I got older – and especially while in another country – I wanted to talk to them every day. I could call them and tell them what I ate for breakfast and they'd be genuinely interested. I had taken it for granted how they'd always answer my calls no matter what time of day or night it was. Maybe they had other stuff going on and I was always too busy talking about myself to give them a chance to tell me? The more I tried to rationalize why I couldn't get a hold of them, the more worried I became. I sent them both a text message asking them to call me ASAP.

It wasn't until 3:15 pm – just before Aidan was coming – that my mom finally called.

"Mom! What's going on? Where have you been?!"

"Hi, peeps. Sorry, just been real busy here. What are you doing? How's Aidan?"

My mom couldn't lie to save her life. My dog died when I was away in college. She would awkwardly change the subject every time I asked how he was doing. I knew for months, but she never told me until I went home for Thanksgiving. I asked her, "Where's Peanut?" and even then she didn't say it. She just pointed to an urn on the mantle and started to cry. It was wrong on many levels.

"Mom, tell me what's going on. You're keeping something from me and it's not fair when I'm so far away." All I heard in response was a sniffle and my heart sank.

With a cracked voice, she stuttered, "Umm, well, your dad…" and trailed off.

I felt sick. I grabbed my dining table and sat on the sofa, my stomach in knots.

"Dad was in a car accident on Wednesday." My eyes filled with tears.

"AND?! Is he okay?! Where is he? I want to talk to him now!" I shouted.

"He's going to be alright. They're keeping him in the hospital to make sure, but he's okay. He was really lucky, Jess." I'd never been more relieved than I was at that moment. I can't imagine what I'd do if anything happened to either one of them. I wanted to teleport home to Florida. What was I doing so far away from my family?

"Why didn't you tell me earlier? I'm so mad at you!" I said, crying and repeating, "I'm so mad at you!"

"We didn't want to tell you until he was out of the hospital. We didn't see a reason to worry you when you were so far away and we knew he'd be okay."

"Didn't see a reason to tell me?! So we're just going to keep stuff from each other now?! I'm booking a flight home tomorrow; I want to see my dad."

"This is exactly why we didn't want to tell you, Jessie. Dad is fine; we're all a little shook up, but he's going to be alright. You can Skype him in a few days and see for yourself. Don't you dare come home," she protested.

She kept saying 'we', which really stung. The whole family knew what had happened and was there in the hospital with my dad except for me. Maybe I wasn't where I was supposed to be after all?

"Okay. I'm sorry for yelling. You promise he's alright?"

"I promise. He'll be out better than new. Honey, we just want you to enjoy your time over there and make the most of it. Stop trying to be in two places at once. Have fun with Aidan and don't feel guilty about it, got it?"

"Got it. But if I can't talk to Dad by Monday morning, I'm coming home."

* * * * *

I tried to calm myself down before Aidan came to pick me up. When he did, it was in a black Audi A5 which looked pretty damn new. Even though we had been dating for a few weeks, I didn't know what kind of car he drove because there wasn't a need for it in the city – we'd always walk or take public transport.

Aidan had just gotten off the phone with *his* mom and supposedly she was dying to meet me. He told me she wouldn't let him hang up until he agreed to a day when he'd bring me over. He was smiling, alternating his head between looking at the road and at me.

I turned toward him in my seat.

"Why, Mr. McGovern, whatever did you tell your mother to make her so anxious to meet me?"

"Awk, I think she was getting worried that I always spend my weekends with Killian. Oh… and she loves that you're American." He changed his voice to imitate either his mother or Richard Simmons and carried on, "I know most people think Americans are insincere when they say 'Have a nice day,' but I think they really, really just want you to have a nice day! God bless them for that!" He was bobbing his head and shimmying his shoulders to really play up the impression of his mom. I laughed hysterically while he continued, "Bring Jessica over so I can get out the photo albums, and I'll make my famous raspberry buns!" He then switched back to normal Aidan voice and explained the raspberry buns were purchased off the shelf from the Tesco supermarket. She heats them in the oven and sprinkles powdered sugar on top before calling them her own.

I debated whether or not I should share the conversation I had with my mom. I decided not to – I didn't want to kill the mood. I also didn't want to bring up the reminder that I was in Dublin on borrowed time.

"I told her I needed to discuss it with you first – what do you say? Will you come meet my parents and sisters?" he asked.

"The sisters too?! Oh, the pressure!" I laughed. "Of course, I can't wait to meet them." I smiled, but I was thinking about my dad, wishing we could go to *my* parents' house for dinner. At the red light, he took his hand from the stick shift and grabbed mine. He leaned over to kiss me, which brought me back to the moment.

After the Lighthouse Cinema, we went back to his place. We saw an old screening of *Citizen Kane*. He suggested it after poking fun at how few American classic films I had seen.

His apartment was very clean and certainly the most modern I had been to in Dublin. Killian was visiting a friend in Munich for a week, so we had the place to ourselves. He put on a record, handed me a glass of wine and went to work away in the kitchen. I was surprised to hear one of my favorite songs, "Try Me" begin to play.

"James Brown? Major brownie points there, Mr. McGovern," I said, walking over to sit on a stool at the kitchen island. "I've been to a lot of good gigs in Dublin, but I noticed there isn't a big soul scene. Same with country music, but I guess I was expecting that one."

"Yeah, we wouldn't be big on country music; that's completely an American thing, but there's plenty of R&B – I'll show you." He paused from chopping zucchini, or courgettes as they're called in Ireland, to smile at me.

"Looking forward to it," I said. "But, you know, there's some really good country I think you'd like. The classics are the best – Patsy Cline, Johnny Cash, Wanda Jackson, Elvis... you know, before the war," I said puffing out my cheeks and curving my arms to imitate fat Elvis. "There's great country artists today too – Keith Urban, Kenny Chesney, Garth Brooks... you'd like Jason Aldean; he's kind of rocker-ish. Guess *I'll* have to show *you*," I teased.

He laughed and shook his head. "Ah, I'm too much of a music snob – I know good music, and country isn't good music. Lucky for me, you can't drag me to a country concert in Ireland because there aren't any; no one here would ever buy tickets to a country concert!"

The pasta and the chicken were both overcooked, but I ate all of it. It had been a long time since someone cooked for me, and he really went out of his way. After dinner, we opened a second bottle of wine and sat on opposite ends of the sofa with our legs tangled in one another's. He kept trying to tickle my feet and I'd pull away laughing. I hate having my feet touched, even during pedicures – which I really needed one at that time.

"So tell me about your religious views," he blurted, causing me to choke on my wine.

What the fuck?! What a topic, especially considering he's probably Irish Catholic or at least comes from a family that is, and I'm definitely not. It never really mattered to me what someone's religion was, but it hadn't occurred to me that he probably did care. I thought to myself: here goes nothing...

"Well, don't tell my parents this, but... I'm not trying to get into heaven." Oops, that sounded kind of slutty. "What I mean is... when I do good, I feel good and when I do bad, I feel bad. I want to be a good person because I truly believe it makes for a better life, not because I'm trying to get into heaven." I could have gone off on a tangent there, but decided to just soften it with, "...but I think it's beautiful when someone is devoted to their religion, as long as they're peaceful about it; organized religion just isn't for me." I nervously waited for his reaction.

"Very good," he said, nodding as if I had just spelled a word correctly at a spelling bee. "I feel the same way. You're just full of surprises, aren't you? Sorry to be blunt, but it's important to make sure there isn't a big disagreement there." I figured it was a good sign he wanted to be so direct about such a fundamental subject. We stayed on the topic and discussed how our beliefs had evolved and changed as we got older and what inspired those shifts. I told him how my views really shifted when I took a Greek mythology class in college (leaving out how that class also inspired me to take up a second degree in philosophy). Learning about all the ridiculous stories of the Greek gods on Mount Olympus – like Zeus, who morphed into an animal to impregnate women, was the explanation for most things the Greeks couldn't explain. What's with all that lightening tonight? Zeus must be angry. That's when I started to think that all religions were essentially a compilation of stories – beautiful stories but made up nonetheless. I had never shared that with anyone in fear of them thinking I was an empty atheist, but Aidan seemed to get it… and to agree.

We covered a lot of other topics that would typically be seen as 'off limits' for a brand new relationship. He asked me my views on the death penalty, euthanasia and what my thoughts were on kids using iPads and other technology at a young age. He let me do most of the talking as he listened intently, nodding at my rambling answers. On several occasions, I joked about feeling like I was on a job interview.

"Look, Jess, I'm almost 33… I want to know the *real* stuff," he said, looking me in the eye. "I like you; I want to know everything about you and as soon as possible. Does that make sense?" he asked.

"Yes. It does," I answered honestly. He wouldn't be asking me these things if he didn't see it going somewhere, and that made me feel better about opening up.

At one point, we were talking about adoption (not together, just in general). I talked about my friend Maggie, who was adopted. I wasn't going to volunteer my desire to adopt one day – how it was my dream to have a house full on Christmas day with tons of grandchildren of all nationalities. As much as I wanted to open up, it was too deep of a confession after only a few weeks of dating. Just after I decided not to bring up adoption, *he* confessed that *he* wanted to adopt one day. I sort of nodded and smiled awkwardly but remained silent. I imagined how much of a psycho I'd sound like if I said that I did too. *Oh my God, I want to adopt too! How perfect are we for each other?!* rang in my head as I sipped my wine instead.

Hours passed and I stumbled through at least five more blunt questions. Aidan came back from the kitchen with the third bottle of wine. He set it on the coffee table and extended his hand for me to stand up. The song "I Want You So Bad" had just begun. The wine hit me when I stood up. We were dancing and he was singing the words, well, some of them. Our conversation (and the wine) made it easy for me to bring up the sleepover rules. "So, I don't want to make this weird, but..."

He interrupted, "Uh oh, there's a but..."

"No, no, no. Look, Aidan... I'm crazy about you and I want to stay the night and all, but... I'm just not ready to..."

"Stop." He put his finger to my lips. "You don't need to say another word. I'm glad you brought it up; yet another way you impress me." He twirled me around and dipped me. "Now that that's out in the open, we can relax." He kissed me and we sat back on the sofa. "I have shorts and a T-shirt you can wear and I promise I won't try to take them off you," he said, smiling as he poured us more wine.

"Well, just not tonight." I made an exaggerated 'WINK WINK' gesture. Maybe a little too much exaggeration, dammit! "Thanks, Aidan." I leaned over, grabbed his face and kissed him hard. It quickly turned into a hot make out session until...

"Ouch! I think I cut my hand on your legs," he joked as he rubbed my prickly legs.

"Oh, you jerk!" Jeez, if I wasn't going to put out, I could have at least shaved my legs up to the knee.

The next morning I had a terrible headache from all the wine. Aidan got me water and Panadol and made an ice pack with his T-shirt. He rubbed my back until I fell back asleep.

I woke to him banging around in the kitchen. I still felt a bit hung over, but a million times better than earlier, so I went out to him.

"Good morning," he said, giving me a kiss. "Why don't you get back in bed and I'll bring you coffee? Soya milk and cinnamon – no sugar – right, missus?"

"Impressive," I replied. We had only been for coffee a couple of times together.

"I pay close attention to you," he said, smiling. "Oh, your phone was beeping earlier but I turned the volume off so it didn't wake you." He handed me my phone and personalized coffee. I unlocked the phone, relieved to see a message from my dad:

Dad: *Hi Sweetie! I'm OK, don't you worry your pretty little face. I'm gonna be around to see my baby conquer the world! Talk soon, LU.*

I had also received a picture from Lindsay. I shrieked in excitement when I opened it.

"What is it?" Aidan asked.

"Lindz got her passport! Look!" I showed him the picture of her holding it up next to her face with a big cheesy smile.

"Brilliant! So she'll come soon, aye?"

"Yeah, next time we talk, we'll figure out when exactly."

"Speaking of… I have two weeks off in September. You reckon you could take your holidays at the same time and we could plan a trip together?"

He asked in way that made it obvious he had been thinking about it. Was he oblivious to the fact that we had only been dating for about two seconds, or that I was supposed to go back to America in September? I was almost certain I had told him the timeline. Nonetheless, I was flattered he wanted to plan a long trip with me and almost three months from then.

I smiled and said, "Yeah, I'd like that."

ELEVEN
July 2013

One month and about 15 sleepovers later, Aidan was picking me up near Merrion Square after work on a Friday. We were going to meet his family. To me, it was a much bigger deal than when we first had sex. Things began to move fast, much faster than it had ever moved for me before, but it felt right.

He had already started to let the stubble grow in for the weekend and had the top three buttons of his light blue shirt undone with the sleeves rolled up. His tie was thrown on the center console.

"You look great; I like your casual Friday look, missus," he said, splitting his attention between the road and me.

"Thanks. You don't look too bad yourself, hot stuff," I said as I leaned in for another kiss which didn't go as smoothly as I had planned. I thought he had seen me coming towards him, but he hadn't. So, when he turned to say something, I was right in his face with puckered lips. He decided to be funny by leaving me hanging there like that.

He gave me a 'what are you doing?' look. I erupted in laughter.

"You jerk! You like making me feel awkward, huh?" I teased.

"So I do," he laughed. "Ah, but the look on your face! I love making you laugh, missus," he said, leaning in for a bona fide kiss at the stop sign. I tucked my right leg underneath my left as I asked, "So this a good meeting-the-family outfit?" I had on dark blue skinny pants and a basic gray t-shirt, pulled together with a khaki blazer and the leopard ballet flats Lindsay got for me.

"You look great; you always look great. But don't worry about that stuff; they're going to love you," he said, smiling. Damn, that's *love* twice in two minutes, I noticed. "But I do apologize ahead of time for dinner. Hide it in your napkin, push it on to my plate, give it to the dog – whatever you need to do. We'll get kebabs on the way home, erm, back to yours."

"Ah, stop! I'm excited for my first Irish mum-cooked meal and... you don't have a dog!"

We parked outside a lovely home in Clontarf, a few boroughs north-east of the City Centre.

"What do you have there?" Aidan asked, looking at the covered dish I had pulled out of my over-sized navy bag.

"Just a little something I made. It's rude to go to someone's home for dinner and not bring something," I replied.

"You are very good. And very American," he said, playfully. He put his hand on the small of my back and opened the door, nudging me to go in first.

"Maaaaaa! We're here!" he shouted. There was loud rustling and banging in the kitchen and we looked at each other with wide eyes and tried not to laugh.

"Ooooh!" she shrieked as she emerged from a doorway, taking off her bright yellow rubber cleaning gloves. She raised her arms and made a beeline toward me. "It's so good to have you, dear! Come, come make yourself comfortable – Aidan, take her jacket," she said in between the kisses she planted on my cheeks. "You two must be *absolutely wrecked* from the drive – and coming straight from a long day of work!"

I silently laughed at the thought of being 'wrecked' from the seven or eight kilometer drive. Although, it was about 45 minutes due to the traffic of the tiny, one-lane each way roads – still, not going to 'wreck' us.

"It's so nice to meet you, Mrs. McGovern; thank you for having me over. Aidan mentioned you always serve cake, or I mean buns, after dinner. So, I made my mom's favorite sweet treat. It's famous in St. Louis where she's from. I hope you like it." I handed her the dish. I had gone to Dunnes to buy the baking dish as the only one I owned had baked-on residue.

"Oh! Bless your heart! You are *actually* the sweetest little thing! We'll have it tonight," she said, taking the dish from me. "Aidan – a girl that can cook, aye?" She winked at him. "But please, call me Barbara, dear."

"Or Babs. She likes it when people call her Babs – don't you, Babsy?" Aidan teased. She rolled her eyes at him.

"It's called gooey butter cake. It's really easy to make; there are only a few ingredients. I wrote a recipe card for you there." Shit! I hoped that didn't come off as: So I heard you suck at cooking and might need a basic, fool-proof recipe. Good one, Jessica, insult her before you've passed through the foyer.

"Ah, you're very good! Come; let's get you a cuppa tea." I would have much preferred a bottle of wine.

"That'd be great. Can I help you with anything?" I asked.

"Ah no, pet – it's gammon; it basically cooks itself. You just sit right here and tell me *all* about yourself," she said, putting my cake next to a package of Tesco raspberry jam filled rolls – her 'famous raspberry buns' that Aidan had told me about. "Aidan, you're getting too skinny; there isn't a pick on ya!" Babs pinched his waist. It was funny because skinny wasn't a word I'd use to describe Aidan's tall, average build.

"Hiya! So Aidan is finally bringing one of his girls home, aye?" Emma said loudly, opening the cupboard and reaching up. Pieces from her messy brown bun fell into her overly made up eyes as she poured two glasses of wine. "You're much prettier than he let on, and your teeth... they're so white!" she said, walking toward me. Although her introduction really caught me off guard, I wanted to hug her when I realized the other glass of wine was for me. It's not a proper meeting of the family if you're not caught off guard or feeling awkward – in that case, things were off to a good start.

Aidan must have dated a lot and told his family about his ladies but hadn't brought many around. That was in line with what he had insinuated to me, so I wasn't too bothered by it. In fairness, I was the same. I had only ever introduced my parents to Brad and one other guy, despite the handfuls of 'relationships' I had been in.

"Ah, you're very kind," I laughed. "I just got prettied up to meet you all."

"Don't be daft. Now Aidan, he's usually a slob. I still can't get over seeing him in an ironed shirt; it's actually so unnatural," she joked.

Kate walked in and quietly introduced herself. She was shy, even more so than Aidan had described. Her light freckles complimented her small face and strawberry blond hair. It was crazy that she and Emma were sisters; they were like night and day. The three McGovern women were all fussing over me – asking me questions and poking fun at Aidan. When he saw I was relaxed and could handle the girl talk, he left to go find his dad.

I really liked his family. At dinner, they all had a lot of questions, so I didn't get to eat much of the overdone, bland meat Babs had made. Kate was talking about the Marian Keyes book she was reading, called *Sushi for Beginners*. I'll never forget the look Aidan gave me when I told her that I had just read *Under the Duvet*. He was surprised because he knew that I had just started *Secret Speech*, the second book of the Tom Rob Smith trilogy, and that I don't read Chick Lit. I'd picked the book up from Dubray a few days after he asked me to meet his family. He mentioned on our first date that Kate was (a) hard to connect with and (b) obsessed with Chick Lit. On another date, he said that Marian Keyes was her favorite author and she had read all of her books. It was a way to strike up a conversation with her and was a nice, easy read.

At one point, Emma said something in Gaelic. Aidan's dad laughed and responded, also in Gaelic. Having no clue what they were saying, I smiled awkwardly and shoveled a bite of food in my mouth, taking advantage of the break from all their questions.

"Have you picked up any Irish words since you've been over here, Jessica?" Babs asked.

Ah, crap.

I knew *sláinte* was used to say 'cheers' although it really meant 'health', and I knew that *anseo* meant 'present', which I only knew because it was the name of a pub Simon and I often drank at. Think, Jessie, think! I tried to remember any other word that didn't have to do with drinking. Then I remembered... the Luas! The voice recording on the Luas said the name of each of the stops in Irish after saying them in English. From all the times I had taken the Luas into the City Centre, I knew I had one nailed.

"I know a few words here and there... some of the basics like Dublin and St. Stephen's Green." They looked at me with wide eyes, waiting for the delivery. I could hear the woman's voice from the Luas as I tried my damnedest to say it just as she did. I even added the gurgling phlegm sound and all: *Awk-stof-dare-nawk.*

I totally nailed it!

"That was perfect pronunciation, Jessica, well done," Babs complimented before awkwardly reaching for her wine. Everyone was exchanging glances with one another, except Aidan who was looking at me with a big grin.

He broke the silence, "Yeah, Jess... it *was* a great pronunciation. But what you just said was: *This is the last stop,*" he smirked. "St. Stephen's Green is *Faiche Stiabhna.*"

Fuuuck!

St. Stephen's Green *was* the last stop, but the bitch on the Luas recording said both – my brain retained the wrong part. I squeezed my eyes tightly and smacked my palm to my forehead, laughing. Everyone else joined in. Oh man, did they join in!

After dinner, we all gathered in the living room drinking tea and working through the entire dish of gooey butter cake. The electric kettle ran nonstop as we listened to Babs share stories of their annual family holidays to Kenmare and some of the genius ideas Aidan and Philip came up with to raise money to save the family dog, Luke. Luke was old and needed an expensive surgery that couldn't be rationalized. The boys went door to door selling Babs' (store bought) cookies, offering to pick weeds, take out trash, anything. When that wasn't raising the big bucks, they decided to try and sell the girls, who were two and four years old at the time. Babs got a call from one of the neighbors explaining that Emma and Kate were on the market for 100 quid – which included a knapsack they had packed with their clothes. It was very entertaining watching all of them interact. Aidan and Emma took after Babs – extroverts who spoke with their hands and facial expressions as much as they did with their mouths. Kate was their father's child. John was quiet and mild-mannered. He sat back and happily let Babs take center stage. I saw a gentle kindness in him that reminded me of my dad. He didn't say much, but I could tell he was a good man.

When it was time to say goodbye, giving the McGoverns hugs and kisses didn't feel awkward at all. It felt like I had been there many times before and knew them all very well. Babs repeated multiple times that I should come back again soon and told Aidan not to let me get away. During the goodbyes, Kate had run upstairs to her room to get *This Charming Man,* one of the novels she recently finished reading. I told her I'd read it straight away and get it back to her, along with *A Thousand Splendid Suns* which was one of my favorite books. While Aidan was arguing about the length of his hair with Babs, Kate suggested we go for lunch in a couple of weeks to exchange and discuss the books. That was my favorite part of the evening.

On the drive back to my apartment, Aidan told me he wanted to show me something. He was explaining Bull Run, the little island not far from his parents' neighborhood that had a golf course on it. I found it weird that they play golf on a relatively small island; wouldn't they lose a ton of balls? I'm sure that was considered in the design and I wasn't coming up with a new concept, so I didn't say it out loud.

"There's a nice view along the Dollymount strand. We'll come back and go running together – you'd love it."

"If you can keep up," I teased. We turned from the main road onto a small access road that allowed us onto the island. A rickety wooden bridge was straight ahead; so narrow that only one car could cross at a time. Aidan pulled off to the side to let the oncoming car cross before we took our turn – this was typical all over in Ireland, even in the 'big city' of Dublin.

"And that's us, just there on the wooden bridge, so we are," he said. I made fun of him for the Irishism overload and repeated the hangnail phrase, "So we are."

Once we crossed, he parked and we got out of the car. As we walked on the bridge, it started to lightly drizzle, but neither of us said anything about it. He pointed out the statue at the end of the run called the Star of the Sea, which was funded by port workers in honor of one of the archbishops. He pointed out Dublin Port, and far, far out in the distance, the faint light shining was Dun Laoghaire.

"We'll go there one lazy weekend; it's close to your place – we can cycle out there."

I didn't feel it necessary to tell him I had cycled to Dun Laoghaire several times before.

"You have a lot of things on the agenda for us, don't you mister?"

"You have no idea." He faced toward me, sandwiching me between him and the railing. "How much time do I have?"

"A couple of months max. My visa expires on September 1st, but there's some time after that where I'm allowed to stay without a visa," I tried to explain.

"See now, that's a problem… I'm going to need *at least* ten months to show you everything I have on the list – and that's just the stuff here in Ireland."

"Hmmm. That is a problem, isn't it?"

"Look, Jessica," he interlocked his fingers with mine. "I'm not very good with this sort of stuff, but … I think you are very special; no one has ever made me feel the way you do. Every time we're together, I find new reasons to adore you." I smiled while awkwardly losing and regaining eye contact. I hoped he wasn't going to say the 'L' word so soon. The first time Brad told me he loved me, I accidentally blurted out, "Awe, thank you!" without reciprocating.

"What I'm trying to say is… don't go back to America yet." He grabbed my face and looked into my eyes. It reminded me of our first kiss on the Ha'Penny Bridge. "Stay longer. Stay with me… please?"

Of course I had thought about it. The truth was, I had already thought about extending my contract even before Aidan came into the picture. But with my dad's accident, the upcoming holidays, my friends' weddings, babies being born and so many other milestones I was missing out on… I did miss home. Plus, I knew Lindsay and Jason were either going to break up or get engaged soon – I wanted to be there for her either way. I *was* ready to go back at the end of August… until Aidan came along. Then, being with him became the only thing that mattered.

"Okay." I nodded firmly. "I'll have to convince my bosses, but I think I can extend it another year." I was surprised at how sure I felt after saying it out loud.

"Really?!" he said, excited.

"Really!" I was smiling like crazy. "But you better not let me down with this agenda of yours," I joked.

Holding both my hands, he brought my left hand to his chest and said, "I cross my heart; I promise." I smiled at the endearing, child-like gesture. He squeezed my hands tightly and kissed me for a long time on the rickety bridge.

TWELVE
August 2013

Another month flew by, it was more than infatuation. Aidan continued showing me parts of Dublin I would have never seen otherwise. In the mornings, down side streets, we'd stop and chat with the delivery men in their small vans bringing fresh goods to the restaurants and pubs. We'd stroll around the city wearing sunglasses and holding an umbrella. We laughed a lot. We'd go from intense talks about the meaning of life to imitating chimpanzees at the flip of a switch.

The best dates were the ones where we'd sit along the canal, drinking cans of beer and talking for hours. It didn't get dark till after 10:00 pm, so we'd often grab dinner from a Chipper and take it back to my place. The brown paper bag of greasy, fried cod and thick-cut chips smothered in vinegar and salt was the best dinner. It was a good thing I didn't claim I was a foodie on our first date when he asked.

During one of those canal-side date nights, Aidan was telling me about going to school in Dublin and how he became a barrister. It was a welcome change to hear him talk about himself versus the rapid-fire interview questions he liked to ask me. The school system is very different in Ireland. They have primary school and secondary school – no middle school. I didn't have much of an explanation for why we have an entirely separate school for only three years, other than that those are the worst three years ever. Kids aged 11 to 14 who are going through puberty are punks and should be segregated from the children in elementary as well as the almost-adults in high school. Clearly, I'm still scarred from my middle school experience. I remember the dorky Wal-Mart clothes and shoes my parents made me wear to school. Aidan didn't have to worry about that because every school in Dublin requires uniforms. I told him how my parents wouldn't let me get blonde highlights, so I had no choice but to do it myself with peroxide. Then, I was the nerd with splotchy orange cheetah hair eating lunch alone. Fuck middle school. It wasn't until sophomore year of high school that I became somewhat cool, thanks to making the varsity track and field team. I had to explain what varsity and junior varsity were to Aidan because they don't have the same emphasis on sports in school as we do. He explained that Irish schools don't play competitive sports against other schools.

After secondary school, he went on to Uni (i.e. college), which is pretty much fully funded by the government, so he didn't have to stress about scholarships or student loans. While he was at UCD – University College of Dublin – he studied commerce. It was fascinating to talk about the differences in Irish and American colleges. University students in Ireland study whatever they want; it doesn't have to be focused the profession they're aiming for. He could have studied natural science those four years, just as long as he passed his law exams whenever he went to take them. It was so different from America, where you'd have to take a big law exam (LSATs) after four years of political science or something similar just to get accepted into law school. After two years of studying nothing but law and taking out $100,000 in loans, you'd start studying for the bar exam, hoping to land an internship. Our grueling process probably has something to do with the fact that Americans are so eager to sue – a mentality that thankfully hadn't made its way to Ireland.

"I always wanted to be the best at everything I did," Aidan said. "When I played football, soccer to you, I was obsessed with being the best on my team. It's a bit of a character flaw, because when I realized I wasn't the best was right around the time I quit," he said, putting his head down. "I had to get the best apprenticeship and join the best law firm in Dublin, I wouldn't accept anything less. I can see that in you too, Jessie. You don't strike me as the type to settle for mediocrity."

It was a compliment and it was something I liked hearing. So why then did it turn my stomach in to knots? Maybe it was because he thought I was the best for him?

"Let's go to Morocco," he blurted. "Did you get annual leave approved for the week I have mine? It's the week before a bank holiday, so we could get away for ten days. Morocco has been at the top of my bucket list for a long time, but I didn't want to go on my own," he said, sipping from the can. "What's on your bucket list?" he asked.

"Well, I've only ever been to London with Simon, but I want to see everywhere in Europe. It's hard to put them in order because there are so many places I want to visit. When I took this gig in Dublin, I was most excited to visit Spain. My grandma lived just outside of Madrid for sixteen years and I loved to hear her stories about it. After Spain, I guess it'd be Rome and maybe Paris – the quintessential charming European capitals."

"Ehh, they're not that great. Not that much different from Dublin – it's still Europe and all the big cities speak English, so there's not much of a culture shock," he said, crapping on my bucket list. "But Morocco... Morocco will be completely different. Something new – somewhere that neither of us has been. It's our first trip; it should be really special. What do you say?"

I couldn't point Morocco out on a map, but I knew I liked Moroccan spiced couscous from Tesco and that my Irish boyfriend wanted to go there with me – that was all I needed to know.

"Okay, Morocco it is," I nodded.

"Really?! This is great! It's going to be an adventure!" He kissed me just as the rain drops started to fall on us. We kept kissing. The rain picked up and within minutes we were drenched. It wasn't until I smelled – and tasted – the hops that I realized he was pouring his can of beer on top of my head.

"Oh, you think you're funny, huh?" I grabbed an unopened can and shook it. He tried to get up and run away, but I opened the top in time, spraying his face before he could escape.

He laughed as he tackled me to the ground, pinning me on the dirt and kissing me hard.

"See? I really am falling for you, missus," he said as I held his head with both my hands.

"No... you're not falling for me," I grabbed his face. "You're falling with me."

We walked back to my apartment soaked in beer, holding hands. We no sooner turned onto my street when the black cat emerged and started weaving in and out between our feet.

"This cat is so creepy, don't you think? I feel like she's going to steal my soul if I look her in the eyes for too long," I said before explaining I wasn't much of a cat person.

"Ah, I reckon she just wants some attention. She looks like Cleopatra with those slanty eyes." He was right; she did look like a Cleopatra.

"That suits her. Cleopatra she is," I nodded at him. "Your sister told me about your family cat, Jinxy. She said you cried for weeks after Jinxy died. I wouldn't have pegged you for a cat person," I teased as we entered my apartment building.

"I'm going to have to put a squash on these lunch dates you've been having with Kate – you're finding out my deepest, darkest secrets," he said, tickling me.

"Ah come on, so you're an emotional cat lover – it's not like I found out you're a cheater or anything." I meant for it to be a joke in response to his 'darkest secrets' comment, but it flopped. He froze and looked at me startled as soon as I said it.

Shit. Maybe he was cheated on? Dammit, Jessie. I changed the subject quick.

"I gave her *The Little Coffee Shop of Kabul* on our lunch date last week – and she gave me this…" I held up *The Fault in our Stars* by John Green.

"That's supposed to be a real tear-jerker – my shoulder is here for you, missus," he joked. Project 'change the topic' was a success.

"It's really nice that you're spending time with Kate; it means a lot to her. It means a lot to me too. My family loves you," he said, taking the book from my hand and tossing it on the table. I was worried that he was going to say he loved me too. Instead, he lifted the wet t-shirt over my head and led me to the shower.

THIRTEEN

Early September 2013

Faiche Stiabhna... Is é seo an stad deireanach.

I laughed, thinking of the dinner with Aidan's family when the voice recording on the Luas informed the travelers that we had reached St. Stephen's Green... the last stop of the Luas.

I was meeting Simon in town for a catch up and some shopping. Even after being in Dublin for almost a year, I still loved walking down Grafton Street. Something about seeing the Stephen's Green park entrance and the cursive branding of Butler's coffee shop always made me say to myself, "I live in Ireland!" I loved the random street performers – my favorite is the guy with the sand sculpture. I wasn't sure whether it was meant to be a dog or a pig. I never asked because I wanted to avoid that awkward moment when he'd nod at the tray of coins next to the mystery animal.

"Dahling!" I heard Simon before he emerged from the crowd with both arms up. "Love the clogs! Are they new?" he asked, looking at my mustard colored ankle boots.

"Better than new. I've had 'em for ages, but they were packed away in my closet – only just pulled them out." He looked again in satisfaction before giving me a hug and kiss on both cheeks. I told him that even though he loved the mustard boots, I still wanted and needed to find my ultimate riding boots. He knew about the search for the boots and had a complete disregard for my criteria by always offering me stripper-looking boots to try on.

"I need to pick up the *Bangerz* album and then we'll find your boots." I loved that Simon still purchased CDs at the record store. I thought he had a great taste in music except for his obsession with Miley Cyrus. I rolled my eyes and locked my arm under his. "Fine; only because it's for you, Simon."

We walked and talked and laughed our way down the busy shopping street and into the record store. It wasn't even five minutes before he asked how Ken was. Simon often joked that I had transformed from 'Florida Barbie' to 'Irish Barbie' and that Aidan was my Ken doll.

"He's so good," I said, blushing. "And I got the final approval from my home office to stay another year, so… it's official!'

"Oh my God! This is the best news ever, J. D.! So is he like… The One?!"

I smiled nervously. "Maybe…"

I was crazy about Aidan, but I felt uncomfortable answering that question, especially since we had only been dating for four months. "He makes me feel like *I'm* The One for *him*. I don't have to second-guess his feelings. Even with this trip to Morocco… he's so excited and is planning everything. It feels too good to be true."

"I'm so jealous of your guys' trip! It sounds so exotic! But I thought you said Spain was on the top of your list of places to go… and Italy?! Didn't you move here to see romantic Europe? I don't think *romantic* is a term often used to describe Morocco." I laughed as we walked out of the record store and headed back toward Grafton.

"Yeah, but he said he'd already been to Spain and Italy and most of romantic Europe, and it'd be better to go somewhere neither of us had been. Since it's been on the top of his list, it made sense. I don't care where we go… it's all new and exciting to me!" Simon didn't look convinced as we walked, my arm still entwined with his. Only then did it occur to me that Aidan didn't really include me in choosing the trip destination decision. He knew where he wanted us to go and only had to do a little convincing.

"I can't believe I haven't asked yet – how was your date with Merrick?!" I wanted to squash any negative thoughts involving Aidan.

"Hmm, about that… We had a really good time. He was funny, sweet, the chemistry was there…"

"But?!" I pushed.

"But he wasn't who he was in his pictures! He's not tan or tall!" he said, making a face.

"What?! So the pictures online weren't of him?"

"They were him… like five years ago when he was super buff and tan because he was on holiday in Ibiza. He's still cute, I guess, but not hot like he was online. Oh! And his profile said 6'2" – in his dreams! I'd say he's 5'10" at best."

"Simon, that's still taller than me and I'm tall – it's certainly taller than you," I said, standing up straight beside him. My boots were off so I could try on a pair from the display.

"Yeah, he might have an inch or two on you."

"I'm confused… what's the problem? Since when do you care about height?" I asked, putting my own boots back on.

"I don't. I just feel deceived," he sighed. "I had this image of a dark and dreamy, tall glass of water. If I were expecting an average height Caucasian, I wouldn't have been disappointed." He picked up a sky-high wedge with crazy embellishments (i.e. stripper heels), insinuating he wanted me to try them on.

"Maybe you wouldn't have felt the same excitement if you *knew* he was an average height Caucasian." I gave my best 'chew on that' face. "Look, Simon, I'm not saying what he did was right, but he wanted to put the best version of himself out there – he just got carried away. If you had a good time with him, then I hope you reconsider."

"Ugh, I was expecting an Avatar when we stood up… but no."

"You know these boots I'm wearing, the ones you love so much?" I shoved my foot out. "I ordered them online in bronzed caramel, which was their fancy way of saying brown according to the picture online. Brown ankle boots would have matched everything. I was so pissed off when they arrived. Clearly this is not bronze or anything remotely in the brown family. They should have called it Plochman's Mustard, or whatever the main mustard brand is here, but you get the point." Simon smiled and rolled his eyes,

117

knowing where I was going with it. "However…" I continued, "I decided to give them a try and I ended up loving them. Surprisingly, they match almost anything that brown would have, but they give the outfits more color. Moral of the story? Give Merrick a chance."

"I don't think I would have liked your boots as much if they were boring brown."

"Exactly! Sometimes you don't know what you like until you try it."

"We're meeting up again tonight. I'll give it a try," he said, reluctantly.

We made our way back onto crowded Grafton Street. We stopped in Aldo where I was almost tempted to buy a pair of jazz shoes on sale but resisted. No luck with the riding boots. We wandered along, talking nonsense, mostly things we'd be embarrassed of if anyone overheard.

Simon interrupted himself, "Ooh, let's check out Oxfam; there's nothing like finding a hidden treasure in a second-hand store." I appreciated his enthusiasm in helping me find my riding boots.

We walked into the Oxfam on Kings Street and rummaged through the hanging pieces – some outrageous, some exquisite. We had made our way to the back of the store. Behind the mannequin in a 1920s flapper dress was a small section of shoes. We both made a beeline for the one pair of boots, slouched over in the corner.

Simon picked one of them up and I caught a whiff of the sweet smell of leather. The leg height was high – holding it next to me, it came to the middle of my knee. On first glance, they looked a rich brown, but up close, they had a hint of burgundy mixed in. It was subtle enough to make them unique but not so much that they wouldn't match the same things a dark brown boot would.

"J. D., these are FAB!" Simon said, inspecting them.

"They really are... and I love the bit of burgundy – I hadn't considered anything other than brown or black before."

"They're high fashion, yet no one would ever say to you, 'Wow! Look at your burgundy boots; you're so BOLD to wear them!'" Simon looked at the bottom of the sole. "300 quid – that's way less than any of the ones you've tried on and they're Michael Kors! They don't look like they've ever been worn."

Had we really just stumbled across the perfect pair of boots in a second-hand charity store? Being designer and costing less than any other pair I had looked at were added bonuses... it was too good to be true. I didn't have a budget in mind, but I was willing to spend a lot more than 300 euro on THE ultimate boots. Although, at that time, I was on a tight budget, especially with the Morocco trip and then Lindsay and Jason coming the week after we got back. I couldn't really manage an extra 300 euro that month, but there was no way I was going to let them go.

They didn't have any excessive zippers or embellishments, no awkward shape... just classic, well-crafted, beautiful riding boots with a bit of sass. "They are perfect – better than anything I had imagined. I must try them on!" That's when it occurred to me that the chances that the one pair would be in my size were slim.

The woman that worked there approached us as I looked for the size. "They're gorgeous, aren't they now? A posh woman from Ballsbridge brought them in last week along with a suitcase full of Brown Thomas dresses," she said in a mild Dublin accent.

"Wow, my closet clean-outs usually only produce bags of stained shirts that should not be donated," I joked. I saw the marking, UK 6.5, inside the top of the boot. "They're my size! It's fate!" I shrieked. I slipped my foot into the left boot with ease despite there being no zipper and with my... umm... cankle issue. There was the perfect amount of space between the boot and my jeans. I stood in front of the full-length mirror in the lone fitting room.

I loved them even more on. I turned to the left, turned to the right, looked from behind, walked toward the mirror and finished with a spin. Even with the outfit I was wearing, they looked fabulous. I was immediately obsessed – head over heels.

Simon hollered, "Work it, girl! Damn, J. D., you look ah-mazing! It's like you walked off the cover of a magazine!" I laughed and twirled again, absolutely loving everything about them. Simon snapped a couple of pictures of me on his phone while saying, "Hashtag shoe porn."

I imagined different outfits I could wear with them as I took the boots off, ready to buy.

"Alright, Irish Barbie, let's cash out and get a coffee. I need something disgustingly sweet too."

I laughed as I took the boots off. "Okay, okay. Can we go to Bewley's and sit upstairs on the terrace? I don't care how touristy it is."

"Fine with me, as long as they have really dirty cakes."

I took my burgundy boots up to the register, not feeling any buyer's remorse or hesitation whatsoever about the purchase. Except, when I went to pay, I realized I had left my wallet in my Pilates bag from that morning's class.

"Ah shit! This is so embarrassing, but I forgot my wallet – can I come back for them tomorrow?" I asked the sales woman. Simon pulled his wallet from his pocket.

"Don't worry about coming back for them; you're going to be with Aidan. Here..." he handed me his card.

"No, no. I appreciate it, but really I'd prefer to get them myself. Aidan's going to leave in the morning to watch the match with his friends, so I'll come into town. I need to get some other stuff anyways." I turned back to the sales woman. "I'm really sorry, I'll be back tomorrow."

"Ah sure, it's no bother. We're not supposed to, but I'll hold them for you in the back, will I not?" she said, in the typical Irish way of turning a statement into a question.

"Perfect! Thank you so much!" I said to her before grabbing Simon's arm. "You will have to pay for our Bewleys though, sugar daddy."

FOURTEEN

The next morning I was awoken by Aidan rubbing my bare back.

"Good morning," I said, smiling with my eyes still closed.

"Good morning, missus. Did you sleep well?"

"Mmm hmm," I nodded and scooted closer, and he kissed my forehead. I felt comfortable waking up to him. I didn't worry about whether or not my face was puffy, if my breath smelled or how pale I was.

"So, I was thinking about what we should do today... there's somewhere I want to take you."

I opened my eyes and propped my head on my hand.

"But I thought you were going to meet Killian and the guys in town for the match?"

"You're my priority now, not the match. I want to spend my day with you," he said, playing with my hair.

"So did the guys sell out on you, or was the game cancelled?" I joked.

"Ah, you think you're so funny, don't you?" He started tickling me. "How funny are you now, huh? Huh?"

"Gosh, now I can't spend the day shopping!" It just encouraged him to tickle more.

An hour later, I got up to make breakfast in nothing but underwear and socks because I couldn't stand walking on my sketch carpet barefoot. My tiny refrigerator had the staples: a mini carton of milk, hummus, a single yogurt, shredded cheese and a half carton of eggs. The hummus predated our relationship, so into the trash bin it went. The cheese passed the smell test, so cheesy scrambled eggs it was. The secret to making the perfect scrambled eggs was to add a splash of milk in the scrambled mixture before adding it to a medium-low heated pan. My mom told me the tips after I had sacrificed countless eggs to a scalding hot pan while in college. No matter how many times I messed up eggs, I never called my mom for advice – I always assumed I knew what went wrong and tried to fix it the next time (which I never did). At one point, I gave up making them on the stove and decided to make a dozen hard-boiled eggs. I googled how to do it and it seemed foolproof… or not. Apparently, you can't just dump them into the boiling pot straight from the refrigerator; they have to gradually heat up with the water. When the 20 minutes were up, I had a pot of cracked eggs with white mucus oozing from each of them. I still didn't want to call my mom and get lectured about how to cook eggs, so I didn't buy eggs for years. Funny how that changed – sometime after college, I started calling my mom all the time for domestic advice and I became quite the chef. The best recipe she ever gave to me is still that cauliflower soup!

After our breakfast in bed, we hit the road, driving to a destination I didn't know. It was a gorgeous day, perfect for getting out of the city. We were on the motorway for 20 minutes when he pointed out the big hills, the ones that could be seen from the city.

"That hill right there is called Sugarloaf because well… it looks like a sack of sugar I suppose." I just smiled, failing to see the resemblance to any formation of sugar. I would have said it looked like the downward-facing dog yoga pose. "Since the Irish are so creative with naming things, can you guess what the smaller one next to it is called?" he asked.

"Ummm… baking soda?" I guessed.

"What the…?! No!" he laughed. "It's called the *Little* Sugarloaf, duh!" he exaggerated.

"I like 'baking soda' better," I said, nodding my head. "So is that where you're taking me… to the Sugarloaves?"

"Not exactly, but we are going to Wicklow. I thought it'd be nice to get out of the city and get some fresh air."

"Will I see sheep like in the movies?"

"I reckon we'll come across some sheep, so we will."

I liked his accent. I liked how he looked when he was driving. I liked that he still made me nervous after four months. The butterflies in my stomach were a feeling I hadn't ever felt before – not even with Brad. Looking back, Brad was my best friend first, boyfriend second. Maybe that was the problem? Ah, it didn't matter anymore; why was I thinking about Brad then?

"Hey, Aidan?" I paused, reciting the words in my head. "I just want to say... thank you for today." He looked confused, probably because 'today' had barely begun at that point. "I know I've been quiet lately, but I'm really happy." I placed my hands between my knees. "I appreciate you taking me out today. I just wanted to say that."

"I know, missus." He took his hand off the gearshift and held mine. I looked out the window at the little town we were driving through. The landscape looked more like the pictures in the Ireland table book my mom got for me. We turned onto a little street behind a pub called O'Neill's. We were in a residential neighborhood and the ocean was in view. He parked on the side of the street just outside a cottage-like home.

"My Uncle Damian and Aunt Suzanne live just down there," he said, pointing toward the bottom of the hill we were on. "We'd come over a lot when we were younger; they have three boys around my age. We'd sneak beers and go drink them on this cliff right over here." He grabbed my hand and nudged his head toward the sea. "Come, missus. I want to show you something."

He held my hand and led me up the cliff, careful not to slip on any loose rocks or to step on any sharp objects. The panoramic view at the top was absolutely beautiful – better than any calendar or postcard of Ireland I had ever seen. The calm ocean went on forever, as did the jagged cliffs off on the right side. The wind whipped my long ponytail in my face as I turned to see a pasture of sheep, most of which were freshly shaven and frolicking about naked. It was quite a 'Holy shit, I live in Ireland' moment – more so than walking down Grafton Street.

We sat on that hilltop for hours, talking mostly about our adolescent years. Teenage Aidan was popular but had quite the temper, which got him into a lot of fights. I couldn't imagine Aidan being angry; he seemed to get along with everyone. The most rebellious thing I ever did, on the other hand, was skipping class senior year to go to the beach. I'd try to get Lindsay to come and sunbathe, but she would never skip school. It was always interesting to talk about how different our upbringings were.

We stopped in the village and had lunch at a proper old man's pub where the only other customers were bald men consuming pints of Guinness in the middle of the day. After the bangers and mash (basically the only thing the pub served), we headed back to Dublin.

"Ah, almost forgot – I made a wee playlist for you." He swiped and tapped his phone before setting it back in the dock. He made a playlist for me? I felt really uncomfortable as I waited for the first song and hoped it was something funny and not cheesy. Loud lyrics without any instrumentals played:

> I've been seeing all… I've been seeing your soul…
> Give me things that I've wanted to know…
> Tell me things that you've done.

It was R&B mixed with an electronic beat. I could see Simon liking it.

"I like this. Who is it?" I asked.

"Chet Faker and Flume. I'll send you the playlist; after all, you are the muse" he said. I didn't care anymore if he saw me blushing – it happened too often to try and hide. A couple more songs played, none of which were cheesy, thank God. He slowed the car down until we were completely stopped on the side of the road.

"Alright, missus... your turn." He took off his seatbelt.

"Oh no, Aidan, seriously... I haven't driven a manual in ten years, and I sucked at it then." It was a white lie because Brad used to make me drive his manual car in college – but I *did* suck at it. The lessons stopped after I kept stalling in the middle of an eight-lane intersection and started panicking. We had to run around the car to switch spots while the traffic honked at us.

"I'm a really good teacher," he said before walking around to my side. He opened my door, but I stayed put, gripping the seatbelt as if that would help. He entered the car and went for the buckle. I started rambling...

"Did I ever tell you my first car was a manual? Which by the way, less than 5% of Americans own manual cars and only another 5% could drive one in an emergency situation. To put myself in that bucket of people would be a stretch. I mean, if it were really and truly an emergency, I could do it, but Aidan, this isn't an emergency! Anyways, my dad took the car away after two months because I kept stalling it; I just couldn't get the hang of it." By that point, he had backed away from the buckle and was standing with one hand on the open door and the other on his hip.

"And I haven't driven any car in almost a year, so I don't think it's a good idea to drive your nice car. Plus, the steering wheel is on the wrong side of the car *and* you guys drive on the wrong side of the road." I was out of breath from my rant. The look on his face revealed how unimpressed he was. I knew I sounded like a baby, but I had no desire or reason to drive and I didn't want to fuck up the transmission for the hell of it.

"No, *you* guys drive on the wrong side. Come on, I taught an ex that had never driven a day in her life," he said confidently.

Buurrn!!

I had told him before that exes make me uncomfortable and I preferred not to discuss them if we didn't have to which he agreed to. The thought of him teaching an ex-girlfriend – and her not carrying on like I was – was the motivation I needed.

"Fine!" I said, fumbling around to get my seatbelt off. I stomped around to the bastard side of the car, sat in *his* seat and got situated. With shaking hands, I adjusted the mirror and pulled the seat forward. I didn't want him to think I was an idiot who couldn't drive, but it was such an awkward feeling sitting on the right side.

"So is first gear still top left or is that backward too?" I assumed it'd be top right.

"Yip, it's still top left, but make sure you push the clutch in first – push it all the way down and keep it there. When you put it in first gear, keep the clutch in or you'll stall." I knew that part – it was trying to make the car *go* that I was dreading.

"When you're ready, release the clutch slowly until you feel the sweet spot and then push on the accelerator at the same time you're releasing the clutch. Don't overthink it." I released the clutch slowly and scrunched my face like I had swallowed curdled milk. When the transmission revved up, my reflexes caused me to give too much gas and I completely released the clutch. The engine made a loud noise and the car jolted forward.

"Jesus, Jessica! Keep your eyes open!" Aidan yelled. "For fuck's sake!" he pounded his fist against the center console. I felt panicky and wanted to cry.

"I can't do this, Aidan! I'm going to break your car!" My hands were trembling.

"Fine," he said. "Sorry I made you do something you didn't want to do." His tone made it obvious he was annoyed. He opened his door to get out.

"No, wait! Let me try again." I grabbed his shoulder. "I want to learn; I just don't want to screw up the transmission." I felt damned if I did, damned if I didn't. I didn't want him to be angry with me and figured it'd be best to just fucking drive the car. "You're right, I'm probably overthinking it. I need to calm down and I'll be fine." I grabbed the wheel, hands precisely at ten and two. He closed his door, convinced.

I heard a bass guitar and upbeat tempo – it was The Coral's "Dreaming of You". Great, he made me a playlist and there I was, falling off the pedestal. I said a little prayer in my head: Please God, I know I said I don't believe in you, but if you can just help me to drive this damn car, I'll reconsider it.

I repeated the process with the clutch and put the car into first. After a few jerks and near stalls, I was able to fully release the clutch and we were in business.

"Ahhh, babe! I'm doing it!" I yelled out, feeling proud of myself.

"See, it's not that hard," he muttered in the same cold tone as before. I figured he didn't like the overenthusiasm – some people find that annoying. I get it. I told myself to tone it down.

"Holy shit! There are sheep in the road!" I screamed when we descended from a small hill.

"So stop the car!" he shouted back.

"I don't remember how! What do I do? Pull the emergency break?" I asked franticly.

"No! Just push the clutch in!" I pushed it in while he switched the gear. "Now break," he added. The sheep were almost all off the road when I stopped, but I still swerved off to the side.

We sat until I broke the silence.

"That was something out of a movie," I laughed half-heartedly. "Actually, it did happen in *Three Men and a Little Lady*." I turned to him, "Have you seen that one?"

"No, never heard of that *film*," he corrected. "But let me get this straight – you haven't seen *American History X*, *Schindler's List* or *The Godfather,* but you've seen *Three Men and a Little Lady*? Interesting…" he said sarcastically.

What was that supposed to mean? Was he insinuating that I was a bad American for not having seen some of the classics?

"I told you I'm not that big into movies – erm, films – especially not violent ones." I looked down and picked my cuticles. "I used to watch that one with my grandma when I was a little girl. There's a scene with sheep in the road in Ireland; it sticks out in my mind." I felt I had to explain myself. Was my not being a movie buff an issue?

"I'm just surprised, that's all. Right, I'll take the wheel now." Just like that, he was out the door and we were switching sides again. His behavior seemed so uncharacteristic. I tried to think if it was something I had done or said. I considered that maybe there was something going on at work, or with his friends. Maybe he was just feeling off; no one can be in a good mood all the time, right? I tried not to overthink it, but it was difficult not to. I felt it in my stomach.

We hardly spoke during the drive back. The playlist had ended and the radio played quietly in the background while I made a few comments about the pretty scenery and thanked him again for the day trip. He responded with polite smiles and a "you're welcome."

It was a long day after a long weekend, so we were both tired. We usually didn't do sleepovers on Sunday nights, but I was still disappointed when he dropped me off at home without bringing it up. The evil black cat, Cleopatra, was lurking on the stone wall behind my apartment complex where we were saying our goodbyes.

"Thank you for a lovely weekend, missus." He put his hand on my leg. "I'll see you this week and we can book some places in Morocco – real nice places. Sound good?"

"Sounds good!" I had a big smile, glad he had brought it up. I told him before I didn't mind staying in hostels as long as we had a private room. I didn't want him to think that since I hadn't travelled before, I was going to be a prima donna. We were going to be in Morocco for ten days, so nice places would get expensive and I needed to watch my funds. We had agreed to split all the costs in half. I was going to bring up the budget I needed to stay within, but at that point, I decided I wasn't going to mention it. I'd cut back on other things or rack up my credit card if I had to, but we were going to stay at nice places for our first real trip together.

"I can look online tomorrow, for nice places." I leaned over to give him a kiss. As I reached to open the car door, he grabbed my arm and pulled me in for another kiss.

Alone in my apartment, I checked my messages – Simon had sent the picture of me wearing the burgundy boots in Oxfam and asked if I had bought them.

Dammit! I thought we would have been back in time to get them, but it was almost 7:00 pm; being a Sunday, the store would be closed. I texted him explaining that I didn't get around to doing it but that I would one evening after work that week. Looking at the picture of the boots, they really were perfect. They were exactly what I had been looking for. I felt the same way about Aidan.

FIFTEEN
September 2013

The following week was extremely hectic at work, so I never made it to Oxfam to buy the burgundy boots. I called and the same sales woman from the day I was there said not to worry; she'd hold them in the back until I returned.

That weekend, Aidan and I had dinner at El Bahia, a Moroccan restaurant in Dublin City Centre. He thought it'd be fun to eat there and then compare it to the real thing the following week. Afterwards, we went to Elys where we shared a bottle of wine in their basement bar. I wanted his advice in planning an itinerary for when Lindsay and Jason came over, which would be just a few days after we returned from Morocco.

"Where should I take them outside of Dublin? I was thinking Northern Ireland – the Giant's Causeway and the Carrick-a-Rede rope bridge. But I feel like they need to see the Cliffs of Moher and Galway. There are so many options!"

"Wait a second there, missus – leave some of the good places for us! Those are great weekend getaways I want to take you on. Which of those places have you been to already?"

"Don't be selfish," I laughed. "I spent last Christmas in Galway with Orla and her family. She and her boyfriend took me to the Cliffs; it was amazing. Jason and Lindsay want to do a trip *somewhere* outside of Dublin, so I need to come up with somewhere good."

"What about Dingle? It's really scenic and you can drive the Ring of Kerry on the way, stopping at all the nice spots. I'll put together an itinerary for you."

"That'd be awesome. Thanks, babe!" I had only recently started calling him 'babe' from time to time, but it felt awkward. Since he always called me missus, I figured I needed to join him with the nicknames.

"Speaking of Christmas, erm… what are your plans for it this year?" he asked.

"My mom was talking about doing Christmas in St. Louis this year, but it's not confirmed yet… why?"

"Well, Babs already brought it up to me, so she did." He switched over to his Richard Simmons voice and shimmied his shoulders as he does when he's imitating his mom. "Jessica can take Philip's spot at the table. Aidan, you're so much more pleasant when she's around; she is such a lovely girl! Oooh, tell her I'm making my famous lamb pie!" I was laughing hysterically as he continued.

"I'd love… no, *we'd* love to have you stay here and spend Christmas with us, but I understand if you need to go home," he said, back in normal Aidan voice.

"Well, maybe I can do Christmas here with you and go home for Thanksgiving instead. I prefer Thanksgiving anyway – it's all about food and football." I debated whether or not I should ask him if he'd want to come home with me; would that be too much?

Fuck it… he started it.

"Would you like to experience a traditional Thanksgiving celebration… with me in America?" I felt awkward asking him but figured it'd be weirder if I didn't. Plus, I *did* want him to come home and meet everyone.

"I'd really like that. I always wanted to see firsthand what it's all about." His smile reassured me that I had made the right decision in asking him.

I thought of all the things I wanted to show him if he came home with me. I'd definitely take him to the USF campus and I'd show him what tailgating at an American football game is all about. We could go to Busch Gardens and purchase the picture of us screaming on the Sheikra ride. I knew he'd love the MOSI museum as much as I did; they always have cool exhibits. Or maybe he'd like the Salvador Dali Museum in St. Pete better. I was certain my friends would organize a big beach day so they could scope him out. We'd rent jet skis and drink Coronas with Bacardi lime floaters at Postcard Inn. Thanksgiving Day would be at my brother's house. I could see Aidan and my dad hitting it off while Dad encourages Sambuca shots after every beer. If Dad really liked him, they'd gang up and make fun of me as a form of endearment. I thought, maybe we could squeeze in a trip to Key West or New York City. I couldn't wait to have him on my turf and be the one to show him around for once.

"Great! We can figure it out when we get back from Morocco. I can't believe this time next week we're going to be in Africa! This time last year, I had never set foot outside of America!"

"I reckon some of the parts we'll see will be quite a shock for you – such a different way of living compared to how you've been brought up," he said.

"I think I'll be alright. After 27 years of Walmart shopping, there's nothing I haven't seen," I joked, trying not to overthink his comment on my upbringing.

"I'm telling you, even a small amount of poverty can be a shock if you've never seen it. It can really pull at different emotions – sort of wears you out actually."

I knew I wasn't well-traveled, but I certainly wasn't sheltered. He definitely needed to come home with me so I could show him how rough some areas of Tampa are. I didn't want it to become a pissing match about how I may or may not react to things we may or may not see. But I also didn't want to keep quiet like I had a tendency to do in those conversations where we had different views.

"I know what you mean." I nodded and sipped my wine debating whether or not to tell him about the little girl I mentored through a program in Florida. She was seven years old when I started the program and after four years, I was still scared to pick her up at her apartment which was in a rough part of town. The crowded apartment smelled of musk and body odor. I'd pick her up every other weekend and help her with homework and spoil the shit out of her. She had never baked cookies until we did at my apartment. It was a sad but fulfilling experience.

The moment had slipped away; I decided not to share that experience with him… not then at least. It'd come off sounding confrontational – better to wait I thought.

"There's bad stuff everywhere. It's even harder when you see it in your own backyard, which I did in certain parts of Tampa."

"Oh really? In Tampa? I guess I need to see that for myself," he winked. "But yeah, it sucks and there's really nothing you can do to help."

But I did feel like I helped. I knew I couldn't solve the problem, but I did feel like I made a positive impact on at least one person's life.

"Yeah," I agreed quietly.

"You seem quiet, missus." He leaned back in the booth and I breathed in that delicious Aidan scent. "I meant to tell you – you can take my car when Lindsay and Jason are here. I can call my insurance to find out if I need to add you to my policy."

What?! Was he out of his friggin' mind?!

"Oh God, Aidan, no! You saw how uncomfortable I was driving. I appreciate it, I really do, but no. I'm going to rent an automatic."

"I can't take the time off work to go with you guys on the trip, but I'll be around all weekend. Or if you want, we can all go over on the weekend and I'll catch a train back Sunday night and you'll only have to drive one way."

"Don't be silly! You don't need to be around the whole time they're here; I just want you to meet them, even if it's just for dinner one night. Don't feel like you need to entertain us, seriously."

"Well, I can't wait to meet them. That's really cool she got a passport just to come see you. I like her already," he winked.

"Funny, she seems to already like you too."

SIXTEEN

Aidan had to leave my apartment early the next morning. Before he left, he had written out an itinerary for the trip with Lindsay and Jason. I found it on my laptop when I woke up. It listed exactly what to do for a great trip around the Ring of Kerry and over to Dingle. I didn't need to stress about where to take them; he had done it for me.

I wanted to do something for him to say thank you and also because he was always the one planning things. I searched online for upcoming events and concerts. I saw that the group 'Everything Everything' was coming to The Academy a few weeks after we got back from Morocco – and after Lindsay and Jason would have left. Between all the song links he had sent me over the months and the playlist he had made for me, I was certain he'd like the group. I'd surprise him with a date night... dinner, concert, drinks, perfect! I bought the tickets and logged into my email to get the confirmation. I was taken aback when I saw the name in my inbox: **Bradley Binx**

Brad had reached out to me just before I left for Dublin, when he heard through the grapevine that I was moving. We met for coffee and talked as if we were old friends. The conversation that day was polite and generic – no mentioning of *us*, the good ole college days, or his new girlfriend. It was just an honest 'goodbye and best of luck'. That's the kind of man Brad is, a genuine one. He was one of the first to check in on me when I arrived in Dublin and to send a Merry Christmas message. He had even sent me a Happy Birthday email at midnight, Dublin time, for my birthday, which was just before I met Aidan.

I opened the email:

From: bbinx84@personalemail.com
To: jess.fun.hour@personalemail.com
Date: 21 September 2013 – 9:27
Subject: Checking in across the pond

Hey stranger,

I'm in Chicago for work and I went to that restaurant we went to before the theatre. It's now a 60s themed diner with drag queen servers on roller skates, you'd probably like it better now than when it was the fancy Italian joint!! How are you doing over there? You're probably engaged to some lucky Irish guy by now =)

Take care you,
Brad xx

I noticed he signed it Brad. To his mom he was 'Bradley', to all our friends and the entire free world he was

'Binx', but to me… he was always 'Brad'. And kiss, kiss? He was not the 'xx' or 'xoxo' type of guy – well, not that I had remembered anyways. It had been a few months since I'd heard from him. I hadn't even noticed since I started dating Aidan. Every now and again, I would think about my decision to let Brad go. It had crossed my mind as recently as the first few months in Dublin. Lindsay would tell me it was only because I wasn't seeing anyone, but I wasn't so sure about that. Brad spent over a year trying to win me back and I wouldn't budge. Then the tables turned – he had a new girlfriend and I was single after a couple of failed relationships. But after reading the email, I felt everything was as it should be. I was happy with Aidan, living abroad and planning to travel all over Europe (and apparently Africa too). I assumed Brad was happy with his girlfriend and doing well at his career in sports marketing. He was probably in Chicago for the Cubs. He was handling their spring training marketing from Tampa when we were together. The first time I went to Chicago and fell in love with the city was when Brad took me along on one of his work trips.

I told myself I'd write him back later.

A couple of hours later, I called Lindsay to discuss her trip to Ireland.

"You don't need to pack warm clothes, Lindz, it won't get colder than 60 degrees while you're here. You can wear my sweaters and jackets; that will save space in your suitcase."

"Good point. I'm so glad to have an excuse to wear sneakers and flats for ten days. My feet are so swollen; I had to buy a pair of black pumps a size big because I couldn't fit my feet in any of my work heels. And I have blisters all over – my feet look and feel like they went through a meat grinder! The Louboutins are not stretching like I thought they would. They're too small and hurt so bad; they're killing me!"

"Lindz, you have got to cut your losses with those things! Stop wearing them now and sell them on eBay or that second-hand clothing store in Ybor while they're still *like new*. If you keep wearing them, you'll pass the point where you can recover any money AND you'll give yourself a bunion."

"You're right; I should sell them before it's too late. I'll lose a few hundred dollars, but it's better to salvage something out of it."

"Exactly. It's a shame the leather didn't give like you thought it would, but now you know going forward to buy a pair that fit from day one – don't count on them stretching. But yes, just bring comfy shoes for this trip – we'll be doing a lot of walking."

"Oh, Jason asked me if Aidan golfs. It's a dream of his to play on one of the nice Irish courses – preferably with a castle or some cliffs. He said he'll treat Aidan the whole day and then we can have that time to ourselves!"

"You know, I don't know if he golfs," I fibbed. "I'll ask him though." I didn't feel comfortable asking him to spend a day with my friend's boyfriend, whom he'd never met. I didn't want to make him feel pressured, especially considering that'd be the weekend after we returned from our trip to Morocco. It seemed like a lot to ask.

"Jessie, what am I going to do if you stay in Ireland with Aidan? When I'm over, I'm going to talk up Florida so much that he'll want to move here."

"Lindz, it doesn't matter where I live – I'm never going to miss out on anything, okay?" I knew full well that Skype was not the same as having martinis in person.

"I just hope Aidan knows what he has."

"He knows." I quickly asked about Cody because my response felt like another lie.

"He's so well behaved compared to the other kids his age, but I still can't be around him on my own." I heard a loud sigh. "Jason went to help his friend move some furniture last weekend when he had Cody. He was only gone for a few hours, but it was just Cody and me – Jess, it was the longest three and a half hours of my life. I know that sounds horrible; I hate myself for it, but I can't be around him on my own. It's so… uncomfortable."

That was the moment I needed to be brutally honest with her. I fished for the right thing to say without pushing her away. I figured she was going to do what she was going to do regardless of what I said.

"Lindz, you guys have been dating for over a year now. He's probably going to propose soon, but he's always going to choose Cody – that's his son. If that's not the life you want, then you're never going to be happy."

"I'm happy with Jason. I know what I want, and I don't want to lose him. I'll just try harder with Cody and it will be fine."

It hurt me to see her doing that to herself – and to Jason and Cody. I wish she could've admitted to herself that the relationship was never going to be comfortable – the way she admitted the Laurence lace-ups wouldn't ever fit.

When the conversation ended, I looked up Oxfam's closing time; they were closed on Sundays. I knew I wouldn't be able to make it any night after work that week and we were leaving for Morocco at the crack of dawn Saturday morning. I called the store on Monday and they assured me they'd keep them for me until I got back from Morocco. That would never happen in an American retail store!

SEVENTEEN
October 2013

Geographically, Morocco isn't that far from Dublin. However, there weren't any direct flights, so we had a seven-hour layover in Brussels. Lindsay had joked on the phone that the long layovers there and back would be our relationship 'test'. I was ready to get away – the week before we left was absolute hell at work. My boss's boss, Declan, was in a nasty mood due to a huge account we had lost. That, in turn, caused my direct boss to be in an equally nasty mood while we worked late every night trying to win over the marketing for a huge packaging company. The worst part about it (besides not getting to go buy my burgundy boots) was that I didn't see Aidan that week. It was stressful, but we wrapped up the project late on Friday so I was able to leave for Morocco the next day without any work guilt.

During the layover in the Brussels airport, we sat in a café and I started *Agent 6* while Aidan read the news on his phone. After the week of sleep deprivation and having to leave for the airport at 5:00 am, I felt a migraine coming on.

That second flight was brutal. There was a lot of turbulence, so I spent the last half hour of the flight trying not to throw up. I'd breathe deep and count to ten and back down to one and then repeat. When the fasten seatbelt sign came on, I started looking for the sick bag; I thought for sure I'd need to use it. Aidan would rub my back from time-to-time, but there wasn't much he could do except remind me that we were almost there.

The pilot made his landing announcement first in French, then Arabic and finally, in English. Aidan had told me that Morocco was predominantly French-speaking, which would be helpful for us, as he knew some conversational French. I didn't know if he had learned it during his six-month internship in France or from the French girl he had dated last year. I didn't want to hear that it was the latter, so I didn't ask.

We had to take a shuttle bus from the plane to the airport. I held onto the pole in the bus, trying to ignore the hot, congested surroundings and the bumpy commute. Aidan took my suitcase and held my purse while I focused on breathing deep and not getting sick. Before we went through the passport check, I went to the bathroom to see if throwing up would make me feel better – it didn't. It only left me shaking and feeling dizzy afterward. I splashed my face with cold water and tried to pull it together.

The warm, humid air when we stepped out of the airport reminded me of Florida. We got into an old, box Mercedes taxi, the driver having a long, thick beard and white kufi cap. He and Aidan exchanged broken French as Aidan showed him the address to our hotel on a piece of paper. I sat in the backseat trying to manage the excruciating pain of my headache.

It was a good 40-minute drive to the hotel, and the scenery during it left a lot to be desired. All the signs were in Arabic, which looked like symbols to me. I saw one sign that had the names of three cities – Arabic on top, French below. It said Casablanca was '13' away. I hoped they used kilometers, not miles, so it'd be a shorter distance.

A family of four, crammed together on a single scooter passed by my taxi window. The man was the only one wearing a helmet. When we got to the heart of the city, there were parts that reminded me of old Florida. It was the way the palm trees (they looked like palm trees, but hey I'm not a botanist) lined both sides of the street, and the cream coloring of the buildings. I figured the light coloring was essential for any hot climate's architecture. There were several groups of women covered head to toe in burqas. Some of the younger women just had the veils to cover their heads, but were wearing outfits similar to what I'd wear on any given weekend. I wondered at what age the women had to start covering up and to what extent. I assumed it depended on the father and/or husband's preference but made a mental note to research it later.

What I found most interesting were the women's shoes. They were on casual Saturday strolls, but many had on heeled sandals. Most of their shoes were a bright color – much brighter than any pair I owned (well, except for the orange Penney's pumps that broke on me). For those women, their shoes were the one fashion statement they were allowed to make on their own. Despite the shoes being uncomfortable or impractical – it was their choice.

We finally arrived at the hotel. I couldn't wait to put my head on a pillow and rest. I didn't want to ruin our first night, so I told Aidan I just needed to shower and lay down for an hour, then I'd be fine to go for dinner. He insisted that I not push it and that we stay in and rest. He went to get dinner on his own and brought me back a bottle of 7-Up and a variety of packaged cookies and cakes.

"I went to three different pharmacies to look for Panadol, but they were all closed," he said, sitting on the bed next to me.

"It's okay. Thank you. The 7-Up tastes good," I muttered.

"Let it go flat; flat 7-Up cures everything, at least that's what Babs says. And eat the cakes – you haven't eaten anything all day; it's no wonder you're sick." He threw cookies with Arabic symbols on the packaging at me.

"Okay, I will. Sorry I'm ruining our first night," I said sincerely.

"Don't worry about it. Judging from my adventure in looking for pharmacies, I think we saw most of what Casablanca has to offer when we were in the taxi. We have two days here. We're not missing anything." He sounded playful and sweet. "I'm just going to sit over there and catch up on the news." He pointed to the sofa.

That night, I woke up freezing cold and shaking. I was covered in sweat and my pillowcase was soaking. My head hurt worse than it had earlier that day. The pain was so intense, I wasn't sure if I could handle it. I thought about what would happen if I needed to go to the hospital while I was there. I flipped the pillow over and tried to get into a position that would hurt the least. I needed water, so I got up as quietly as possible to get some – stumbling around to find the bottle we had bought earlier.

I tried again to get comfortable, curling up on my side in a fetal position. That didn't work, so I moved to my stomach, but then decided to go back to my side. I was thinking I needed to see a doctor when Aidan awoke.

"Hey… Jessica?"

Weird, he never called me Jessica.

"Yeah?" It hurt me just to say the word.

"Will you stop moving around? I can't sleep." He sighed loudly, keeping his back to me.

Suddenly, my head didn't hurt so badly because all I could focus on was the horrible pit in my stomach. I didn't say anything back. I lay there, startled by the coldness of his request. Sure, he didn't know I was contemplating whether or not I needed to go to the hospital, but he knew I was sick and he knew that me rustling around like that wasn't something I'd ever done before. That combined with how good he had been to me when I had a headache the first time I spent the night made me feel like the honeymoon was over.

I waited for him to turn… to ask if I was okay… to do *something*. But something never came.

I stayed awake for over an hour to make sure I didn't move in the slightest and upset him. I didn't even move to wipe the tears falling down my face.

EIGHTEEN

The next morning, only small traces of the headache and nausea remained. Aidan was super playful, tickling and groping me. He joked that we had to get all our affection out while in the hotel because P.D.A. wasn't allowed once we were out in public. We weren't sure exactly what was or wasn't allowed, as we'd read mixed things on the travel sites. We chose to play it safe after reading several stories of Western women being harassed and spit on for holding their boyfriend's hand in Morocco. It was as if what had happened during the night hadn't actually happened. I figured Aidan must have been in a coma when he said it and didn't even remember. I still wanted to bring it up.

"Hey babe?" I asked nicely.

"Yes, missus?" He walked up behind me and wrapped his arms around my waist while I put some cheap earrings on. I giggled when he blew in my ear and covered my neck with kisses.

"I know you didn't mean it, but last night... you hurt my feelings when you told me to stop moving around. I was feeling so sick and couldn't get comfortable." He took his arms off me and waved them about.

"You were making such a commotion and I needed to sleep! I was this close to pulling out the sofa bed and moving to it," he said as he made a small space with his thumb and finger.

The pit in my stomach returned.

"Well, sorry for interrupting your beauty sleep, but you knew I wasn't tossing and turning for the hell of it! I'm usually a good sleeper and you knew I was sick. I just *assumed* you'd want to ask your girlfriend if she was okay." It came out really defensive. I didn't want to start a fight on our first real day of the trip. "But maybe I'm just overreacting? Being a girl..." I said more softly, trying to retract the previous statement.

"Yes. You are definitely being a girl," he said in a condescending tone. "Are you done now? Can we go get breakfast?"

He gathered up his things while I stood frozen, telling myself: Pick your battles, Jessica; this isn't worth it. Drop it, don't be a nag. I didn't want to ruin a trip to a country that neither one of us would likely visit again.

"Yes, we're done. Let's go, I'm starving!" I faked a smile. He grabbed my hand and just like that, the discussion was over, but I wasn't sure if that was a good thing or a bad thing. I was overthinking it – it was definitely a good thing that we hadn't argued.

We walked along a coastal road on our way to check out the Hassan II Mosque – the largest in Morocco. Neither of us were big fans of guided tours, but it was really the only site to see in Casablanca, so we did it.

We saw a man in a wheelchair sitting at the top of the mosque's stairwell. We thought it'd be nice of us to pick him up in his wheelchair and carry him down the steps so he could pray to his God. It was going to be our good deed for the day, or so we thought. We were on the third step when the guards ran over and yelled at us. It turned out that the bottom of the stairs was not for worship; it was the men's toilet – which, of course, I was prohibited from going near. We were laughing at the incident while Aidan took selfies of us on his phone.

"We'll use this one for our wedding announcements," he said, viewing them. It was an inside joke where he makes fun of America's fascination with over-the-top milestones. He couldn't believe the amount of invites, holiday cards and thank you cards with professional photos that I had received from friends back home. They don't have engagement parties, bridal showers or baby showers in Ireland. They certainly don't have gender-reveal parties. Basically, the Irish, Aidan in particular, think my people are nuts.

"Or the homepage of the wedding website," I countered.

During the walk back from the mosque, we passed Rick's cafe, made famous by the movie *Casablanca*. I had seen the movie, so I wondered if it met Aidan's criteria for being a classic American film.

We made fun of the things our guide from the mosque tour had said and discussed what it'd be like to grow up in Casablanca. We'd ask hypothetical questions such as, "What would it take for you to relocate to Casablanca for work for… six months? A year? Forever?" There was nothing sexy or glamorous about Casablanca besides its name. The buildings where people lived were shabby at best, and clothes hung from a line outside almost every window. Children ran around without shoes, and it didn't seem like there was much to do except wander the streets – and drink mint tea.

"Want to check out the medina?" he asked.

"Absolutely!"

"Just stay close to me because it's going to be very crowded; people are known to get lost in these things," he warned.

"Okay, got it. I'll stay close, but won't actually touch you – who knew there'd be so many rules involved in visiting Morocco?" I joked. He must have not have heard me because he didn't react.

We walked down a narrow alleyway. The left side looked like a housing building with the familiar sight of laundry hanging out of the windows. The right side of the alley was a terracotta wall with nothing but closed doors and scooters lining it. The traffic was organized chaos. We dodged people on bikes; most were carrying someone either on the handlebars or on a self-made backseat. We entered the crowded outdoor marketplace which was the medina. Colorful umbrellas represented a store where you could buy goods – typically produce or spices, but some had scarves, shoes or other clothing. It wasn't the typical knick-knacks you'd expect to see as a tourist. Although there were other tourists, it was evident that was where the locals did their shopping. I had accidentally let Aidan wander away from me. He was walking about 30 feet ahead with his hands in his pockets and head straight forward.

As I weaved in and out of the crowd to catch up to him, cages of chickens distracted me. A Muslim woman in full headdress walked up to the chicken handler with four small children following behind her. I couldn't turn away as I watched him grab a chicken and snap its neck. He chopped off its wings, then its head and plucked the feathers out – right there on a makeshift tabletop in broad daylight. When I saw the blood covering his apron and gloveless hands, I knew what the unidentifiable smell had been.

"They face Mecca when they do it," Aidan said from behind me.

"I can't believe this! It's friggin' nuts!" I exclaimed, turning to him.

"I think this here is death row," he said, nodding in the direction we were walking. "There are loads more chicken stands, lamb ones too. Two men walked past me carrying a huge camel head just there a minute ago."

"A camel?!" I didn't realize people ate camels, but I didn't want to say it and look dumb.

"Yeah, it was pretty wild." He grabbed my shoulders, "Are you okay, missus? Let me know whenever you've had too much and we'll leave, okay?" He sounded genuine and concerned.

"No, I'm fine. I actually love this. Well, aside from the slaughterhouse part. But if you can't come to terms with an animal being killed, then you shouldn't eat it – and I like eating chicken so…"

He chuckled. "Alright well, just let me know. Here, you need to drink more water." He handed me the bottle. He

154

was right; the breeze from the ocean disguised how hot it really was and we had been outside all day.

* * * * *

We heard the call to prayer faintly in the distance as we walked to dinner. On the way, we saw Muslims kneeling on small blankets on the side of the streets – some next to their carts of fruit and nuts. After dinner, we sipped mint tea and watched the world go by.

At one point, he brought up how he wanted to one day open his own law firm – maybe have an online service for giving quick legal advice on the fly. I was impressed with his desire for entrepreneurship and honored that he was telling me his goal. I had always been very private with my goals and rarely stated them out loud until I was 100% sure I would follow through. I wanted to find out how serious Aidan was about his goal of opening his own practice.

"That would be amazing! To get to have your own practice and call all the shots," I said enthusiastically, stirring my tea to bruise the mint leaves. "Have you looked into office space? To get an idea of the availability and what the initial investment would be?"

"Nah," he shook his head. "Although, there are a couple spaces I saw for let just north of me, closer to Phibsborough, that I reckon would be better value compared to the City Centre or south side."

"Well, when we get back, you should ring them and get information. Just to see, ya know?"

He didn't respond to the statement. "What about you? What are your goals?"

Ah, my goals were complicated because they ultimately lived in America. I was in Dublin on borrowed time – who knew what would happen in the upcoming year? I didn't feel it appropriate to mention how I dreamt of transferring to my company's Chicago office for the promotion I wanted.

I didn't want to mention anything about how the main reason I'd agreed to take the year in Dublin was because it'd be a stepping stone to help me get to Chicago. He didn't need to know that I hadn't signed up solely for my raw interest in Ireland – although I did want to do something big, on my own. We had been together long enough that I should have told him some of it, but I wasn't ready. I didn't want him to think that my staying in Dublin was giving up on a dream because that wasn't the case. Goals change, and at that point, my main goal was to focus on the present and my relationship with Aidan. But saying that to him didn't seem appropriate either. I decided to respond safely and generically.

"Well... right now, I can only think about the next year because, clearly, plans change. It was never my goal to live in Dublin or to vacation in Morocco, but I couldn't be happier than I am right now." I leaned back in my chair, hoping to find a great follow-up statement, but I didn't. "My goal this year is to travel. That's the main reason I moved to Dublin in the first place, so I want to visit as many places as possible." He sipped his clear glass of mint tea, bored by my answer.

"Yeah, but... what's your *passion*? Your career doesn't seem to be your passion in life, so what *are* you passionate about?"

What's my passion? Did he think I wasn't a passionate person? I felt the pit in my stomach return, as I felt myself falling from the pedestal he had put me on.

I ran through my accomplishments and hobbies in my head. I was ahead of my peers at work; I got my master's degree in marketing a year early and a second degree in philosophy. When I wasn't working my ass off or spending time with him, I was running, reading or doing something in Dublin with the new friends I had made from scratch – I wasn't exactly sitting on a rock waiting to die. And passion? I was passionate about my family, my friends and... HIM! What more did he want for fuck's sake?!

I felt defensive. Was it because he was onto something? Could it be that despite my hobbies, I wasn't passionate about any one thing in particular? My boyfriend's simple question caused me to spiral into an early mid-life crisis right there.... over a mint tea in Morocco... at the age of 27. I had fucking lost it and didn't know what to say to him. I'm sure my face screamed that I was a loser without a passion.

"Hmm, I'll have to think. I never really thought about it. But there's nothing wrong with having a job that isn't necessarily a *passion* as long as it allows you to do the things you do love. Right now, I'm doing everything I ever wanted to and I'm genuinely happy, so I think I'm living passionately – isn't that enough?"

He didn't look enlightened. We sat silently for a while before starting a new conversation, but I couldn't stop thinking about it. The conversation left me feeling insecure the entire night. What if he was right? After all, wasn't that the real reason I moved in the first place... to find *something*, to get out of a rut?

In that short amount of time, I had convinced myself that I had no passion in life.

NINETEEN

The following two days of the trip were incredible. Aidan and I had similar travel personalities – we both liked to sleep in, but tried to make the breakfast, which usually lasted till 11:00 am. It wasn't until breakfast that we'd give the first thought to what we wanted to do that day. He had looked up the main sites and whatnot before the trip, but we never made an agenda; we just figured it out together. Casablanca wasn't the sexy city we had envisioned, but we found things to do. We enjoyed sipping mint tea and people watching in the Place Mohammed V Square. We'd pass hours talking about anything – from how leather was made (which is a huge Moroccan export), to how turtles breathe through their butts, to my hatred of beetroot. Time and conversation passed effortlessly. I had learned more about Aidan in those first couple of days than I had in the previous five months. Even after discovering some of his flaws and him discovering my lack of passion, I continued to like him more and more.

The pit in my stomach had stayed away. A small bit resurfaced only when I noticed many couples walking by – all tourists – holding hands, which I thought was not allowed. Aidan saw them too, so I wondered why he hadn't tried to hold mine like he usually did in Dublin. I quickly dismissed those thoughts; he was clearly just being cautious. Overall, our time in Casablanca was a good introduction to Morocco with a mix of relaxation and culture shock.

After three nights in Casablanca, we took a train to the capital, Rabat, for two nights. Aidan's research prior to the trip informed us that it was easier, and cheaper, to fly into Casablanca and take the one-hour train to Rabat than it would be to fly directly to Rabat.

The best thing we did in Rabat was exploring the Kasbah of the Udayas. I wasn't sure if Aidan thought I was adorable or an idiot when I told him I thought the song "Rock the Kasbah" by The Clash was "Rock the Cash Bar". I defended it by explaining how the song is often played at American weddings, which have cash bars. "Get it?" I'd ask him. Of course, cash bars are inferior to open-bar weddings; nonetheless, people rock out and drink up when that song comes on. He laughed, but I do think he thought I was an idiot for not knowing what a kasbah was.

We walked along the crescent-shaped beach while I told him what it was like growing up on the beach in Florida. How there was no feeling quite like driving over the bridge that connected the island to the residential coast. How there was no better smell than the salty wind that carried the sound of the waves. How only a beach baby can appreciate the sting of broken seashells on their feet and seaweed tangled in their hair. How we had mastered the art of packing up our belongings when it was time to leave without covering our neighbors – or our cars – with sand. How I tried but never fully got into surfing. I did, however, love snorkeling at Bathtub Beach. I left out the part that Brad loved it too when he'd come home with me to visit my parents. I wanted to tell him that I swore I had saltwater coursing through my veins, but I didn't want him to know I was homesick. The beach would always be home.

After our relaxing two nights in Rabat, we took another train to Marrakech – the vibrant highlight of our vacation. That train was old and looked unfit to make the four-hour journey. It was very crowded and there weren't enough seats, so Aidan and I stood in the dirty narrow aisle with all the gap-year backpackers. The train moved slowly, incredibly slowly. The view outside was desert-like, but everything was a reddish-clay color. Aidan pointed out that the trees we kept seeing were olive trees.

We stood for two hours until a herd of passengers got off at the Settat station, leaving two seats available in the box car. Aidan insisted I take one and an elderly lady in a full burqa take the other. He remained in the aisle, sitting on one of our suitcases, playing with his phone. I took out my book. It was the first time I had read since the Brussels airport layover.

I was completely immersed in my novel when Aidan's hand emerged from behind the plastic barrier between where I was and the aisle where he was. In his hand were white headphones. He wanted me to listen to something. I pushed the buds into my ears, smiling back at him through the cloudy divider.

I heard an instrumental piece and then some muddled words that I couldn't understand. I heard a deep, baritone voice, but couldn't make out a word until the chorus began. That part was crystal clear:

> *I wanna hurry home to you and*
> *put on a slow, dumb show for you;*
> *and crack you up.*
> *So, you can put a blue ribbon on my*
> *brain;*
> *God I'm very, very frightened that I'll*
> *overdo it…*

I melted. When I heard the part about wanting to "put on a slow, dumb show for you and crack you up", I thought of the previous weekend, just before we left for Morocco…

> After the wine at Ely, we went back to my place. We picked up a case of beer and chatted away on the sofa. I mentioned one of my favorite childhood memories was playing Mortal Kombat with my brother. I asked him if Mortal Kombat ever made it to Ireland and whether or not he had played it. Instead of answering me verbally, he set his beer on the table, stood in the open space of my living room and began hopping and kicking about like a

Riverdancer having muscle spasms. He pretended to throw a lightning bolt just like Raiden would have. It was comedic genius! I wanted to get off the couch and join him. I even thought about attempting Sub-Zero's famous sliding kick, but I was paralyzed in a fit of laughter. He continued on with the tirade until pausing to say, "Finish him!" in the video game announcer's voice. Tears rolled down my face as I cracked up at the slow, dumb show he was putting on for me.

The song was nearing the end... the tempo had slowed to just the piano and drums. The lyrics again were clear:

> *You know I dreamed about you;*
> *for twenty-nine years, before I saw you.*
> *You know I dreamed about you;*
> *I missed you for twenty-nine years.*

That part repeated a few times before the song ended. What a beautiful song.

"Who was that?" I asked as I handed back the headphones.

"The National," he answered.

I titled my head and stared.

"You don't know The National?! But they're American!"

No, I don't know all nine million American music groups, I thought to myself.

"I might have, I just don't recognize them," I answered. He shoved the phone and headphones into his pocket.

"What do you think about the part where he's saying he missed her for twenty-nine years?"

I didn't know if it was a trick question or not. I thought the message was pretty obvious. Before I could articulate an answer, he answered himself.

"I guess he's saying to his woman that he knew he had been waiting for her his entire life..." he paused and looked in my eyes. "He knew she'd come along because it never felt right with any of the girls he dated before her." His lips raised into a small smile, his eyes still locked on mine. I smiled back.

The song dedication had me thinking about Brad again. He had dedicated several songs to me over the years, but the one that stuck out was Brad Paisley's "She's Everything". He didn't like country music until he met me and I introduced him to it. He'd play that song at random and ask me to dance with him. One time, he sang it at karaoke despite the overwhelming boos from his friends. He even used it as a way to get out of, or end, arguments – sheer man genius really.

Aidan pulled both our suitcases while we made a beeline for the exit in the crowded Marrakesh train station. His choppy French was enough to get a taxi to drop us off just outside the general area of where our riad was. Based on our taxi driver's hand motions, we gathered that the only form of transportation that could fit in the maze of the medina either had two wheels or four undernourished legs. We paid the 60 dirham, which Aidan insisted was price gouging. I told him that was about five euro, which is what it would cost just to sit in a Dublin taxi before going anywhere. He reminded me that we weren't in Dublin.

About 20 minutes later, we were properly lost. Using a map in Marrakesh was more confusing than it was helpful. The majority of the winding side streets didn't exist on the map and many of the streets we walked down didn't have names.

Aidan was frustrated, but I was reluctant to recommend that we ask directions from a local. The guy selling fried eggs from his fold-up table was not the same as asking someone at a convenient store. He turned the map every which way, trying to make sense of it.

"We are here… I think, and our riad is… there," he said, pointing at two spots on the map. "But I can't tell how far that is without a legend – I need a legend…"

I jumped in front of him, raised both my arms, flexed my biceps and said in a deep voice, "I AM A LEGEND!!"

He laughed hard and kissed the top of my head which might have been a risky move. "You are a friggin' nut; that's what you are," he said, still laughing.

A young boy came up to us and offered to take us to the door of our riad. We believed he knew where it was, so we followed him, trusting he wasn't just going to scam us.

We would have never, not in a million years, found our riad if it wasn't for that boy. We probably should have given him more than 30 dirham.

The riad door was camouflaged against the clay wall. An iron sign, not much bigger than a sheet of paper, stuck out from it with the name chiseled in cursive. It might as well have been written in symbols because it certainly didn't look like the 'Riad I'Heure d'Eè' that we had booked online.

We knocked several times, but there was no answer. Aidan must have been thinking what I was thinking – that we had been set up and were about to get mugged – because he moved closer and pulled me to him. I was scared but felt safe at the same time.

After what felt like ages, a short, round Muslim woman opened the door with the biggest, warmest grin that I had seen in Morocco. She had a wicker basket with gently folded cream-colored linens inside. We gave our best attempts at *marhaban*, which means 'hello'. It was one of the few Arabic words we had committed to memory.

I said, "Uh, check-in? Uhh… reservation… Aidan… McGovern," as if saying it slowly meant she'd suddenly understand English. She kept smiling, having no clue what I had said, but I didn't know another way to say it. Aidan handed her the wrinkled confirmation that we had printed out weeks prior. She glanced at it, opened the door and encouraged us inside.

I went in first and holy moly… it was beyond impressive! It was like we were in a Princess's palace. Sheer drapes hung from the third, or top, floor and embellishments tastefully accentuated everything.

A man slowly emerged from a doorway. He exceeded the 'tall and thin' description that I had come to stereotype Moroccan men as. He wore a light colored robe with a matching cap and sandals that resembled Birkenstocks, or Jesus sandals.

"Ah, Mrs. McGovern." The man bowed his head while grabbing both of my hands. "Mr. McGovern," he repeated the bow to Aidan.

"Jessica, please. And this, this is Aidan." I took my purse off my shoulder but didn't correct him on our marital status, knowing they'd frown on the whole unwed bed-bunking thing.

"Yess-ica and A-don," he repeated. "Mustapha," he said, raising his arms up. I wanted to say *Ka-passa*, like from the *Lion King*. "From Eer-landes?" he said, looking at our confirmation.

"We live in Ireland… uh, Eer-landes. But, she's American," Aidan said, clarifying my accent.

"Amer-eee-ca!" he said, overly excited – they clearly must not get many American guests. "Where in America?" he asked.

"Florida," I replied.

"Ah, Flor-ee-dah! Veryyy nice!" Mustapha smiled and nodded. "Tariq!" he called out. A short, average-build man probably in his mid-twenties ran out from an entryway behind us. Tariq had on dark, baggy jeans and a short sleeve polo shirt – standard Western dress, I thought.

"Come, come! Sit. I will bring you tea and biscuits," he said in broken English. He took our bags and led us to the center of the room. It was equivalent to a hotel's lobby but was more like the palace living room. We sat on a plush, white loveseat and observed the beauty of the place while we waited for Tariq. He brought over a silver serving tray with a carafe of tea and two clear, handle-less glasses on it.

Accompanying the tea was an assortment of cookies – two of each variety. I first went for the one with toasted sliced almonds painted on top with a honey-drenched brush. Aidan went for the moon-shaped, sesame seed-covered one. The table they were served on was an old, refurbished treasure chest. I wondered whether it was actually old or just made to look old for the tourists.

Mustapha emerged, bringing with him the forms we were required to fill out using our passport and other personal information. We had completed them in Casablanca and Rabat as well.

"What did you put for your occupation?" Aidan asked.

"Fortune cookie writer – obviously," I answered without hesitation. My love of books and my multiple subscriptions for daily quotes made it a good alter ego profession. Back in Rabat, I was a running shoe designer and he was a football/soccer coach. We took the forms very seriously.

"What about you?" I asked. "Golf ball diver?" I nudged him with my shoulder playfully.

"Nope. I'm a puppet master," he said firmly. I didn't know what it had to do with his alter ego, but it was funny nonetheless and I laughed at the thought of it.

"Hmmm… marionettes or hand puppets?" I asked, raising the pen to my chin and squinting.

"Ah, I do both, but I much prefer marionettes – you should see the way I can pull those strings. I can put on quite a show!" I thought of the "Slow Show" song from the train.

I completed the form and sank back into the cushion with a bright green pistachio cookie in hand.

Mustapha took our forms and led us up the stone stairs. I kept a close eye where I stepped, making sure not to trip on the uneven, spiral steps. After three flights, we had reached the top. We followed Mustapha through a huge wooden door and then we were out on a terrace. It was covered with planted cacti and bright fuchsia flowers. The view of the off-white and clay-colored architecture stretched as far as the eye could see in all directions. It was serenity in the heart of the chaos and madness of the medina.

"It's going to be an early morning wake-up call, missus," Aidan whispered in my ear, pointing out the minaret just a stone's throw away. I quietly did my best impersonation of the call to prayer, making sure Mustapha didn't hear.

Mustapha told us that we could have our breakfast served at the table behind us or on the terrace above. Aidan and I looked at each other with faces that said: We have *another* terrace upstairs?!

He handed Aidan an iron skeleton key along with a map of the old city and traced the easiest way to get to the main square which we planned to check out that night. Mustapha left and we excitedly entered into our Moroccan oasis.

I swatted back the flowing cream-colored curtains that covered the entryway. The walls were a textured maroon in the main living room. The walls complimented the L-shaped sofa and the vibrant turquoise and gold decorative pillows. The terracotta floor was covered only in the living room by a patterned carpet with gold tassels. The misshapen clay fireplace felt out of place because it was so hot that time of year. Not only did it seem unconventional, it was the only orange eyesore in the entire place.

We checked out the bedroom – the walls were light lavender and the bed was a rich plum. A veil hung from the corners of the four posts in another shade of purple.

"Pretty romantic, huh, missus?" Aidan said, wrapping his arms around me.

I pulled away and put my hands on my hips. "There are no rose petals on the bed, no champagne and from what I can gather, no his and hers robes – they *will* hear about this on my Trip Advisor review!" I said, trying to keep a straight face.

"Awk, you're a tough one to please, Mrs. McGovern! I reckon we can find some champagne or wine somewhere. We'll ask Tariq – don't want Mustapha to think we're raging alcoholics."

I was thinking the same thing. Mustapha was older and probably more traditional, whereas Tariq probably more modern-thinking. We hadn't come across any alcohol since we'd been in Morocco, but they'd have to have some for the tourists, right?

We decided to relax for a couple of hours before venturing out to the main square for dinner. While Aidan was in the shower, I lay on the elaborate sofa while I logged onto the Wi-Fi to check my messages. Simon had sent me a picture of him and Merrick in a sloppy, drunken embrace, followed by the message:

Simon: *Wish my favorite dancing partner was here to meet my future husband! Have fun in Morocco with Ken... don't drink the water!!!*

I laughed when I read it. I was glad to see things were going well with short/tall Merrick.

Aidan walked out of the bathroom in a towel. He lifted my legs and sat on the sofa, putting them across his lap.

"Whatchya reading, missus?" I had just finished reading a message from Lindsay. It was her response to something I had wrote her the night before we left for Morocco – when I was up late packing. The message mentioned how excited I was for the trip with Aidan.

I handed the phone to him, with only her response visible on the screen.

Lindsay: *Jess, I have to tell you, my eyes stung with tears to read what you wrote about Aidan. It makes me so happy to know that you're happy. Any guy that can make you talk like that must be truly amazing. Basically, I already love him for making you feel the way you do. I'm so excited to come see you! I don't care what we do because I know we'll have a blast. I love you so, so much and I can't wait to meet Aidan! Have an amazing time in Morocco! xoxo*

He handed the phone back to me.

"So, what did you say to her?" he asked with a smirk, rubbing my leg.

"Wouldn't you to like to know?" I said, blushing. Showing him Lindsay's response was my way of letting him know I was crazy about him – by letting my best friend say it for me. "What I said to her is a mute point," I smiled.

"Did you say a *mute* point?" he asked, narrowing his eyes. I was confused. "It's a *moot* point Jess… did you really think it was mute?"

"Well… yeah… I did." I didn't know what else to say but the truth. Mute – silent, not worth mentioning, pointless... I thought mute fit just fine how I used it regardless of what it should have been. "Moot? It's a funny word, but I got it now," I said awkwardly.

"Right, okay," he said, slapping my leg and changing the topic. "Let's get dressed, missus; it's time to explore Marrakech." He stood up and headed to the bedroom while I tried to decipher the look on his face while he read the message. It seemed like he was annoyed after reading it. Then I reminded myself that we were in an exotic paradise and I was overthinking things.

"Alright, alright!" I called out to him. "But we better see a camel – a living one and not just a head!"

We set out to Jemaa el-Fna, which is the Main Square and heart of Marrakech's old city. The twenty-minute walk from our riad was sensory overload. We were staying on one of the quieter streets, but as soon as we ventured a few minutes from our paradise, we were bombarded by tradesmen trying to lure us into their shops. They'd say, "Just a look my friends," or, "Come into my shop my friend." The insides of the cafes were filled with men – only men. They were consumed in thick clouds of smoke, all watching the one 1980s box TV hanging in the corner. They'd sip their coffees and mint teas while blankly staring at us as we walked by. I tried to keep a neutral face and to appear like it was all very normal to me, which was far from the truth.

We didn't see many women, and the ones we did see were always fully covered and escorted by a man. Men zoomed by on scooters beeping their horns. It was more to say "hi" to one another and not "move!" Aidan told me several times to get on the pavement and off of street and always made sure he was on the side closest to the traffic.

There was a wide, well-paved road leading into the square. It was basically the parking lot for the horses and donkeys. The frequent gusts of wind carried the smell of homemade macaroons that were sold on blankets all around us; it masked the smell of horse dung. We purchased a few of those macaroons from a woman with a baby secured to her back with a shawl. We didn't object when she blatantly overcharged us. After Aidan handed her the money, she put two more macaroons in the bag and said, "thank you," to which we both replied "shokran" and bowed our heads.

We entered the square of Jemaa el-Fna. It was everything I thought Marrakech would be and so much more than I could have imagined. It was truly another world.

We unintentionally drifted apart, turning in circles, taking it all in on our own. After a few minutes of observing the chaos, we looked at each other and laughed. I couldn't tell where the beating drums were coming from, but they blended well with the mesmerizing song from the snake charmer's flute. Laughter from the small groups having fireside chats in the open square erupted over the clanking pitter-patter of horse- (and donkey-) drawn carts breezing by. The smell of horse and macaroons had been replaced with intoxicating spices – cardamom and turmeric prevailing. It was the Islamic adult version of Disney World. I remembered when my dad took me – just him and I – and my imagination was awoken when we watched the night parade. The same was happening again, there in Marrakesh.

"This is absolutely unreal," I said, holding the strap of my small purse across my chest.

"Tell me about it; I've been to a lot of places, and I have never seen anything like this."

A man with a monkey emerged from behind Aidan. Before I could get the words out of my mouth, the monkey leapt onto his right shoulder, causing him to jump. When he realized that a monkey was on him, he panicked – waving his arms around while I laughed hysterically. When the monkey's owner saw that we did not want to pay for a picture with the monkey, he took him back and walked away.

I was still laughing as I put my arm around him and said, "Awe babe… you're afraid of baby monkeys."

He flailed his arms and said, "That monkey didn't even have a nappy on!" I couldn't handle how adorable he looked when he was annoyed – as long as it was with the monkey and not with me.

There was a mall of about 50 tents so closely set up next to one another that it basically created one huge tent. Under the tents were countless picnic tables and several clay ovens and open fire pits for cooking. We decided to eat there for dinner. After seeing first-hand the hygiene of the chicken slaughtering, we stuck with vegetarian tagines. Of course, the meal came with a bowl of olives and flat bread just as every meal had.

Aidan asked, "Do you think you could ever explain to someone, just in words – no pictures allowed – what this place is like?" He tore a piece off the bap we were sharing. "To be able to place someone right here, in this crazy

174

square?" He tapped his finger on the table with the bread still in hand.

I looked beyond the tent and into the night. A monkey (this one on a leash) walked in front of my view of a man selling lanterns on a blanket. Neon glow sticks shot across the sky from all directions. I felt I could remember enough details to make my parents feel like they were there.

"No, I don't think I could," I fibbed. After all, it was a rhetorical question.

"Me either," he shook his head. "Me either."

I knew what he really meant was, "Me *neither*."

TWENTY

I hit the power button on my phone: 4:22 am.

The blaring call to prayer on the loud speaker woke me as it had the previous two mornings as well. Aidan had awoken too; I could feel him moving around behind me. He shuffled over, pulled me in to his chest and mumbled his sleepy rendition of the prayer song while I giggled. It went on for about ten minutes. When it ended, Aidan would say "one down, one to go" because there'd be another call a few hours after. That had become our morning routine.

That morning, I couldn't fall back asleep after the second call to prayer. Around 8:00 am, I went up to the top terrace with my book and phone. I curled up in one of the half-moon shaped hammocks and read while my music played beside me. The glowing sun was beginning to peak through the morning clouds.

It was two hours before Aidan came moseying up the stairs.

"What are you listening to?" he asked, yawning. The song "Bitter Poem" was playing.

"It's my favorite band, Cold War Kids," I answered, turning the volume down.

"Cold War Kids aye? Interesting name." He sat in the hammock next to the one I was in. His legs were crisscrossed and he started spinning himself around in circles like a child would do.

"Their lyrics are really unique and thought provoking... at least I think so," I explained.

"Hmm, never heard of them. They American?" he asked, still spinning and spinning.

"Yeah, they're from California. I saw them when I was visiting my friend, Amy, in Los Angeles before they even had an album out. I'll make you a playlist of their best songs."

I didn't want to sound like I was lecturing and I didn't want to venture into my philosophy background, so I decided not to tell him the main reason I loved the group so much. It was because their second album, *Loyalty to Loyalty,* was inspired by a lesser known philosopher, Josiah Royce. He was the first to publically challenge Nietzsche's views on community. Nietzsche said that people need to rise above their community if they want to succeed – to be the best of the best – just as Aidan had once said he wanted to be. Royce came in and said that wasn't how to do it. He said that people need to build their own community from within – not try to rise above it. The Cold War Kids made a pact to build one another up as a group, not as individuals.

Aidan was more interested in the hammock than the band – couldn't blame him there. It was better that I didn't go on my tangent about Nietzsche and Royce while he was having a ball.

"Yeah, I'll check them out." He stopped spinning. "Should I let Tariq know we're ready for breakfast?"

"Yes, please – and ask him for extra of those pancake things!"

It was 11:15 am when we finished our breakfast of thin pancakes, yogurt and a display of jams and breads on our private terrace. I mentioned how our disregard for time on this trip combined with the Moroccan backdrop made me feel like we were trapped inside Dali's *The Persistence of Memory*. I told Aidan how Dali was my favorite artist and I'd been to his museum in Florida many times. That turned into a conversation about surrealism, which led to a discussion on crazy dreams we'd had. Naturally, that led to a long discussion on circus performers and ultimately, which kitchen gadgets are worth having. Our conversations tended to go all over the map. We were discussing one of the business proposals we had seen on the TV show *Shark Tank* when he made a joke about how Diana Nyad would not need to ever go on *Shark Tank*. He laughed alone.

"I don't get it, who is Diana Nyad?" I asked.

"Come on, missus, have you been living under a rock? She's been all over the news – especially Florida news I'd imagine!" he exclaimed.

"Well, I haven't been interested in the news since we've been here – wanted to shut off while on vacation," I explained. "So what'd she do?" I asked, pouring another cup of tea.

"She was the first person to swim from Cuba to Florida without a shark cage. And she accomplished this weeks ago

– well before we left for our *holiday*." He looked at me with judgment.

"Oh, right. I heard about that, but didn't know that was her name," I said truthfully and laughed, finally understanding his joke. "Yeah, she'd have no need for the 'tanks' on *Shark Tank*."

He held his stare. Right when it felt uncomfortable, he nodded and looked out at our awesome view. I couldn't tell if he didn't believe me that I had seen the news story, or if he was thinking of something entirely different.

I started to think that between his 'passion' for the news and classic American films, I really needed to spend a lot of time in front of a TV screen to keep up with him.

It wasn't until Tariq came to clear our plates that we started discussing what we wanted to do that day. Tariq recommended a couple of different day trips – we both agreed on the one to the Atlas Mountains.

As we got dressed, I asked Aidan if he was going to keep his flip-flops on or change into the sneakers he wore on the flight over. He insisted it was too hot outside and that we'd be much more comfortable in our sandals.

"Are you sure? I know I'll look ridiculous with sneakers and flowy linen pants, but it's unsafe to wear sandals while hiking on a mountain," I said. I had only brought long pants, sleeved shirts and maxi dresses with cover-ups for my shoulders. I was trying to respect the Muslim culture while not sweating profusely or having to buy new clothes. I wasn't very fashionable during the trip.

"You'll be fine. It's a tourist trail, so it's going to be extremely easy. We won't be the only ones in sandals," he ensured.

"I can bring my bigger bag and keep both our sneakers just in case. We can change into them just for the mountain trail part," I recommended.

"You're overthinking things like you always do. That will be a hassle to carry around." He put his hands on my shoulders and looked me in the eyes. "Wear your sandals – you'll be perfectly fine, I promise." Then he made a crisscross motion over his chest, reciting "cross my heart" as he did that night on the wooden bridge at Bull Run. Then he leaned in for a kiss.

"Okay," I smiled. "Sandals it is."

We laughed every time we heard the 'click-click' of the camera coming from the couple behind us on the bus. They easily took a hundred pictures on the way to the Atlas Mountains. Aidan gave me the window seat and I peered out at the men in bright robes, leading small herds of camels up the mountain.

When the bus stopped, we had an hour to get food in the little town before starting the trail. An hour into the excursion, there was more climbing than we had imagined, but we were doing okay in the sandals.

We made it to a waterfall with a breathtaking view overlooking the mountains. Our tour guide gave our group 30 minutes to take pictures and get a drink at the hut that existed solely for the tourists. The couple who had sat behind us on the bus, taking a million pictures, offered to take a picture of us in front of the waterfall.

"We look like we have to poop," I said when he showed me the picture on his phone. He was startled by my comment but agreed – it wasn't our best picture.

We found an observation area and soaked in the beautiful view – and the fact that we had climbed so high in sandals. I began to reflect on the trip up to that point... it had been a wonderful experience overall and part of me was sad to be leaving in two days. But a bigger part couldn't wait to get back to Dublin. There had been one too many 'off' moments between Aidan and me, but I figured being in a strange new country had a lot to do with it. When we got back to Dublin, without the added stress of the trip, I would find a way to talk to him about it – but not there, not during our trip. I didn't want to be the girl that had to say, "Is something wrong? Are you mad at me?" No way, Josè!

My thoughts were interrupted by Aidan saying, "Smile!" He leaned in and took a selfie of us... and another. They came out much better than the one of us looking constipated in front of the waterfall.

He put his phone back in his pocket and said something I couldn't make out.

"What's that babe?" I asked.

"That guy over there," he pointed down by the waterfall, "He has on a Che Guevara shirt. Even in the Moroccan mountains... Che is everywhere!" he laughed. I didn't know who he was talking about, so I looked at him blankly.

"Che Guevara?" he repeated slowly with wide eyes. I gave him a look that said I didn't know who or what he was talking about.

"Jesus Christ, Jessica – don't tell me you don't know who Che Guevara is either."

I hated that he called me *Jessica* again instead of 'missus'. And *either?* The way he said it pinched a nerve. Were there numerous other times where he thought I was an idiot? Shit, there were… I had thought the lyrics were rock the *cash bar* instead of *kasbah*, I thought *moot* was *mute* and he might have thought I never watch any news since I didn't know who Diana Nyad was. Those had all come up during the trip, in a period of a few days. Was he beginning to think I wasn't very smart? That I was a dumb blonde? Maybe I was too young and the five-year age gap was showing? Or that I was a naïve and sheltered American who couldn't keep up with his worldly experiences and knowledge?

I felt like shit. I thought I had regained my grip of the pedestal, but with that one comment, I had lost it and continued plummeting. The pit in my stomach had returned yet again.

Not wanting to make a big deal over it, I decided it was best to say nothing – which was becoming a trend. I thought I was the outspoken, confident American I was always pigeonholed to be, but around Aidan, I realized I often kept quiet.

"Jess, he's only the father of the Cuban Revolution! His image is arguably the most recognizable in the world." I looked at the ground, wishing I could go back in time and redo the part where I let him know I didn't know. "I can't believe you don't know who Che Guevara is... its actually appalling."

I never wanted to slap someone as much as I wanted to slap him at that moment. I mean, the *Cuban* Revolution?! Earth to Aidan: I'm American and we were banned from all things Cuban! Nothing about Cuba was ever a part of my school's curriculum, and I would know because I was always a straight-A student. How am I supposed to know about something I wasn't taught about and wasn't aware of?!

He continued on and on with a condescending rant – I zoned out for most of it. I was too humiliated to listen, so I walked away from him and toward our tour guide. I tried to watch carefully where I stepped, but it was hard through the tears that had welled up. Aidan followed behind, lecturing on about 'The Che.'

The second half of the hike after the waterfall break had a lot more rocks than on the way up. I was still in front of him from when I tried to escape the Che lecture. I was glad that topic was laid to rest soon after we began the path down the mountain.

The trail had turned into quite the hike and we had to really focus on foot placement at all times. I wished I had worn my damn sneakers. Actually, I really wished I had my old Converse sneakers – they would have been perfect for that type of climb and wouldn't have looked too silly with my linen pants. I wore those shoes almost every day of college. Brad used to say I slept in them.

Brad!!

I had never responded to his email. I wasn't going to reply in Morocco, but I didn't want to leave him hanging. I wondered if I should bring it up to Aidan first. I didn't want to go behind his back, but at the same time, was an innocent email even worth mentioning? I'd worry about that when we were back in Dublin along with the "Did I do something wrong?" talk. There'd be none of those conversations during our trip.

The trail led into an area of rocks – rocks that were made extra slippery by the stream of water running over them. I kept an eye out for the driest, flattest ones to plant my tractionless sandals on. Despite my caution, I chose the wrong stone. I screamed, "Noooo!" as my ankle twisted and I fell in slow motion, scraping the side of my right leg. The only thing worse than the pain was the embarrassment of knowing everyone behind me saw it.

Within seconds, Aidan was helping me onto a nearby boulder and looking at the injuries. Blood had soaked through my white linen pants. He rolled up my pant leg to look at the damage. My ankle was already swollen and there were deep cuts on my knee. He took off his shirt to clean the cuts using the water from our water bottle.

Aidan, looking more worried than me, asked our tour guide for a first-aid kit, but he didn't have one. He explained there wouldn't be one available until we got back to the village where the bus was. Aidan wasn't impressed with that answer. The guide recommended that he run down to the village to get the first-aid supplies and ask someone to help carry me the rest of the way. I insisted that I could make it down on my own; I wanted to get back to the riad as soon as possible.

It was a slow process down the mountain. I had my arm around his waist while I limped from rock to rock, allowing him to carry me where necessary. He told me at one point, "You really have to be more careful."

"Yeah…" I responded. I didn't want to hear it. If I had worn the sneakers like I wanted to, then I wouldn't have slid. Instead, I wore the sandals because he promised I'd be fine in them. There was no point in playing the blame game.

I fell asleep on Aidan's shoulder during the two-hour bus ride back to the riad. When I woke up, he was rubbing my head, staring at me. The ice pack he got in the village at the foothill of the mountain was on my swollen ankle.

Since it hurt to put weight on my foot, we decided to stay in that night. While I showered, Aidan ventured into the New City to the one store where he could purchase alcohol. He came back with a bottle of wine, a huge bottle of water and some cookies that Mariam gave him when he told her about my injury.

"Sorry to keep us in tonight." It was the second time on our trip that I had kept us inside. "We could rent a scooter and go out?" I suggested.

"Don't be silly, missus. It's exhausting out there! It'll be nice to stay in and relax, plus we're both beat from today." He rubbed the leg that I didn't have propped up on a pillow. "We'll go out tomorrow for our last night… if you're up for it, of course." He patted the leg where he had been rubbing and grabbed the wine out of the black plastic bag. "Let's drink our first bottle of Moroccan wine and try to find something on TV in English." He twisted off the cap and filled the glasses from the bathroom, handing me one of them.

We toasted and I took a large sip. "Mmm, the bouquet is sweet, but there's a bitterness from the tannins after you swallow," I said in a tool-bag, wannabe wine connoisseur kind of way. "Ah, it's not bad for a twist off wine... made in a country that doesn't drink alcohol," I added.

"Yeah, but they still export a lot of wine due to their natural resources – the high mountain range keeps the vineyards from getting too warm," he said.

"Ah, interesting. You're so smart, babe." I smiled and took another sip. He flipped through the channels – the only options in English were: *Terminator 2*, African sports news or *My Strange Addiction*. We agreed on T2.

"Speaking of smarts... I'm still really surprised that you didn't know about Che Guevara." He couldn't see my face the way I lay on the couch, but I rolled my eyes. "You're so intelligent – you read books on communism and Stalinist Russia for crying out loud!"

What was he trying to say? I couldn't keep quiet any longer.

"Okay, that's enough." I sat up and faced him. "Wanna tell me how exactly this makes me any less intelligent?" My blood was boiling, but I tried to stay calm. "I can Google this clown right now and in 20 minutes know as much about him as you do. That's just memorizing facts – it has absolutely nothing to do with intellect, so let's not confuse the two, okay?" I lay back down, facing away just in case I started to cry.

"Jessica... the movement he led, the rebellion, is such a significant part of world history. You really ought to care more about history; he was an important revolutionist."

I pulled myself up and turned toward him again. "Well, guess what, Aidan? I don't care." My heart was racing as I looked him in the eyes. "I don't give a flying fuck about this guy. And apparently, he's only *important* to a country that hates mine" I said, using air quotes around the word important.

He fell silent. I should have dropped it then, but I didn't.

"Aidan, I can't go back in time and change what I know and what I don't know... or what information I've been exposed to and what I haven't. I'm only human for fuck's sake. I don't know everything and I never pretended to. Sorry if that bothers you."

He took a deep breath and rubbed his chin.

Neither one of us said anything for a while after my outburst. I thought he was going to walk away – go out on the balcony or to the bedroom. He didn't.

After what felt like an eternity on the couch, I took a few deep breaths myself and scooted closer to him. I knew that no matter what I said, Che would always be 'that thing' we had a fight over. Che Guevara had stained our trip.

Aidan stared quietly at me. I would have given anything to have known what he was thinking, what he wanted to say.

"Next time, I won't be so honest. I should have just nodded and smiled and never said a thing. Then you could continue thinking I'm SO intelligent." I looked away and kept telling myself not to cry; that it'd only make things worse.

"Oh stop it, Jessica! That's not what I think. I just can't believe that you wouldn't have learned about him in school, or at least have seen the image of his face before. He is the most recognizable figure in the world." I rolled my eyes again; that time Aidan saw. "I'm sure even my little sisters know who Che is, and they couldn't be bothered with knowing anything outside their own little worlds."

"Kate isn't in her own world!" I blurted on impulse. "She's sweet and thoughtful and smart and she adores you, in case you didn't know." I felt defensive of my Kate.

I tried to imagine if our roles had been reversed. I pretended I had just discovered that he didn't know who Elvis Presley was. I'd be surprised, yes, but I genuinely wouldn't give a shit. I know Aidan's a smart man, so it'd be exciting to explain to him who Elvis was. I'd play him my favorite Elvis songs and we could watch a documentary on him or something. That's when I realized, after all that, I still didn't know exactly what Che did that made him so remarkable. I spitefully told myself Aidan didn't know either. Quite frankly, I had no desire to find out; I never wanted to hear the name again. It wouldn't be hard considering I managed to go 27 years without ever hearing it; I figured I could go another 27.

I looked him in the eyes. "Look, Aidan, I don't want to fight. This is absurd." I studied his face for a sign… I wished his face was as easy to read as he said mine was, but all I saw was blankness.

"Sorry to disappoint you, but we grew up very differently, so we aren't going to know the same things. I'm

sure there are a lot of things I don't
surprise you."

I placed my hand on his leg. "I'll r
we get back to Dublin and we can have a.
dedicated to intellectual conversation on his wo.
contributions – I look forward to it." I grabbed his hand.
"Cross my heart," I smiled playfully, trying to lighten the
mood. "But for now, can we please, please, pretty
pleeeeassse just drop it?"

"Yes." He leaned over and kissed me. "I'm sorry,
missus," he said before kissing me again.

And just like that... it was the last we ever spoke of
Che.

We watched the movie, but before it ended, Aidan got
up and left unannounced. I finished the film and the wine
on my own. I tiptoed to the bedroom, careful not to wake
him. When I saw that he wasn't sleeping, that pit in my
stomach returned again. Why did he scurry off into the
room alone if it wasn't to crash? He was on his side, with his
back facing my side of the bed. His table lamp was on and
he was fiddling with his phone. He didn't move or say a
word as I crawled into bed. I didn't know what to do – I
didn't want to annoy him if he was reading an article or
streaming a match, but I also didn't want to go to bed
without saying something. I turned on my lamp and
decided to read my book until he was finished.

After a half hour, I couldn't keep my eyes open. He still
hadn't turned or muttered a single word, but he was still
playing with his phone. I didn't know what to do. I was so

to asking the dreaded, "Are you mad at me?" but I ιdn't bring myself to say it. I shut the book and turned ιf my lamp, assuming that would encourage him to say something. Nope, it didn't.

A few minutes later, he put his phone on the bedside table and turned his light off without a word. I scooted closer and put my arm around him. Still nothing. Feeling rejected, I took my arm away and turned so my back was facing his.

What had I done? I debated again about whether or not to talk to him about it. Everything in me said it'd only make things worse.

For the second time that trip, I lay awake in the darkness while silent tears streamed down my face.

TWENTY-ONE

The following morning, I wasn't expecting Aidan to snuggle up to me when the call to prayer blared at the crack of dawn, but he did. I wasn't going to question it; I just giggled as he hummed along to the intercom like he had the days prior.

It was our last day in Morocco. We'd have to leave at 5:00 am the next morning to catch our flight, so we lingered on our terrace that morning, knowing it'd be our last Moroccan breakfast.

"I was thinking, for our last day... we should go to a hammam, one of the nice ones. What do ya reckon?" he asked, eating the spongy pancake-like bread with his fingers. It kind of bothered me that I had said numerous times that those were my favorite part of the breakfast, and he had never offered to give me his. We were only given one each and although there was an impressive assortment of other breads and biscuits he liked, I didn't eat much other than the pancake and yogurt. *Stop being a girl* – I thought to myself. If I wanted his damn pancake, I should have asked for it – maybe they were his favorite too?

"Is that where they cover you in mud, scrub you down and throw buckets of cold water on you?" I asked, eating a biscuit instead of the pancake I wanted.

"Yip. That'd be it. But I reckon if we go to a nice one, it will be more relaxing. We can ask Tariq for recommendations."

"Sounds good to me," I said, as he pulled up the right leg of my pants.

"How's your leg feel?" he asked, inspecting the dressed cut. I winced when he touched it. "We don't have to go out today, missus. I'm happy enough staying in and enjoying our riad."

"Ah, come here, don't be daft!" I said, trying not to laugh. "Did I sound Irish there? I'm becoming SO Irish," I giggled. It was forced, but I had begun slipping Irishisms into my sentences on a more regular basis.

"No. You're not Irish." He finished his orange juice. "You eat way too slow to be Irish," he said before standing and announcing he was going to take a shower. He asked me to look up hammam reviews online as he walked away.

I sat alone at the table, wondering what the hell had just happened. I again told myself not to overthink it and to just find a good hammam to spend our last day at. I did just that.

During the walk to the hammam, the shop owners were extra aggressive in trying to get us to come into their shops. My limping made it more difficult to blow by them when they barked at us in broken English, "My friends, my friends! Come, come… is beautiful carpet and is jewelry for lady, one of kind!"

"Aidan, I want to get something for Kate... uh... and Emma." I tried to cover up that I had a favorite sister. "Something small – any ideas on what they'd like?"

"Ah, you're very good. Hmm... something tiny, we don't have any space in our carry-ons. We'll grab something at the airport or tonight when we're out for dinner." As he responded, I was distracted by six men, three on each side, carrying a wooden board with a body on it. They were walking toward us. Aidan turned to see what I was looking at. As they approached, I became nauseous, realizing the body was a deceased woman. Just her bottom half was covered with a frayed, dirty blanket. Four more people followed behind the body.

Aidan stepped in front of me, trying to block my view as they walked by. "That's a funeral for a woman. The family is carrying her from her deathbed to the burial ground."

"Oh my God," I whispered. That was her funeral? Walking through the medina, only a few people in attendance, none of which even look sad?

"It's horrible; I'm sorry you had to see that. Are you okay?" he asked with his hands on my shoulders.

All the extremes we had seen flashed before me: the poverty, the women having to cover themselves from head to toe, camels and donkeys in place of cars, the overwhelming and constant smell of spices and cigar smoke, chickens butchered on stumps in the street and then... I was limping though a woman's funeral. It was a lot to take in. Aidan's mood swings didn't help either. I couldn't wait to get back to Dublin the next day; I couldn't pretend it was all okay any longer.

"Yeah, I'm okay," I nodded. "It's all part of the experience, right?"

"You amaze me, missus. I don't want to sound condescending, but I'm really surprised at how well you've done here. I've been to a lot of crazy places all over the world, and this is probably the biggest culture shock of them all. But you…? This is your first trip and it hasn't fazed you! I'm really impressed," he smiled.

"Compliment accepted." I nodded once.

But there was no culture that could ever shock me as much as he did when he shut me out the night before. If I could survive that part of the trip, I could survive anything Morocco had to throw at me. Bring on the chicken massacres and public funerals, but do not go to bed without saying goodnight.

At the hammam, we were taken to a dressing room where we changed into robes and slippers – I opted to keep my underwear on and he, his boxer briefs. We were led up three flights of stairs and into a room that looked more like a jail cell than a place for a spa treatment. The floor was drenched and all there was inside the room were two stone blocks that we were to lie on. The two Moroccan women used charades to instruct us to take off our robes and lie facing up. I used *my* charades skills to tell them to be careful with the cuts on my leg. We did as told; we were lying perpendicular with our heads near each other's. The women left us there in silence for about ten minutes. They returned, picking up a hose from the ground and squirting us with cold water. It was real fun. Especially when she sprayed my face and water burned inside my nose. I regretted putting on a coat of mascara as I probably looked like a drowned raccoon.

The women talked amongst themselves as they coated us with a black, gritty mud mixture. I smelled coffee and maybe cinnamon as my lady worked away with her hands, covering every inch of my body – even behind my ears and my forehead, but steering clear of my injury. It tickled and I squirmed, noticing how slippery the stone I lay on was. The next step was a deep scrubbing. I couldn't see what she used to do this, but it had to have been either a horse-grooming brush or a Brillo pad because it fucking hurt. Any bit of tan I had gotten on the trip was scrubbed off, along with several layers of skin. We flipped onto our stomachs to repeat the fun.

After the scrubbing was over, we were still covered in the mud mixture – they actually added more and then left us there. A few minutes went by before I turned my raw, muddy, mascara stained face toward Aidan. He was already looking at me.

"They kept looking at you the whole time – they both were. Especially when you were sitting up facing the wall and your hair was down your back. I wanted to tell my lady: "Hey, I know she's beautiful, but look at me! Over here, hello!" he joked, keeping his voice to a whisper.

"Ha! Well good, I don't want them staring at my man in his skivvies," I said, my cheek pressed against the wet stone bed.

"How long do you think they'll leave us here? Most of the reviews said at least 20 minutes – what do ye reckon I come over for a snuggle?" he joked.

"No way! We'll get in trouble if we get caught!"

It was too late; he was already slipping all over his wet, muddy stone, trying to get up. "Be careful! Oh my God, oh my God!"

"Here comes trouble," he whispered as he tried to lie on my stone beside me. I turned on my side and grabbed him so he didn't slide off. Our slimy bodies reminded me of those jelly toys where the more you try to hold them, the more they slip out of your hand.

"This is very tricky," I whispered, trying not to laugh. When we finally got settled, he stared at me as if he were looking at me for the first – or last – time. He brushed his hand across my bare chest and stroked my face.

"Tricky, huh? Someone told me the first time I met them that *love* was a tricky word," he said, breaking the brief silence.

"Simple wisdom, that person," I smiled.

"Thank you for coming here with me, missus. Thank you for… everything. Thank you," he said and kissed me sweetly.

'Thank you' sounded funny to me. It was *our* trip – an important one as he said… the first of many. 'Thank you' sounded like he was glad I could join him on *his* trip. Maybe he meant 'thank you' for agreeing to Morocco as opposed to somewhere like France, where they don't kill animals in public or haul dead bodies around as if they were furniture. Either way, I decided not to ruin the nice moment by overthinking again.

"You're welcome." I smiled.

"You have made me really happy, missus. I'm so in *tricky* with you." He kissed me hard. "Right, I better get back to my block before we spend our last night in a Moroccan jail."

"Ah, the US embassy would be on me like white on rice. You, on the other hand... would be waiting a while – all the Irish people are on holiday this time of year."

He laughed and squirmed over to his stone bed.

Was that his way of saying he loved me? I didn't know, but that became my favorite part of the trip – superseding the "Slow Show" song.

That night, we went back to the intoxicating Jemaa el-Fna square for our last Moroccan meal. We chose a nice, overpriced, touristy restaurant – mainly because those are the only ones that serve beer and wine and we could sit on a balcony, overlooking the commotion. From our bird's-eye view, we could see just how many vendors there were – so many more than what could be seen from the ground. I was trying to make out what was in the wagon cart being pulled by an anorexic donkey when I heard Aidan say, "Smile, missus."

He took so many more pictures than I did. I was glad, because I wanted a lot of photos but felt awkward taking them. I didn't have to worry with Aidan around – he was constantly snapping selfies of us together.

After dinner, we wandered around a bit – slowly as my leg still hurt. We practiced our negotiation skills to get some trinkets for Kate and Emma before heading back to our riad early to pack for our morning departure.

After I finished packing, I walked into the bathroom where Aidan was brushing his teeth. He looked at me through the mirror as I walked up behind him in only my panties and a tank top. I wrapped my arms around him. He didn't acknowledge me – just rinsed his mouth, wiped his hand on the towel and slid out from my embrace.

Rejected, I stared in the mirror, taking deep breaths. What was going on? How did we go from our muddy make-out session at the hammam to him running away from me on our last night in our fairy tale riad? Again, I wish I had known the right thing to say or do, but I didn't.

I crawled in to the bed, and he immediately scooted over and spooned me. There were no words exchanged, not even goodnight, but we fell asleep tangled in each other.

TWENTY-TWO

The first call to prayer, the one at the crack of dawn, served as our wake-up call.

"I don't wanna get up and go to school today," I joked. His arm was still around me, exactly as we were when we fell asleep. "Ugh, we should get up. We don't have a back-up alarm and it'd suck to miss this flight," I mumbled, half asleep.

"Just a minute – one last snuggle," he said, squeezing me tighter. "You were farting in your sleep, missus."

Ah, fuck! God dammed Moroccan spices. "I was? Uh... sorry."

"It's fine; I've gotten used to it. You did it almost every night here. I just thought I'd wait till the end to tell you."

"Ah, you jerk!" I sat up and began hitting him with my pillow. "Why didn't you tell me?! Do I fart in my sleep at home?" We started wrestling and he eventually pinned me down and held my wrists.

"Nah, you only drool at home... no farting. I don't know how those came from you; they kept waking me up!" I squirmed, trying to get out from under him. "I was hoping you didn't shit your pants. No more Moroccan food for you, okay?" He released my wrists and I reached to turn the lamp on.

"Ah, you're exaggerating now. Get off me… or I'll fart on you."

Mustapha and Mariam had coffee waiting for us when we went downstairs to check out. They hugged and kissed us goodbye as if we were family. Tariq grabbed our luggage and we followed him outside. We said our final goodbyes in the dark and Mariam sent us off with a bag full of assorted cookies and biscuits. I was so over the damn cookies… I wished it was a bag of the spongy pancake things.

We had been in Morocco long enough that we didn't bat an eyelash when Tariq, who we were following, started arguing with another man in Arabic at 5:30 in the morning. After a few minutes of a heated debate that we couldn't understand, the strange man gave Tariq a set of keys. The keys were to a gutted minivan – our ride to the airport. We sat on the floor of the seatless van, clutching on to our luggage. Maybe it was because it was too early or maybe because events that resembled being kidnapped had become normal to us by that point, but whatever it was, we didn't even exchange worrisome glances. We simply listened to Tariq tell us where the best nightclubs were for the 'next time' we came to Morocco.

Twice on the way to the airport, we were stopped by men on the street. Both times Tariq would argue with the men in their foreign language before speeding off. I assumed the van was either stolen or was used for transporting drugs or something scandalous like that. That morning was very odd, but neither Aidan nor I would ever mention it again.

We went through the virtually non-existent security check and boarded the first of two flights back to Dublin. First stop: Brussels… for seven hours just like on the way there. Another horrifically long layover – the relationship 'test' as Lindsay called it.

Aidan went to get us coffee and breakfast while I watched our bags in the open café area. I sent my parents an 'I'm alive' message with a few pictures of Aidan and me – the ones with the most Moroccan-looking backgrounds.

"I practically had to wrestle a guy for the last bacon and egg croissant. You're welcome, missus."

"My hero! I've been dreaming about protein." We had stayed away from meat after seeing first-hand the chickens being butchered in the medina. "It's been quite the carb-overload." I nodded toward the bag of cookies peeking from my purse. "Speaking of wrestling… have you ever been in a fight?" I figured if we had a half a day sitting in the airport, we'd be sharing a lot of stories.

"Babe, I'm a 32, almost 33, year-old man… of course I've been in a fight. But in fairness, it's been about seven or eight years since I was in a proper fight."

I looked at my watch. "Well, we have six and a half hours – spill it!"

He told me the story about how he was out with the lads and a group of guys were being obnoxious and looking to start trouble. Aidan said something that triggered one of the guys to pull out a knife and come at him. He showed me a scar on his forearm, which I hadn't noticed before. It reminded me of the night Brad beat the crap out of a bad drunk who wouldn't leave me alone on a night out. Brad won, but the guy cut his arm with a broken beer bottle. We spent the entire night and next morning in the hospital. I had never seen so much blood in person as I did that night.

"It was mental – a stupid night that got out of hand. But nowadays, I would walk away from a fight; it's just not worth it." He placed his hand on mine. "Unless it involved you," he added. "If anyone ever touched you... even *looked* at you the wrong way, I swear to God I'd fight them." He paused and added his other hand. "Jess, I need you to know that I want to protect you." I held our stare, searching his eyes for something. I responded only by raising the corners of my lips into a smile.

"So, how many olives do you think we ate in the last ten days?" he blurted out.

I gazed up at the ceiling and tapped my finger to my chin. "Hmmm, I'd say..." I did some quick math in my head – every lunch *and* dinner started with a bowl of olives, roughly 50 total per day. 50 times eight (eight instead of the ten days – to account for some of the meals when we didn't get olives) was 400. 400 between the two of us was 200. No way.

"200 each," I replied. "As much as I love olives, I don't want to look at another one for a while – unless of course it's garnishing a Ketel One dirty martini."

"I like that you have a signature drink, right down to the brand of vodka. It's very sexy."

"What's your drink? The only cocktail I've ever seen you drink was that fruity concoction on our first date at Fitzsimons. That can't be it, can it?" I joked.

"Ah, the fuzzy navel! I didn't know it was going to come out with so much fruit and a twisty straw – I just picked one with a cool name."

"Ohh, so is that why you ordered two more after that instead of switching to beer?" I laughed.

"You caught me… I don't really drink spirits. I only did that night because I used the 'wanna go for cocktails' line to get you to stay out, so I *had* to order cocktails. I was nervous!"

"Oh. My. God. Did you just say that *you* were nervous?! I've told you so many times that you make me nervous – you always just tell me not to be." I looked at him with widened eyes. "I guess it would ruin your image. It's okay, babe – it'll be our little secret," I winked.

"I was nervous. Why do you think it took me so long to ask you out?" he asked.

"Because you were seeing someone else?" I responded.

"That's not the reason," he replied. "You were intimidating – waltzing into my life with a pink boa and ridiculous sunglasses."

"Ah, so you were judging!" I laughed.

"No, just observing. But the more we emailed and texted, the more I liked you. Then, when you backed off and stopped, I thought I had blown it – until you sent that picture of the coke bottle. I knew I had to ask you out so… yes, I was nervous on the first date."

"How many times were you nervous on the trip? Like, that something bad might happen?"

"31 times," he responded without much hesitation. "No wait, sorry… 32."

"What the…? Alright, explain," I insisted.

"The first 30 is from the three meals a day on our 10 day trip. I was nervous that it'd be the one to give me, or you, food poisoning. I'm shocked we made it out of there without getting sick."

"We didn't get sick thanks to living off of olives, couscous, bread and cookies for those ten days," I pointed out. "Can we cook steaks one night this week – before Lindz arrives?"

He just smiled and sipped his coffee.

"So that's 30... what about the other two times you were nervous?"

"When we first arrived in Marrakesh, I thought that boy showing us to the riad was a con artist," he said with widened eyes.

"Oh yeah! Me too, but I was so tired at that point – he could have robbed us if it meant getting to sit," I said.

"Then, the time I was most nervous was back in Casablanca – the first medina we walked in. When I couldn't find you I... well, I sort of panicked. You were my responsibility. The way the Moroccan guys looked at women, especially you, I assumed the worst. I was never as happy as I was when I saw you standing in the front row at the chicken massacre. You were fine – the only thing you needed was a bucket of popcorn." He said it all with a straight face while I laughed.

"Gosh, I almost forgot about Casablanca and Rabat – it feels like we were there ages ago! Marrakech kind of overshadowed them." I took my last sip of cold coffee.

"What are you going to remember most about Morocco? What will be the first things to pop in your head about this trip years from now?" he asked, in the bluntness that I had grown used to.

"Definitely the olives," I answered straight away. "And being in the square that first night in Marrakesh. I think I'll always be able to imagine myself there – even if I can't describe it well enough to place someone else there."

He was waiting for more. I couldn't say what I feared I'd really remember most about the trip – his mood swings that left me feeling like a crazy person. I'd never tell him that I'd always remember the two nights I cried myself to sleep or how humiliated he made me feel about the Che Guevara thing.

"Oh! I'll remember the big smile we'd always get from Mariam when she opened the door – usually after 10 minutes of waiting," I added.

"Oh, that's a good one... I'll remember that too. I really liked her and Tariq. Mustapha needed some more warming up to."

We continued reminiscing about the trip as if it were years ago. We then played our beloved people-watching game. I scanned the airport cafeteria and selected a couple – they looked about 60 years old and in a grumpy mood. I started it off by saying they were the Harrisons, an American couple. The last of their four kids had recently moved out, so it was their first trip outside of America – they hated it. She's going to hold it against him for months that they didn't go on the Carnival cruise to the Caymans like she had suggested. Aidan added on that she's upset they didn't make it to the Tulip Garden and he's more upset they didn't make it to the restaurant Anthony Bourdain recommended – those damn European streets are just too confusing and filled with cyclists. They'll go back to their home in a Midwest suburb, where next week they'll fight over who was supposed to pick up the ketchup for the steaks – because they can't have steak without ketchup. The game went on for a while until eventually I read my book and he read the news on his phone.

After an hour of reading, Aidan went to get us another round of coffee.

"So, Lindsay and Jason are pretty serious, I reckon?" he asked, blowing into his cup.

"Yeah, I wouldn't be surprised if he proposes soon. I just hope she snaps out of her denial about becoming a step-mom. I thought she'd be a great mother figure, but it's not happening. It's hard to state the obvious to her – she loves him and she's just being hopeful… ya know?"

"How long have they been together?"

"Let's see… they started dating a few months before I moved here, so almost a year and a half," I answered.

"And you wouldn't be surprised if he proposed after only a year and a half?!" He was surprised about that timeframe. I was well accustomed to the Irish dating for four or five years before even thinking about marriage. A year and a half would be pretty standard for Americans – it's probably a major factor in our high divorce rate.

"Well, he is 35 with a kid and she's 29. They both know what they want, so I think they can skip the years and years of testing the waters. Jason would have proposed by now if she wasn't so slow to warm up to Cody." I sipped my soy cappuccino and debated whether or not to ask the next question.

"Have you ever come close to proposing? Or have any ex-girlfriends ever put the pressure on you to get married?" I asked, setting my coffee down.

"Every single one of them," he laughed nonchalantly. "It's funny, after about a year, year and a half, they all brought it up – a couple gave ultimatums. But to answer your question… no, I never actually considered proposing to any of them."

He leaned back in his chair and crossed his arms. Part of me was glad to hear that he had never wanted to propose to anyone, but a bigger part of me was turned off from the way he said it. I didn't know anything about any of his exes except that by virtue of them being his ex, I automatically didn't like them, but something about his cavalier attitude made me ask the follow-up question on their behalf.

"Why did it take them bringing up marriage for you to end it? Clearly, you would have known it wasn't working long before that discussion – why did *you* drag it out?"

"You're right; I should have ended it earlier, but I guess I was just… hopeful. Jess, relationships go through phases – highs and lows, various life events, changes and whatnot. I wanted to make sure I didn't end something because we were going through a phase. Maybe it was selfish to drag it out, but when marriage was mentioned, it was kind of like: no, this has gone too far."

It was a good answer. No, it was the perfect answer. I felt silly for ever worrying that something was wrong during the trip. He was right – relationships aren't perfect and even in the beginning, it's not all puppy dogs and rainbows. People have mood swings, off days and us being in a developing country hadn't exactly created a romantic backdrop for our new relationship. But Aidan knew this – and to be fair, he had done and said so many sweet and reassuring things during the trip. Why had I been focusing on the few one-offs? I had wanted to talk about things after Lindsay left, but I knew then that there was nothing to talk about. I needed to deal with my insecurities.

"What about you? Have you ever been engaged?" he asked.

Ah, crap. I knew that Brad had bought a ring, but I broke us up before he actually proposed.

"No... I haven't."

I regretted the words as soon as they came out of my mouth. Technically, it wasn't a lie, but withholding the truth was the same as lying. I would tell him the full story later on, but an airport layover after a rollercoaster trip was neither the time nor the place.

"Well, Brad and I kind of assumed we'd get married one day, but I was just shy of 25 when we broke up – we were too young to seriously talk about marriage."

Dammit Jessie! Why on Earth did I say that? *That* was definitely a lie.

"Right, I know what you mean," he said. "What about any other guys after him?"

"Well, there were only two years between Brad and my move to Dublin. The few relationships during that time were never more than three, maybe four months. I think that's the time when you know if it's working or not – no need to continue on if you know it's not right."

I didn't mean for it to come out how it did, and I hoped he didn't take it as a dig at him because he took a year to figure out it wasn't working with his exes.

"I just feel that although you may not know if someone's 'The One' after a few months, you certainly know if they're not. I think it's always better not to drag things out."

He jerked his head back, slightly, as if taken aback. Then there was a small smile.

"Right," he said, finishing his coffee before grabbing our suitcases. "Shall we head to our gate, missus?"

TWENTY-THREE
Mid-October 2013

We arrived back in Dublin late Sunday night, making Monday a tough transition back to work. I only had to manage a four-day week as I had taken off work that Friday for Lindsay and Jason's arrival. I also took off the following Monday and Tuesday to bring them on the mini side-trip that Aidan had created an itinerary for. Taking a total of eight workdays off between Morocco and Lindsay's visit was no big deal in Dublin. In fact, some co-workers even asked why I wasn't taking the entire week off when Lindsay was in town. It was because they were taking a separate romantic trip alone. That Wednesday after Dingle, I'd go back to work (for good) and they'd be off to Kinsale before going home.

Aidan and I spent Monday evening in our respective apartments, unpacking and doing laundry. We both had to work late on Tuesday and Wednesday, but we met for lunch at Joe Burger on Wednesday to catch up on the protein. That week was all about getting back into the real life routine – so much so that I never made it to Oxfam to get my burgundy boots. I wasn't too worried about it because I called again and they were still there, waiting in the back room for me. Plus, I knew I'd bring Lindsay and Jason to Grafton Street, so I could just get them then.

That Thursday, I left work early to clean my apartment and pick up some goodies to have on hand for Lindsay and Jason's arrival the next day. I bought a loaf of soda bread, Superquinn sausages, baked beans and tomatoes so I could make them an Irish breakfast. I made a separate trip to Redmond's, for a selection of Irish craft beers – mostly for Jason.

I sent a picture of the care package to Aidan and asked if I was missing anything. He responded: "Olives!" But, of course, I already had those for the martinis.

The next morning, I was playing on my phone, leaning against the oven as I watched for Lindsay and Jason's cab. By the end of my second cup of coffee, all I had seen out the window was Cleopatra the cat, lurking around like the she-devil that she was.

When I finally saw their taxi outside my building, I opened the window and yelled out to them. I ran out and tackled Lindsay while Jason paid the taxi driver.

"Oh my God, Jessie! I'm here... in Ireland!" she screamed. I pulled back to see her face filled with excitement. She pulled me back in and whispered, "I've missed you so much."

"Me too, Lindz. I'm so glad you're here; we're going to have so much fun!" I squealed.

Jason came over to give me a hug as well. "You look stunning as ever, Miss Dunhour – more European than when you left us, but it looks good on you!"

He was the stunning one, dressed as if he'd just walked off a Tommy Hilfiger shoot – one of the ones where everyone is fully dressed on a yacht and laughing at the sunset. He's tall, muscular, has dirty blonde hair, blue eyes and a scruffy beard – Lindsay had done well for herself. He snatched the luggage from me when I tried to take one of the bags.

"Welcome to my little Euro flat!" I exclaimed as we entered my apartment. It was awkward trying to fit their three huge suitcases in my tiny living room. *So typical of Americans to over pack,* I thought. "It's a bit different from our place in South Tampa, huh?"

"Aww, Jessie, it's fabulous! You've really made it your own; I was nervous when you sent the pictures back when you first moved in, but you've fixed it up. I'm so proud of you!" Lindsay said, setting her purse on the chair.

I made them a quick, mini Irish breakfast while they told me about their taxi driver and the stories he told them about Dublin. Lindsay caught me up on all her work events she'd organized the past two weeks and I told them about Morocco – showing them all the pictures and talking up how great Aidan was.

"You are fearless, Jessie! I don't think I could go to Morocco," Lindsay said, handing me my phone back.

"I'm not fearless; I was with Aidan. I wouldn't have gone otherwise, but I trust him. I'd go anywhere with him. Well... almost anywhere," I laughed.

"Will we get to meet Aidan tonight?" Jason asked.

"Yeah, I need to meet this guy – he's taken my stubborn Jessie and made her talk like a girlie-girl," Lindsay said, leaning against my kitchen doorway. "I was starting to think that every guy was going to be cauliflower to you," she added.

"That was harsh!" Jason said in my defense.

I laughed. "Nah, he makes me forget that vegetables exist. I don't think I'll want to ever make cauliflower soup again." The joke sounded much better in my head.

"That's a bold statement!" Lindsay exaggerated.

After they ate, they napped for a few hours to adjust to the time difference, while I went for a run. I took them into town for a whistle stop tour of the main sites in City Centre – Stephen's Green, Dublin Castle and Trinity College – and to take some cheesy pictures with the Molly Malone statue. Between the jet lag and all the walking, they were beat, so we headed back to my neighborhood after a few hours.

Aidan had texted me to let him know when we were back from sightseeing so that he could call me. I was going to tell him to meet us the next day, since they weren't going to last much longer than dinner.

We walked through the Ranelagh village before heading back to my place to shower. Out of nowhere, Lindsay blurted, "I meant to tell you – I ran into Binx a few days ago at Walgreens. He wanted to talk, but he was with his skanky fiancée, so it was weird."

Fiancée?!!

"Oh really?" I laughed awkwardly. "I didn't realize they were that serious," I said, casually. It had been over three years since we broke up, so I wasn't expecting the news to sting the way it had. I was with someone that I knew fit me better, but it still stung.

"Yeah, it was only like two weeks ago that he proposed."

Two weeks ago? When did he send me that email? Fuck! I remembered I had never responded to him! He probably thought I was such a bitch. I had received the email a couple of weeks before we left for Morocco, so the email was sent about a month earlier – well before he proposed.

"Rumor has it that he wasn't ready, but she gave him an ultimatum – pressured him into it."

Oh shit, Brad, NO! Was *that* why he sent the email? Was he breaking the ice so that he could talk to me about it? Get my perspective? And I just left him hanging. I wondered if I should respond back with apologies for the delay and congratulate him on the engagement. Or was that no longer appropriate now that he was engaged?

"Of course he asked about you. I told him I was coming to see you, and he said to tell you 'hi' and all that."

I wondered if she told him I was seeing someone – it'd be right up her alley to. I felt guilty for hoping that she didn't tell him.

"When he hugged me goodbye, he whispered quietly so the skank couldn't hear, 'Please look after *our* Jessie.' Good Lord, he still loves you, Jess… even the skank knows it."

I shook my head at her.

"I could tell by the looks she gave me that she knew exactly who I was – the best friend of the girl she'll never live up to. It's no wonder she had to force him into marrying her." Lindsay was waving her hands as if she were Italian.

"Ah, stop it, Lindz! That's water under the bridge. It was so long ago; we're completely different people now," I replied.

"Maybe you are, but Bradley Binx will always love *every* – and *all* – versions of you."

"As I will you," Jason said playfully, putting his arm around Lindsay.

"Aww!" I exaggerated, ready to change the subject away from Brad. "Hey, how are your feet feeling?" I asked, wondering how she was holding up after a day of walking around.

"Oh, they're fine; I could walk for days in these flats," she replied.

"Are the blisters from the Louboutins all better?" Lindsay gave me a look of death as soon as I said it.

"The Louboutins gave you blisters, sweetie?" Jason asked, confused. "But you always tell me how comfortable they are."

Ah, so she wanted Jason to think that wearing five inch, strappy stilettos a size too small didn't hurt at all – that it was like clouds caressing her feet.

"They are comfortable; they just gave me a little blister the last time I wore them. But I had them on all night, so it was expected," she smiled through the fib.

"Okay, just so you're alright," he replied, satisfied by her explanation.

It was evident that Laurence the lace up stiletto and Cody the child had a lot more in common than I originally had thought. Lindsay wasn't just lying to herself – she was lying to Jason too... about both. He was under the impression that she and Cody were moving in the right direction, not regressing. Just like he didn't realize how painful the shoes really were to Lindsay.

Back at my apartment, I showed them my hand-picked variety pack of Irish craft beers. We did a little taste test, splitting each bottle amongst the three of us. They both liked my favorite, Belfast Blonde, but when we got to the Dark Art's stout, Lindsay gave her portion to Jason and scurried off to take a shower. Jason and I moved to the sofa, drinking the beers and catching up.

"Jessica, a big reason why I wanted to come here with Lindsay is because, well...." He trailed off and bent over and fiddled with one of the suitcases. He sat up, holding a tiny grey box. He opened it to reveal an enormous, cushion-cut diamond ring.

"Sweet baby Jesus!" I exclaimed, low enough that Lindsay wouldn't hear. "Wow! Congratulations, Jason!" I hugged him. "Are you planning to pop the question when you guys go off on your own trip next week?"

"Yep – I booked three nights at The Carlton in Kinsale. There's a really nice view close by, so I'll ask her there. I hope it will be really special for her," he said, smiling like a fool.

"Oh, Jason, she'll love it... really, she will." I couldn't remember her ever telling me that they had mentioned or talked about marriage. I wondered if it would catch her off guard – if she really *would* love it.

"She's The One, Jess... I know this is my second go at marriage, but I want you to know that I love her so much. I felt more for Lindsay after a few months than I ever did for Cody's mother. I know that sounds horrible, but it's the truth."

I forced a smile and placed my hand on his wrist and said, "I know you love her – she loves you too." It certainly wasn't my place to bring up the Cody/step-mom situation, especially not while he sat there with a two and a half carat ring in his hand.

We heard my loud electric shower turn off, so Jason put the ring back into its hiding place. I hollered through the bathroom door that the hairdryer was in my room as there were no outlets in the bathrooms. I told Jason I was going to step outside to call Aidan. I wanted to tell him not to worry about coming out for dinner that night, but without them hearing.

As I walked outside, my phone rang. I smiled when I saw a picture of Aidan and me outside one of the mosques in Morocco. I had set it to be his contact picture after he sent me all the pictures he took of us on the trip.

"Happy Friday!" I said, extra bubbly. He liked to make fun of my enthusiastic greetings.

"Hey there, Jessica, how are you? Did your friends get in alright?" he said, stiffly.

Jessica? Why was he beginning to call me 'Jessica' more and more instead of 'missus' or 'Jessie'? And *my friends?* He knew their names – we had talked about them numerous times.

I continued on, telling him they got in fine and I told him what we did during the day. He muttered a few 'yeahs' to show he was listening, but I could tell he was distracted. I began telling him about how I saw Cleopatra kill a mouse and then leave it on the street – the evil cat didn't even eat it! As I was in the middle of the story, he interrupted me…

"Erm, Jessica?" he paused. "Look, the reason I need to talk to you right now is… well, because…"

When he paused, I thought that something bad had happened to him. I had been selfishly thinking he might have been annoyed with me and failed to consider that something might have been going on with a friend or family member, or with work.

"Jessica… I don't want to continue this relationship."

TWENTY-FOUR

I was dizzy and nauseous. Everything started to spin. I felt trapped inside a kaleidoscope with all the colored doors on my street swirling together. I sat on the pavement before I collapsed.

Was he really saying he wanted to end our relationship? Why? He had asked me to stay another year... then with one sentence, he took it back. I had no say; I felt completely blindsided.

We had just gotten back from Morocco a few days prior. In that time, we met for lunch and everything seemed fine. What had happened to cause such a sudden change? I quickly replayed the entire trip in my head. Was it being with me all day and all night for ten days that made him realize I wasn't what he wanted after all? I felt so insecure.

Then it occurred to me – he knew *before* Morocco. I thought back to the weekend before we left, searching for a triggering moment that I failed to see at the time. But that didn't make sense either. The weekend before we left was when he invited me to spend Christmas with his family and said he wanted to come home with me for Thanksgiving. That was also when he mentioned letting me take his car to drive around the country and he brought up all the plans he had for our own weekend trips in Ireland. Did he realize he was committing himself to too much too fast? Or was he bullshitting the whole time?

Maybe it was because I was venting and complaining about work all week? Maybe he thought I was a miserable, negative person… with no passion? In about 30 seconds, I came up with dozens of possibilities as to why he was breaking up with me. None of them really made sense.

Despite all the thoughts and questions running through my mind, I had remained silent. I didn't know whether to scream, cry or plead. I chose silence. Neither of us said anything for what felt like an eternity. Part of me wanted to say, "Goodbye," and hang up, but I couldn't bring myself to do it. I didn't want to appear weak or immature.

He broke the silence. "Ah, Jess, it's just that I feel…. I don't know… I guess I feel indifferent about you."

Indifferent? Indifferent?!! Did he really say he felt *indifferent* about me?

I hate that word. Indifferent is how I feel about the color of the socks I wear to bed, not about a human being. I thought we were crazy for each other? Even if it changed for him, how could it have completely changed to indifference?

What if he never really felt what I felt – well, what he led me to believe he was feeling? Maybe for him, it was just infatuation and I was no longer something new and exciting? Maybe I was just a travel buddy so he wouldn't have to go to his bucket list country alone? No matter what I *was* to him... I had *become* cauliflower.

Cauliflower – that was it! He saw that I was holding back – all the times he asked me those deep questions and I hid behind a polite answer? Did that make me boring? Not passionate enough about anything? If that was the issue, it'd be an easy fix – I could show him more, I could put the guard down.

There were so many things I wanted to say to him, but where would I start? How could I talk about it without sounding desperate? I decided I'd ask him if we could talk in a few days, so I could think through what I wanted to say and not be an emotional mess.

Before I could muster up the words, he sighed loudly. "I feel like... like it wouldn't matter if I were to see you this weekend or not. And that's not fair to you."

I could physically feel my heart breaking.

"I didn't want to have to go through meeting your friends and *then* have this happen after they've left. I figured that'd be even harder for you. I just couldn't do that to you, Jessica."

OH MY GOD, STOP TALKING!! I may not have known who Che Guevara was, but I fucking knew the definition of 'indifferent' – there was no need to elaborate. Did he want me to think he was sparing my feelings? To think the option he chose was so much less cruel? I wanted to scream hurtful things to him, but I was still paralyzed.

"Jessica?" he asked, making sure I was still on the line.

"Yeah," I muttered.

"Can you say something, please?"

I tried to take a deep breath, but it was hard with the knife stabbing me in the chest.

"Umm… well…" Fucking pull yourself together, Jessica! Don't sound like you're devastated, but don't sound like you don't care. Say goodbye, sleep on it and then call him in a few days to talk in person. Yeah, that was a good plan.

"I'm… umm… I'm really sad to hear this, but I… I can't make you feel something you don't. Thanks for being so… honest?" I closed my eyes tightly and recited: stay strong, stay strong, STAY STRONG! "I don't want to keep you any longer – goodbye, Aidan." I was shaking and my head was in between my knees. I was going to be sick.

Just before I hung up, he interrupted. "Ah Jesus, Jessie! Look, I wanted it to work out, I really did. We have so much fun together and I think you're a lovely girl, but… I think you're feeling something more than I am."

I was feeling more than *he* was?!?! I didn't create the relationship up in my head! If anything, I was following his lead! *He* asked me to extend my contract, *he* took me to meet his family, *he* told me that Morocco would be the first of many big trips for us, *he* invited me to spend Christmas with him, *he* dedicated the "Slow Show" song to me and *he* said he was in 'tricky' with me just the WEEK before! How was any of that a sign of *indifference*? But yet, I was the confused one? Fuck him.

Was it all a game?

How long had he led me on?

I was furious at that point and decided to get the one answer I wanted and then scrap the idea to meet up after few days to talk.

"Hey, Aidan?" I paused, he didn't respond. "Did you feel this way before we left for Morocco, or was it the trip that did it for you?"

The first time I really felt the shift was on the first night in Morocco, but everything was great before that. What could have happened in that one day to cause such a change? If he had been feeling indifferent before Morocco, he sure had me fooled. If he would have told me he felt indifferent during the trip, he knew I would have left which would have messed up his vacation. Either option made him a coward in my mind – to keep me there in a strange country, feeling insecure, only to break up with me a few days later, on the phone.

"Erm… uhhh… uhhh, I think I started to feel it a couple of days before we left. Then, in Morocco, I'd go back and forth… trying to decide if things between us felt right or not."

Yeah, no shit he was going back and forth. Glad I could be his emotional yo-yo while he figured it out. I wanted to end the conversation; I couldn't take it any longer. I remembered the money I owed him for the trip. I knew it'd kill me if weeks later I got a call or text from him only so he could get his money. I wanted to be the one to bring it up.

"But then, when we were at the airport – you said that after a few months of dating someone, you might not know if it's right, but you know when it's not right. It struck a nerve and that's when I knew I needed to end it."

Shit, I wasn't expecting that. I couldn't take any more surprises.

Would he still be breaking up with me if I hadn't said that at the airport? Would he have strung me along like he did with the other girlfriends before me? What about what *he* said at the airport? He said he had remained in relationships because he was *hopeful* – knowing relationships and feelings go through phases. Was he so sure that I wasn't The One that there was no reason to try and see it through any longer – not even a few days until my best friend left? Awesome. Really fucking awesome.

I had a million more things I wanted to ask him, but why? Why drag out a conversation with someone who was indifferent toward me? That one word said everything. After a long silence, I managed, "Well, umm… it's Friday night and there's nothing left to say, so… just text me what I owe you for the trip when you've figured it out." My chest burned thinking of our relationship being boiled down to a monetary transaction. "Goodbye, Aidan."

"Jessica, wait!" I couldn't imagine what hurtful thing he was going to hit me with next. "I want you to know that I feel sad about this. I don't feel relieved or anything – I really did want it to work out."

He didn't feel relieved? What did it matter? He had just broken my heart. I didn't give a shit whether or not he was relieved to have done it. I couldn't handle another minute of the conversation – with every word, *he* was falling off the pedestal I had put him on.

"Goodbye, Aidan," I repeated. I didn't want to believe that it'd be the last words I'd ever say to him.

"Have fun with your friends and enjoy the rest of your time in Ireland."

He might as well have said: Have a nice life.

I quickly hung up so he wouldn't hear me cry.

TWENTY-FIVE

I never ended up crying when I hung up the phone. I was too numb and too much in shock to produce tears. I started to call my mom, but as my luck would have it – the rain came pouring down. There was definitely a God, and He was pissed at me for ceasing to believe in Him.

I pulled myself up from the pavement where I was sitting and headed back to my apartment. Although the conversation had only lasted about ten minutes, it was long enough for me to completely forget I had visitors back at my place. I hated Aidan for causing me to wish they weren't there. Not only were they there, but they were happy, in love and waiting for the fun-filled trip I had promised. All I wanted to do was to lie in bed for days and not talk to a soul.

I opened the door and Lindsay, with her hair wrapped in a towel, asked how dressed up she should get for dinner.

"I want to look just right for the first time I meet Aidan – don't want him to think your best friend is a slob," she said, holding a sweater dress with a geometric print. "Jessie? What's the matter? You look like you've seen a ghost."

"Aidan just broke up with me," I said, staring at the ground.

"What?! Just now *on the phone*?!" she exclaimed.

It hadn't occurred to me until then that it was shitty of him to do it on the phone.

"Yep. On the phone, just now," I said, toneless. I went to sit on the sofa; I had to sit.

"What a dick! Seriously, what's his deal?" she said loudly, emphasizing each word. "He could NOT have picked a more inconvenient time – and you guys just got back from your trip!" She waved the dress about. "What was his reason?"

"I don't know," I responded, putting my head in my hands. "I didn't ask. I don't want to know."

"Jess, he went from hot to cold in like two seconds and you didn't ask why?" She knelt on the floor in front of me. Jason sat on the sofa with me, rubbing my back.

"He told me he doesn't want to be with me. What more of a reason do I need? He said he feels indifferent toward me – and it wouldn't matter to him if he were to see me this weekend or not."

"Did he *really* say that to you, Jessie?" Jason asked. The tone of his voice validated my hurt feelings.

I nodded. Tears began to cloud my vision.

"That was really unnecessary. It sounds like he wasn't such a great guy after all," he said.

"I don't know who he is. I can't believe my heart and my judgment were so wrong," I whispered.

"You deserve someone so much better than that, Jessie. I know that sounds really generic, but as an outsider looking in… I could never say something so hurtful to a woman I was seeing. If he realized he no longer felt the same way he did before, he didn't need to say that. It sounds like he needed to convince himself of his decision," Jason said calmly.

"Jess, I told you… in the beginning, when he was playing games and not asking you out that something was off. He's way too old to be playing those games." Lindsay went on and on, but my mind was spinning out of control.

"Come on, Jess, let's be real… you were out of his league anyways. Now, after this little stunt, it's clear you two weren't even playing on the same field."

I knew what they were trying to do, but I didn't want to hear any of it. If I was such a great catch, then why was I rejected… basically told I was cauliflower… by the guy I was crazy about… *on the phone*… five days after a big trip together… on the day my best friend arrived from 4,000 miles away?

"Thanks, Lindz," I muttered. "Do you guys mind if I go for a walk? I want to call my mom."

"Of course, take as long as you need. We can order pizzas; we don't need to go out," Jason said.

"Don't be silly. It's your first night in Dublin and you came all this way. I'm so glad you guys are here," I lied.

I put on my wellies and rain jacket and went outside. Walking past the lamppost where I sat just minutes before was hard. That area had become stained.

My mom answered on the second ring. "There's my little world traveler! What's up, peeps?!" I wished she hadn't sounded so cheerful.

"Hey, Mama. Not much, just getting ready to go out to dinner with Lindsay and Jason."

"Oh good, so they got in alright? Is Aidan going out with you guys?"

"Umm... Mom? Aidan just called and... he broke up with me." I didn't believe the words as they came out of my mouth. "He said that I was feeling more than he was. I don't know what happened; I'm just so confused, Mom."

"Jessica, listen to me," she said sternly. "You stay far away from him. Don't you contact him and do not respond if he contacts you – do you hear me?"

Her reaction really caught me off guard.

"I wasn't planning on contacting him, but why do you say that?"

"Jessica, something doesn't add up. He put on this big show – said and did all the right things – and then POOF! And he's done. I don't buy it and I don't trust him as far as I could throw him. He kept you around long enough so that it wouldn't ruin *his* trip to Morocco but he had no problem ruining yours with your friends. Stay away from that selfish bastard."

Dad piped up in the background, "I'm gonna hunt that little weasel down and give him a swift kick in the ass!"

"Ugh, I know why he did it, Mom – it's all my fault. I wasn't opening up. I had a guard up, I kept things from him."

"What do you mean? What did you keep from him?" she asked, confused. Several examples came to mind – when we were talking about poverty and I didn't tell him about my four years of mentoring, when he asked about my goals and passions and I didn't tell him about Chicago or the promotion I wanted, when he mentioned adoption and I remained silent, hell – even when he asked if I was a foodie and I gave some generic answer. I had opened up a few times but not enough for someone I was so crazy about. Shit, I didn't even tell him about what had happened with Brad – I'd swept it under the rug. He probably thinks I've never had a serious relationship. He didn't really get to know me... and apparently, I didn't really know him. In being reserved and agreeable, had I pushed him away? The Jessica I was presenting to him was a watered down version of the real thing – or was it? I didn't even know who I was anymore.

"Well, there were a few times we talked about philosophy and he'd ask me how I knew about it... Mom, I didn't even tell him I have a second degree in philosophy. I wasn't ready to be questioned on why I wasn't doing anything with it." I sighed, feeling annoyed with myself. "There were lots of things like that." I told her some other examples as well.

"So maybe you held back a little, but so what?! Jessie, you were only dating for what... four? five months? It *should* take a while. If you want to learn about someone, you nourish the relationship... you don't end it. You only get to know someone over time and experience, not by interviewing them."

"Yeah, you're right." It was easier to agree. "But there are two sides to every story. I'll never know his side... and he'll never know mine. It's a sad story really."

I had been walking during the entire conversation, so I sat on the pavement. In front of me was the Canadian Embassy – it was the same place where I had cried on the phone to my dad, wanting to move home. It had been almost exactly one year after I had my melt down on Labor Day, the previous September. What a difference a year can make. Although the breakup was so much worse than a series of annoying mishaps – I wasn't crying like I did when my bath towels fell on the ground. Nor did I want to run home to America waving my white flag. I had grown a lot in that year.

"Peeps, I know this is hard, but please… don't beat yourself up over it. He wasn't the one. Like I always say to you… everything happens for a reason." I rolled my eyes – I knew that by calling, I had asked for the cookie-cutter breakup advice, but I couldn't take any more of it. "You have the best friends in the world. They adore you – and Lindsay came all the way out there to see you. Don't let this take away from your time with her, okay?"

"It won't, Mom, I promise. We're going to have a good time… really," I lied again. "I should get back to them."

"Okay, good. We love you, peeps. Call us any time – day or night; we'll always be here for you, sweetie."

"Thanks, left wellie," I managed.

"Left wellie?" she asked.

"Yep. Left because you're left handed – Dad's the right one. You guys are my wellies; that's what Irish people call rain boots. You guys are both always so dependable, the only ones I can count on – just like my wellies," I explained.

"Wellies, huh? I like it! And, yes... your wellies are always here – rain or shine!" I could hear her smile through the phone.

"Thanks, Mom, I love you," I said before hanging up.

I walked home, waiting to be woken up by the call to prayer – to have Aidan snuggle behind me while he sang along and I realized that it was just a dream.

TWENTY-SIX

Lindsay was doing her makeup while Jason watched golf when I returned. I went straight to my room, kicking off my wellies as I climbed into bed. I felt so empty.

I lay on my right side, staring at the ground. I started counting backwards from 100 to keep myself from replaying the conversation in my head. I hadn't even gotten to 90 when Aidan's voice interrupted… *I feel indifferent toward you.* I continued the useless exercise and by the time I reached 70, Lindsay was sitting on the bed.

"Jess? I know you don't want to think about this, but do you think he met someone else? Or maybe someone from the past came back into the picture?" she asked. Yes, of course I had thought of that.

"I hope so," I said quietly.

"Why in the world would you hope that?!" she exclaimed.

"Because... then it'd be out of my control and not because I wasn't smart or funny or interesting enough," I answered, still staring at the same spot in the corner.

"WHAT?! Are you kidding me? If you're not interesting, then the rest of the world might as well be a cabbage. And smart enough? Coming from the nerd who cried when she got a 'B' one time in advanced physics?" She scooted closer, putting her hand on my back. I saw her feet on the ground in front of me. I could see the blisters and red marks from the Louboutin lace-ups.

"Jess, where is this coming from? Did something happen that is making you so insecure?"

Oh I don't know, maybe because the guy I was crazy about feels INDIFFERENT toward me!

"Nothing specific, just thinking that maybe I was a boring travel buddy – I wasn't as talkative as I usually am." I sighed. "And I was sick the first day and a half... and then I fell and cut my leg... he probably thought I was a drag." I wiped a tear hanging from the corner of my eye. "Maybe he thought I was ugly without makeup?" I lifted my head toward her, "Did I tell you... I didn't have a hair dryer or a hair straightener the whole ten days?" I smiled, trying to lighten the mood. Lindsay would find even a weekend without hair gadgets to be unfathomable.

"Oh my God, Jessie, STOP IT! You sound like a crazy person! You are beautiful inside and out – with or without makeup. You could shit your pants and you'd still be gorgeous. People's feelings don't just change that easily!" she yelled.

Oh my God, Lindsay had nailed it – shit. Maybe the farting in my sleep had something to do with it.

"Jess, I think there's someone else – I'm sorry, but I do."

I remained silent for a while. "Lindz? Do you know who Che Guevara is?" I asked, unaffected by her outburst the moment prior.

"I have no friggin' clue – is he that crazy French designer who sent his models down the runway in airtight bags?" she asked. I saw her shrug her shoulders from the corner of my eye.

"Yeah, something like that." I laughed.

"What does he have to do with anything?" she asked.

"Nothing. He has nothing to do with anything. Or maybe he has something to do with everything. I don't know. I don't know anything anymore," I rambled, still staring at the same piece of pulled up carpet in the corner of my bedroom.

"Jesus Christ, Jess! Did he make you feel bad for not knowing about some stupid guy?"

I remained silent and closed my eyes.

"You know, on the flight over, Jason laughed at me because I had no clue who some Congressman that he mentioned was. He explained to me who he was and that was that. I still don't know who he is and Jason couldn't care less. It doesn't affect my ability to be a good girlfriend or a good person. No one gives a shit who this Nakey-Vera, or whatever, guy is. I hate him, Jess. I really, really hate him for doing this to you."

"You said in your message last week that you loved him without even meeting him. I think you *would* have loved him, Lindz," I muttered quietly.

"Well, it turns out he's a massive dickhead. He played you, Jess. It's like it was some sort of game for him – like you

234

were some sort of puppet," she said angrily. There was that damned pit in my stomach again. I thought about Aidan's pseudo occupation in Marrakesh – a puppet master. Was he alluding to what was to come? Jesus, everything she said brought on a new possibility as to what might have gone wrong. I couldn't escape my own head.

"Jess, you are amazing. He's going to have a hard time finding someone who even compares. If he thinks otherwise, then he's got another thing coming."

I couldn't stand to hear any more of her trying to make me feel better... it wasn't going to happen. "Thanks, Lindz. But I just want to be alone right now. Would you be mad if I didn't join you guys for dinner tonight?"

"I'm not leaving you here to sulk over some self-absorbed asshole. Get up and wash your face."

"There's a restaurant called TriBeca; I know you'll like it. It's in the village – just down the street. Please... go without me, I'm not hungry."

"Oh no, no, no! You're not gonna start this not eating bullshit! I refuse to watch you waste away again. Get up... now!" She was referring to the breakup with Brad, when I just couldn't eat. She had never brought up how skinny I had gotten, until that moment.

"Lindsay, I'm begging you... please leave. I'll get up and I'll eat tomorrow. But for tonight, please... I just want to be left alone."

She stood and playfully pulled my arm, trying to coax me out of bed. "Come on, get up!" She pulled harder. "You are going to find a better, hotter guy in no time and Aidan will always just be a dick."

I pulled my arm back and sat up to scream, "I don't want anyone else!! And I don't want to fucking eat!! JUST. LEAVE. ME. ALONE!!" I regretted it the moment I said it. Our eyes were locked and tears were streaming down my heated face.

She stood, her face showing hurt. Without saying a word, she left my room, slamming the door behind her. I felt like shit, but I couldn't get out of bed to apologize. I heard her and Jason talking quietly, but couldn't make out their words.

An hour passed, and there was a knock at my bedroom door.

"Come in," I mumbled, still frozen on my side staring at the corner. It was Jason.

"Hey Jess, we're gonna head out in a bit. What would you like us to bring you back?" he asked.

"Nothing, thanks."

"Alright, but just in case, I'll pick out something small – a fudge cake with whipped cream and chocolate sauce – you know, something light like that."

I managed a giggle. "Sure, that'd be great."

He sat on the edge of the bed and awkwardly patted my foot. "Jessica, I want to tell you one thing, and then I'll leave you alone, okay?"

I nodded.

"A few months after Lindz and I started dating, we were in my patio, a couple bottles of wine in, asking each other all sorts of random questions. I asked her who her role model was – who she looked up to and admired the most in the world, living or dead. Without any hesitation, she said *you*."

My nostrils tingled and I bit my lip to keep from crying. Jason continued…

"She listed out all the ways she admired you. She said, 'Jessie always does what she says she's going to do – even bigger than she plans.' She said you're the kind of friend everyone wants to have but only the lucky ones actually do have… and that she was a lucky one because she had you." I shoved my ugly cry face into the pillow to absorb the tears and snot.

"She was right. I'm 35 and I don't have a friendship I feel that passionate about – I don't think I ever did," he paused. "I just wanted you to know that – to know how important you are to her." He squeezed my foot which was something my dad would do. I could feel him stand to leave. "We'll take the spare key so we don't wake you if you're sleeping. Goodnight, Jessie."

A few minutes later, I heard them leave.

I pulled my head back from the pillow – it was drenched. I flipped it over, got up, washed my faced and put on some mascara. I threw on jeans and wellies and headed to TriBeca. Aidan may not have given a shit if he were to see me that weekend or not, but I had two people who had traveled a long way (and spent a lot of money) to spend theirs with me.

I walked through the door at TriBeca and quickly spotted them. From across the room, Jason's warm smile caused Lindsay to turn around. I mouthed the words "I'm sorry" and stuck out my bottom lip.

She just smiled, yelled "Jessie!!" and ran over to hug me. She led me to the table, and we never mentioned what happened in my room again. It wasn't to avoid confrontation; it was because best friends don't need to say the things they already know.

TWENTY-SEVEN

The next morning, I checked my phone, hoping to have a message from Aidan – one saying that he had made a mistake. I'd settle for any message as it would give me a reason to respond.

There were no messages. It wasn't a mistake.

I didn't know what I was going to do with Jason and Lindsay that day. Aidan had planned to take the four of us to Howth, but I didn't feel up for taking the train out there. I went to the living room where Jason was returning with coffees, bagels and muffins from the shop down the street, Itsa Bagel.

"Soy cappuccino, extra shot of espresso for the lady," he said, handing me a cup. "The guy looked at me like I was crazy when I asked for creamers. Apparently, that's not an Irish thing."

"Nope, just milk here," I said, snuggling up to Lindsay on the couch. "Thanks, Jason, you didn't have to. We could have gone out somewhere."

"Not today, there isn't enough time. A taxi is coming in an hour to get you ladies," he smiled.

"Huh? A taxi? We don't need a taxi to get around Dublin. And what do you mean *you ladies*? What about you?" I asked.

"I figured you two needed a day to yourselves, so I booked massage packages at The Dawson Spa. I'm sure you could get there easily with public transport, but the taxi is to make sure you actually go," he said, smiling devilishly.

"Jason! And what about you?" I exclaimed with wide-eyes.

"One of my old college buddies, John, has an uncle who lives nearby in Blackrock – I'm going to go golfing with him. The course he's taking me to is supposed to be really nice. I can't wait!"

"See, Jess? Everyone is happy! Come on, let's go get pampered and have mimosas," Lindsay said, grabbing my arm, looking as if she were going to start bouncing on the couch.

"Would you judge if I went straight to a dirty martini before noon?" I asked, raising an eyebrow.

"Are you kidding? I'll have one with you!"

After our massages, we remained at The Dawson Spa to get pedicures. We sat side-by-side in robes, drinking martinis while our feet got some TLC. It would have been a great Saturday with my best friend if I weren't trying to mask the sadness.

I looked at Lindsay's feet soaking in the water and asked, "Are you going to stop wearing the Louboutins? Your feet look like a pit bull got ahold of them."

"Hey! It's not that bad! Jess, I wanted them for so long and I get so many compliments – I can't just stop wearing them."

"So, they look fine to the outside world, but only you know they're actually killing your feet? That's logical," I said sarcastically, sipping my briny vodka. "By the way, how's Cody?" I winked.

"Yeah, yeah, I see what you're doing – but hey, we don't need to talk about me... how are you feeling?"

"Confused, depressed, heartbroken, deceived." I pulled my mouth to the side. "It doesn't matter; I really don't want to talk about it, if that's okay?"

"Talk about what?" She smiled and grabbed my hand. "Love you, Jess."

I smiled back. "I'm glad you're here." I squeezed her hand and we sat in silence for a few minutes.

"Jess? Do you think Jason will leave me when he realizes I'll never be able to be a good mom to Cody?"

Oh shit, the engagement ring, I thought.

"First of all, Jason is never going to just walk away, okay?" She gave a slight smile in agreement. "But if you want a life with him, it means a life with Cody too. He loves you, but he's always going to love Cody more. If you can't accept that, then you have to be honest with him. It's one thing to fake it with your heels but not with this. You can't live your life as a picture perfect family image on the outside if it's tearing you up on the inside. You're eventually going to resent him."

She was looking off in the distance, thinking. I let her ponder without interruption. After a few deep sighs, she said, "I'll talk to him when we get back. I don't want to lose him, but you're right – I can't keep pretending without letting him know how I feel." Her tone sounded dismissive, like she wanted to drop it just how I didn't want to talk about the breakup. "I am trying, Jess, I really am," she added, her eyes beginning to water.

"I know you are." I wanted to tell her about the ring so she'd stop tiptoeing around and make a decision. But I couldn't betray Jason like that and I didn't know if it'd really make a difference. "How about when you guys go on your trip to Kinsale, you can bring it up then, when it's just you two?"

"I will, I'll talk to him about it then." She smiled. "Okay, can we talk about celebrity gossip and Pinterest projects?"

"Oh, thank God!" I laughed and finished my martini. I didn't have a Pinterest account, but I was delighted to talk about DIY projects. I tapped my empty glass. "Can we get two more please?" I asked to the lady scrubbing my feet.

We left the spa and wandered around town with a respectable buzz. We popped into a little restaurant where we shared chicken goujons and each got tomato basil soup. She fell in love with the homemade soda bread and Irish butter that came with it. I mentioned I wanted to stop at Oxfam to pick up the burgundy boots. I kept thinking about them and I had called twice that week to make sure they were still there. Both times, the saleswoman assured me they were. When I showed Lindsay the picture of them, she agreed they were amazing and very 'me.'

On our way to the charity store, we stopped in Carroll's for some souvenirs. We goofed around with the silly hats and wigs before she eventually got some gifts for Cody, including an Aer Lingus airplane set and an Irish flute. I'm sure his mom would love him practicing the flute in the house.

By the time we left the souvenir store, Oxfam was closed. Dammit! I wanted them so badly, but getting them had become a hassle. I would have to wait another four or five days because we were leaving for Dingle the following day and would be there for three days.

I wanted to go somewhere other than Dingle solely because it was the trip that Aidan had planned on my behalf. Plus, changing the trip destination would be too much effort as I had already booked our B&Bs and had a legit itinerary. I couldn't be bothered to change it – I guess one could say I was *indifferent.*

TWENTY-EIGHT

Our trip to Dingle went smoothly, barring a few scratches on the rental car. Although it was an automatic transmission, it was hard to adjust to driving on the left side. Jason drove most of the time, but I insisted on taking the wheel during the more scenic parts of the Ring of Kerry on the way there.

I was a robot during the trip, just going through the motions. I tried to stay focused on the conversation, tried to enjoy the quaint town and the company, but it was useless. All I could think about was Aidan. I read through our text messages and looked at our pictures over and over. It was toxic and I felt like a crazy person, but I told myself it was fine as long as I wasn't contacting him. There were several times when I almost called him, but I'd think about how desperate it would sound, especially if he *was* seeing someone else. The more I tried not to think about it, the more I thought about it. I wasn't eating much and was sleeping even less.

On our second night in Dingle, after watching Lindsay and Jason dance to the live pub music all night, I went back to the B&B early. I wanted to be alone. I calculated the hours until they left for their trip to Kinsale. If they left at 9:00 am on Wednesday morning, it was 81 hours. I told myself that in 81 hours, I'd be free to lie alone in bed and not have to pretend I was okay.

The next and final day of the trip, the three of us were walking along the port. Seeing all the sailboats, Lindsay mentioned she had never been on one. Jason put his arm around her and said, "I'll take you on one... and I'll teach you how to steer." I thought about Aidan teaching me to drive. Everything triggered an Aidan memory. I needed to get away from them for a little while, so I announced that I was going to get coffee and I'd meet them in 30 minutes.

In the coffee shop, I called my dad. He answered, cheerfully as usual.

"Hey, Dad. How are you feeling? Fully recovered?" It had been months since his accident, but I still asked him about it every time we spoke. He blew me off and asked what was wrong – he knew.

"I uh... I don't know why I'm calling you. I guess I just want to be sad and alone right now, but I can't in front of Lindz," I choked.

"It's okay, baby. You don't have to be so strong; she's your best friend. You can fall apart a little bit – just not too much because I kinda like you how you are."

I got that tingle in my nose that I get right before I cry. A girl isn't supposed to talk to her dad about the mushy love stuff or the heartbreak that follows, but Mom was so angry with Aidan; I don't think she cared to hear his name ever again. Dad at least sounded more understanding on the phone.

I was stirring my coffee with the wooden stick, but hadn't taken a sip yet. "I'm just so confused. I don't know what happened. I'm mad at myself for feeling like this. How did I not see this coming?"

"I know, baby, but as hard as it is, try not to overthink this. As someone who did some pretty careless things as a young whippersnapper, I'm telling you… his real reason for breaking things off is a poor reflection on his integrity and personality, so you'll never get a straight answer from him. He's a deceitful individual, but baby doll, some things are better left unknown… buried in the sand."

I stopped stirring. "Oh my God, did you just say whippersnapper?" I giggled and sucked back snot. "And thanks, Dad, but… you're biased."

"Biased you say? To the max!! I've known you for 27 years and you were perfect the last 25 of them. The first two were bad… all you did was scream. My God, did you love to scream! I wanted to leave you on the side of the road, but your mom wouldn't let me."

I kept laughing and crying at the same time. I'd heard what a bad baby I was so many times that it had to be true.

"What I'm trying to say is that after the stunt he pulled, he has 'Loser' written large across his forehead… no class, no consideration for anyone but himself. You are too genuine for such a flawed shite-head. Real commitment scares weak people – don't you dare let anyone ruin your beautiful spirit!"

246

"Oh my God, now you said *shite*?! I can't handle this!" I couldn't stop laughing. How did he know the Irish word for shit?

"I picked up the word 'shite' at Barnes and Noble a few weeks ago – there was a book of things Irish people say and do. Your mom and I sat there for an hour reading it; we got a real kick out of it. Now, she calls me a *shite-head* and I tell her that her cooking is *rubbish*."

"I love you, Dad. I don't know how you do it, but this was perfect. I feel better, I really do," I said smiling.

"Wonderful! Now get back to your friends and go enjoy all this time off… jeesh don't you ever work?!"

"Overtime… it's another perk of the European experience," I responded. In reality I only took five days off for Morocco as it fell over a bank holiday, and then I took three more off for Lindsay and Jason. That's nothing in Ireland; most the people in my office took at least three consecutive weeks for vacation.

"It's a good one!" he said. "I love you, baby, and remember… trash isn't worth thinking about, except that it takes a while to clear the stench it leaves behind. Have a GREAT day!!" he said casually, as if he never slipped in the jab.

The conversation with my dad raised my spirits and got me through the night and next day, until we were back at my apartment. But when Lindsay tried to make a joke by saying, "On the bright side, this means you'll move back home sooner, right?" I felt sick all over again. Moving back home would make it so officially over. Not just the relationship, but also my time in Dublin. Part of me wanted to go back to Florida, where I could be an ocean away from Aidan – out of sight, out of mind. But I had fallen in love with Dublin – with my new office, my friends, my life abroad. I told Lindsay I didn't know what I was going to do but that I would definitely be home for Christmas.

TWENTY-NINE

The Friday evening after Jason and Lindsay had left, I went for a long run. I hadn't been running in weeks and needed to clear my head. It had been exactly one week since the breakup call. It felt like it had just happened because that weekend was the first time I had been alone since. I had moved beyond replaying every conversation in my mind and focused only on associating everything with Aidan. Every restaurant, pub or shop we had so much as *walked by* together felt tainted. During my run, I saw an advertisement on a bus that stated: Share a Coke with Friends. It reminded me of the serendipitous Coke I got at the concert that told me to: Share a Coke with Aidan. I wanted to take a picture and sent it to him, but I could no longer do that. He was indifferent and didn't want to share a Coke with me.

Back on my street after the run, Cleopatra the devil cat emerged and followed me to my apartment. She was circling around my cankles, probably trying to trip me. Of course Cleopatra made me think of Aidan because he had named her. Even the songs on my playlist reminded me of him simply because I listened to those songs while I was dating him. The entire playlist had to be deleted, especially the "Slow Show" song, which I had added after I heard it.

My apartment was a mine field of Aidan bombs. In my cupboard was a big box of Jaffa Cakes and granola, kept on hand for him. Three shirts, a hoodie, two DVDs and a book he lent me were scattered around. I couldn't bear to see him just to do the exchange of belongings. When I thought about contacting him to give him his stuff back, his voice saying, *it wouldn't really matter if I were to see you this weekend or not*, rang in my head. No, I wasn't going to contact him over some stupid shirts, so I put all his shit in a Zara bag and tucked it away in my closet.

My phone buzzed and I checked to see the text message:

Simon: *Serial Mom, cheap champagne and dirty takeaway tonight?*

Simon always knew how to make me laugh. *Serial Mom* is our movie; we had seen it at least five times together. There's nothing better than the dry, twisted humor of a 1980s suburban housewife turned serial killer. I considered accepting his offer, knowing human interaction was supposed to be better than sulking alone, but I wanted to sulk... alone.

Me: *Maybe tomorrow? I'm exhausted from playing hostess all week. Thanks though xx*

He responded:

Simon: *Fine. Let me know if you change your mind, pussy willow.*

I laughed at his use of pussy willow – a reference from the movie. I was content to spend that Friday evening curled up on my sofa with a cup of tea and a book, trying not to imagine Aidan out having a good time meeting new girls he didn't feel indifferent about. I texted Simon:

Me: *Am I boring? Be honest.*

After two hours of reading my book and no response from Simon, there was a buzz at my door. I figured it was for someone else in my apartment block. There were only eight apartments in my building, but the numbers on the buzzers were so worn that people always messed them up. I pushed the button to let the possible intruder into the building and stuck my head outside the door.

In the dark hallway, I could make out the silhouette of a man's body walking toward me. I quickly recognized the delicious scent.

It was the special garlic chili sauce from Zaytoon, covering their signature doner kebab. Simon had reached my front door and looked me up and down. "You're wearing white after Labor Day?!" he joked. I had on an oversized white sweater – it was another reference from *Serial Mom*.

He gave me a hug with his free arm while I replied, "Suzanne Somers! This is my bad side!"

He laughed and said, "J. D., you are the most non-boring person – don't ever ask such a ridiculous question because clearly, I won't respond," while pulling back from our hug. "Now this sweater on the other hand... should be burned immediately."

"Hey, I like this sweater! Although, no one is supposed to see me in it," I replied as he barged into my apartment and put his bag on the coffee table. He picked up my coffee cup and looked at it as if it were a foreign object. He set it on the dining table, replacing it with a bottle of wine.

"You don't have to do this, Simon; I'm fine, really. I'm so numb that I won't even need Botox for another 15 years," I said, locking the door.

"Pshh, seven years honey – and that's a compliment! Most people need Botox by age 30," he called out as I went to get a bottle opener, wine glasses and forks from the kitchen.

"Listen, dahling, you're my girl and we haven't spent time together outside of work in three weeks. Why else would I be here?" he winked. "Plus, Merrick is horrifically sick. Poor thing – today was the first time in three days that he's been able to keep anything down. He's at my place sleeping like a baby."

"Bringing him to your place to take care of him? Must be getting serious, huh?" I said, pulling the onions off my kebab.

"Nah, he's just sick and lives on his own; I'd do the same for you." He nudged me and reached for the wine.

"Look, Simon, I'm sad, yes. But, that doesn't mean I can't hear about your relationship happiness – I want to know; I'm dying to know! Tell me all the mushy, lovey dovey stuff," I insisted.

"Okay, fine," he said. "I love him. I really love him. He's everything I never knew I wanted. He laughs at my jokes, he makes me feel important and loved, and when we're together, everything is right. Life is just better with him in it. It's that simple really. There's nothing more to it."

"And there shouldn't be." I raised my glass and clicked it to his. "I'm glad you didn't write him off because of the height thing. Look at what you would have missed out on. I think I'll wear my mustard ankle boots to the wedding in honor of the symbolism."

"Please do!" he exclaimed. "Hey, speaking of boots, did you get your burgundy boots?" he asked.

"Ugh, no," I said, rolling my eyes.

"What?! J. D., that was a month ago. Are they even still there? I would have gotten them for you," he said.

"I know; I was going to go the next day, but Aidan took me driving in Wicklow and then things were so crazy at work before the trip that I couldn't leave before they closed. Then there was Morocco and then catching up at work, and this past week I was with Lindsay and Jason and it just got out of hand!" I sighed after my long-winded explanation.

"Well, we will go tomorrow after Orla's brunch," he said, popping *Serial Mom* into my DVD player.

"Oh shit, I completely forgot about that." Orla had celebrated her birthday at home in Galway the previous weekend, so some of us in the office were taking her for a birthday brunch. I didn't want to go, but I couldn't sell out on Orla – she was my first friend in Dublin. Plus, she had been talking about moving back to Galway to be closer to Gearoid.

"Thanks for coming over – this is great. Now, let's watch Kathleen Turner beat a woman to death with a leg of pork roast."

He topped up our wine, mumbling, "I know who I'd like to beat with a leg of pork roast."

THIRTY
Late October 2013

Odessa is my favorite brunch restaurant in Dublin. I love its ability to transform. The building used to be a house, but now it's divided in half and there are two separate entrances. The one on the left is modern décor – more dark and cozy, with oversized leather seats and candles throughout. The right side entrance was preserved to keep the original look of a flat. We were seated on the left side.

Although I had fun with Simon the night before, the brunch was a lot like my time with Lindsay – putting on a happy face and going through the motions. I politely smiled as I listened to whoever was talking and I contributed a few mindless comments, but inside I was still thinking of Aidan.

Orla talked about her upcoming trip to Portugal, where her parents had a vacation home. I ordered the full Irish breakfast, despite still not having an appetite. I reached for the salt without tasting my food first. I thought of how Aidan always made fun of my salt obsession. Stop it, stop it!

Stop thinking about him! I was becoming extremely annoyed with myself.

"You did good, J. D.," Simon said before kissing the side of my head. He was looking at my plate, which had only some mushrooms and half an English muffin left on it. It had only been eight days, but the weight I had lost was noticeable to Simon.

I smiled and replied, "Well, the food was absolutely gorgeoussss," exaggerating the word. I still found it hilarious that Irish people use the word to describe food. It could be a grilled cheese sandwich and it'd be gorgeous – just like Kate Moss.

We said our goodbyes to Orla and the gang and moseyed along Exchequer Street with our arms interlocked.

I listened to Simon tell a story about his old flat in London as we dodged the tourists who stopped to look at everything. When we came up to Oxfam, I saw the boots on a small display table near the front of the store. They must have assumed I wasn't going to come for them and moved them back onto the floor. I remained standing outside the window, just like the tourists. A woman inside the store picked up *my* boots and inspected them. They really were beautiful. The kind of boot any woman would like to have in her closet.

"That bitch is looking at your boots; come on, let's go get them," Simon gestured, walking toward the door. I didn't move. "Hello?! Earth to Jessica! Get your skinny ass inside; it's starting to rain." I remained cemented in the same spot. The woman put them down upon seeing the size inside the boot leg.

"I don't want them anymore," I said, pulling my polka dot umbrella from my handbag. I walked over to Simon so we could share the umbrella. "Those aren't my boots. I thought they were, but they're not. Let's go get a coffee at that Italian café we like." I walked away from the store.

"WHAT?!" Simon yelled. "You were *crazy* about them! Hell, I was crazy about them for you! You're not going to find better boots anywhere – certainly not ones that check all your boxes and for a better price," he protested.

"Maybe I won't, but maybe I will. Maybe it will take five years. It doesn't really matter because I don't want those boots. At least not right now. Maybe I'll change my mind again and come back for them."

"Someone is going to scoop them up; they won't be there for long!" Simon exclaimed.

"If they're not, then it wasn't meant to be. Simon, listen to me… I'm not buying those boots. I have too many boots at home that I never wear; I don't need to add another pair. I'll wait for a pair that I can buy without any hesitation."

I finally convinced him that I wasn't going to budge. We walked around the corner, onto Chatham Street to Il Fuoco. Simon ordered me a soy cappuccino and a caramel latte for himself. We sat at a tiny table and again, he brought up my sudden change of heart about the boots.

"Simon, you mean to tell me that you've never changed your mind about something you thought you wanted but then just felt… ya know, nehhh," I asked, making a face.

"Indifferent!!" Simon blurted. "Oh my God, J. D., you feel about the burgundy boots how Aidan feels about you! Sorry, that sounded harsh, but it's true."

I thought about it for a minute and laughed.

"Yeah, I guess you're right. Gosh, I hope I'm not breaking the boots' heart like he did mine."

"No, you're not a dick," he said on impulse. "But the point is – these things happen. Feelings *can* just change, and sometimes you don't know exactly why. Do you still think the boots are amazing? Do they still check all the boxes? Do you know exactly what it was about them today that made you not want them anymore?"

"They're still amazing and no, I don't know what it was exactly that made me change my mind. There's nothing wrong with them… it's me."

"Exactly! Those boots didn't change – they are still the same lovely boots they were last month. Just like *you* didn't do anything wrong or change from when you first met Aidan – but his feelings still changed. It's no one's fault."

I thought about it.

"You're right. He didn't break up with me for any one of the reasons I've come up with in my head – it might have been a bunch of small things or maybe he did meet someone else. Maybe he doesn't even know the real reason himself – like how I don't know why I no longer want the burgundy boots. Thanks, Simon, this is empowering!" Our coffees arrived and Simon dropped three brown sugar cubes into his already sweet latte. I couldn't say anything after I had put a full day's sodium allowance on my breakfast.

"And what's really funny – well, maybe not to you – is how you couldn't even go inside the store to try them on one more time. If nothing else, you could have gone in just to get out of the rain. But your mind was made up and that

258

was it. You wanted to get away from them as soon as possible."

"Yeah. Like how Aidan couldn't even speak to me in person or wait a few days until my friends had left – he wanted to be done with me as soon as possible." No matter how much I was beginning to see things from Aidan's shoes, that part would never make sense to me… the part where he couldn't even wait a few days in order not to ruin my time with Lindsay.

"It sucks on both sides. I wish Aidan a lifetime of impotence, but as much as I dislike him… I didn't think he wanted to hurt you, and I'm sure he knows how amazing you are. You can feel that way about someone or something and still not want it – you just experienced it first-hand. So please, bloody please, stop being so hard on yourself. Just let this go, okay?"

I thought about the similarities between my short-lived relationship and my fickle infatuation with the boots. No one was going to change my mind about the boots that day – not Simon, not a 50% off sale, not every soul in Dublin telling me how great they looked on. My mind was made up. Aidan's mind was made up. Simon was right – there wasn't anything I could do, but move forward and let it go.

"You're right. I'm done trying to make sense of it; it's out of my control. Who knew a pair of boots would give me the closure I needed? Okay, I've let it go." I felt a small smile develop naturally. "Hey, want to split a piece of cake?" It was the first time I genuinely wanted to eat since the breakup.

"Yes ma'am! Go pick out the biggest, dirtiest piece!"

THIRTY-ONE

The next morning, the ringing of my phone woke me. It was a random number. I thought maybe it was someone I knew calling from jail… certainly not a normal reaction as that had never happened before, but just in case, I answered.

"WE'RE ENGAGED!! WE'RE ENGAGED!!" Lindsay screamed. I hadn't heard from them the previous two days, as their phones were turned off. Plus, I knew Jason had planned the elaborate romantic weekend, so I didn't even try to check in.

"Ahhhhh! Congratulations! How did he do it? I want details!" I said excitedly, still lying in bed.

"Yesterday morning! He told me that the hotel had recommended to him that we go to some spot to see the sunrise, so he played it off like 'oh we *have* to go do this' because he knows I hate waking up early." I thought about how I do too – especially on a Sunday, which it was. "He had horses for us to ride there, but I ruined it because I was too scared to ride by myself, so we shared one. It was so awkward trying to get him on behind me; it took like five tries and two men helping to get him up." I laughed at the thought of charming, sophisticated Jason draped over a horse's ass, kicking his limbs like a cockroach, praying the horse didn't take off running.

"When we got there, he gave this speech about how the sunrise was a new beginning to the day just like I brought a new beginning and meaning to his life. He said he doesn't want to ever see a sunrise or sunset without me in his life."

Oh come on, Jason! I rolled my eyes, thankful she was on the phone and I didn't have to keep a straight face for that shit in person. Brad and Aidan both used to tell me how readable my face is.

She continued on, "Then he knelt down and I kind of blanked out when I realized what was happening. Whatever else he said, it was all a blur – I just said YES!"

"Did you mean to say it?" Ah shit, that came out wrong. "I meant... did you mean to say it *then*? Or did you cut him off early because you were in a daze?" Good cover up, I applauded myself. She'll never know what I really meant was: Why are you marrying him when his kid gives you hives?

"Yeah, he said I cut him off, but he's glad I did because he was so nervous," she responded.

"Did you get to talk to him about Cody before? About the idea of being a step-mom – how it's tough for you, but you are trying?" I tried to sugar-coat it as much as possible.

"Umm... not exactly. It just didn't feel like a good time – here on vacation and all. Plus, I don't exactly know what I want to say; I'll just work through it on my own. I love Jason and that means I love Cody too. Plus, we'll only get him

261

every other weekend; I can handle that!" I noticed her use of *we'll,* as in she will actually be with Cody the entire weekend every other weekend when they move in together. She practically lives with Jason now, but she conveniently goes back to her apartment for most of the Cody weekends.

"I agree. It will all be fine. I shouldn't have brought that up now; I'm still half asleep. But hey – YOU'RE GETTING MARRIED!!" Two cover-ups in two minutes, jeesh!

"Ahhh! I'm getting married! Oh my God, the ring is gorgeous, Jessie! I'll try to send you a picture. You're the first person I called. I haven't even called my mom yet."

I wasn't sure if I was supposed to say that I already saw the ring, so I didn't. "Well, hang up and call your mom, and then go do whatever newly engaged people do and enjoy your last day in Ireland. What time do you fly back tomorrow?"

"We fly out of Cork at 7:30 at night. Hey, how are you doing, Jess? Have you heard from Aidan yet?"

"No, I haven't. But it's fine; I'm okay. I'm moving on… there's plenty of fish in the sea and all that bullshit."

"You're such a guy sometimes. I worry about you over here in a weird country all by yourself."

"Hey now, give me some credit! And it's not a weird country – you think it's weird?"

"I meant foreign. Although, it was weird all the guys I saw wearing colored skinny jeans – they're tighter than my jeans! You know what I mean, Jessie… it's not home."

"I'm fine. The only thing you need to worry about is finding me a bridesmaid's dress that doesn't make me look like Gumby." I had been aware for years that Lindsay's wedding colors would be *Sea Foam Dream* and *Rustic*

Eggplant, more commonly known as light green and dark purple. Her vision was for the bridal party to be in tight, long, green dresses with full-length green gloves – a flock of Gumbies at her side.

"Well, you'll be my maid of honor. We'll find a dress you like, I promise."

"Thanks, Lindz, I'd be honored to be your maid of honor," I said genuinely. "Now, go call your mom and give Jason a kiss for me. Let me know when you guys get home."

I couldn't fall back asleep, so I got up and went for a run. When I came back and checked my mail, I got double bitch slapped. My new registration card came from the Immigration office, stating I was permitted to be an Irish resident for another year. I had applied for it just before Morocco. Then, there was an envelope from Ticketmaster. It was the tickets for the 'Everything Everything' concert I had gotten for Aidan – the surprise date night with the guy who didn't want anything to do with me.

I called Simon to see if he'd go to the gig with me. It was for the upcoming Saturday night, so I was prepared for him to say he already had plans with Merrick. He swore they didn't and that he'd be happy to be my date.

I kept wondering when Aidan was going to text me about the money I owed him. I wanted him to get it over with so I could stop dreading every text might be it. Mom and Dad both told me not to contact him to remind him about it, and that if he was a real man, he'd never ask for the money. Dad also said that if he *did* ask for it, I should tell him to stick it up his indifferent asshole.

Oh, my right wellie!

THIRTY-TWO

Being back at work for a full week was the first sign of normalcy in a month. The work hadn't piled up like I thought it would have – a few days off work in America, and I'd spend half of my first day back responding to people who knew damn well I was gone.

When Claire and I were making tea in the kitchen, she mentioned she heard that Aidan and I had broken up. My silence confirmed that it was true. She rolled her eyes and shook her head. "That boy will never change – you're not the first girl he's done this to." She looked me in the eye before throwing her tea bag away. "It's a shame; they all thought he was going to finally settle down with you. I swear that boy has an allergy to commitment."

He had done it before? An allergy to commitment? I suddenly remembered his reaction when I jokingly made the comment about him cheating on an ex. *Had* he cheated? Was that what Claire meant? I was just about to ask her to elaborate when Orla and a few others came in, so I didn't.

On Saturday, I was getting ready for the gig when Simon called to tell me that he had caught the bug Merrick had the week before. He was deathly ill, so Merrick would be going as my date. I didn't want Merrick to feel like I was some sort of charity case, so I told Simon it was fine if we just cancelled. That was when Merrick took the phone from him.

"Is this THE J. D. I've heard so much about?" Merrick asked.

"If it's the one with the sweet dance moves, then yep, it's her."

"Oooh, you sassy little thing, you! Look, I told Simon I wanted to go with you when you first asked him, but tickets were sold out so I couldn't tag along. I had to conduct a lot of make-out sessions to give him this bug so I could take his ticket."

"Ah, you're evil! We are going to get along very well," I joked.

"I think so too. I can get all the juicy gossip on Simon without him around."

"Ha! Deal. The main act is at nine, so let's meet for pizza and pints at Cassidy's on Westmoreland at half seven and we'll walk up together." Saying 'half seven' instead of 'seven thirty' was natural at that point.

"Brilliant! See you then."

Merrick was a trip. He kept me laughing and talking the whole time, and most importantly, he kept my mind off Aidan. His infectious and constant smile turned his good looks into great looks. I couldn't believe Simon almost wrote him off because he wasn't as tan or as tall as his online profile stated – especially considering he was more tanned than the average Irish person and taller than the average male!

At Cassidy's, we played Jenga with a couple of tourists from Germany. Merrick ordered the four of us a round of Jäger bombs, which I don't particularly care for but slammed back anyways. It was the first time since the breakup that I was having fun. After a couple of pints, we walked across the O'Connell Bridge and over to The Academy.

We were standing at the bar waiting to order our drinks before the band came on when a woman caught my eye. She wore a funky graffiti shirt underneath an olive leather jacket and the perfect distressed jeans were tucked inside of... MY burgundy boots?! She swept back her angled cropped hair that had fallen onto her face. She held a big smile, laughing at whatever the guy next to her was saying. I couldn't take my eyes off her and the boots really made the look. I was so jealous of the woman for wearing *my* boots (that I had passed up) in my presence.

"Heineken for the lady," Merrick said, handing me the pint glass.

"Thanking you!" It was another small Irishism I had picked up. "Hey, Merrick, what do you think of that woman over there with the short hair? What's the first thing that pops into your mind?"

"Deadly! Killer boots! But you're much prettier, if that's what you want to know," he said, turning back to me. "Why do you ask? Bitch stole your man?" he said, zigzagging his neck with attitude.

I laughed, almost spitting my beer. "Oh, I'd kick her ass – I work out," I teased. "No, I was actually admiring her boots too. I like her style, that's all."

The lights were dimmed and the crowd started cheering. "Oh, they're coming on!" I turned to face the stage.

The band was fantastic. Merrick and I danced and swayed, and the beers went down like water. I couldn't stop smiling, which was something I hadn't done in what felt like forever. During the song "Armourland", their slowest song, Merrick pulled me close and we danced like awkward teenagers. He pushed his forehead to mine and sang along, changing the lyrics to make up his own hilarious version:

> *I wanna take you home*
> *Take off your blindfold*
> *And show you my big cock…*

I laughed hysterically at his ad-lib skills. When I threw my head back in a fit of laughter, I saw Aidan.

He was staring at me with stone cold eyes. He looked shocked.

I didn't know what to do. I certainly wasn't going to tell Merrick, "Hey stop having fun with me because my ex (who feels indifferent toward me) might think we're together and I don't want to hurt his feelings just in case he isn't *really* indifferent."

I considered going over to say 'hi', but we weren't old pals and I didn't want to shoot the shit with him, so I squashed that idea fast. I looked at Merrick and fake laughed so he didn't catch on that anything was wrong.

"I'm gonna get us another round. Same thing?" he asked.

"Umm, I'll go with you," I said, not wanting to be left there by myself. The bar was behind where Aidan was standing. The positioning allowed me to scope out who he was with. I was sick to my stomach at the thought of him being there with a new girl on a date – the very date I had planned for us. He was with a group, no one I recognized. There was a girl in the group, but judging by their interaction, it was clear she wasn't *with* Aidan, she was just a friend.

Merrick handed me a fresh beer and grabbed my hand to lead us through the crowd. Out of the corner of my eye, I could see Aidan had turned to watch us. I was thankful that our spot was in front of him so I didn't have to look at him during the entire show. I wanted to talk to him. Maybe not there in the midst of the concert, but I wanted him to grow a pair, look me in the eye and say he was sorry for how he chose to end things. Everything inside me told me I'd never get that closure.

After the gig, Merrick and I went out for another drink. I gave him the summary of my rise and fall with Aidan and how he was there that night at the concert.

"This is brilliant! He broke up with you and there you were... two weeks later, having a laugh with a rather handsome young chap, if I may say so myself. It's absolutely brilliant, it really is! I bet he was raging with jealousy!"

"Nah, he wasn't. You can't be jealous of someone you feel indifferent toward. He doesn't give a shit about me or who I date – he made that clear on the phone."

"Jess, I may be gay, but we're all the same." He placed his hand on mine. "He *was* jealous, and I assure you… he's *not* indifferent about you. It simply isn't possible," he smiled.

We chatted through two pints before calling it a night. I took a cab home – Merrick insisted just like Simon always did.

I slept in till noon the next day. When I awoke and checked my phone, my stomach sank. I had a text message from Aidan.

THIRTY-THREE

I read and reread the message several times:

> **Aidan:** *Jessica, I tallied up our expenses from the trip and you owe me €540 for your half. Let me know how you plan on getting it to me. Hope you had fun last night, sure looks like you moved on quickly...*

I wanted to throw the phone against the wall as hard as I could.

He broke up with me, he felt indifferent! What would it have mattered if I were with Merrick or not? I gave him what he wanted... I had left him alone so he could move on, and he was going to pull that shit because he saw me having fun? How had things gotten so fucked up so fast?

I went to take a shower. As I washed away the smoke smell from my hair, I thought about how I'd respond. I teetered between two completely different options: 1) Explain that Merrick was Simon's boyfriend and that I hadn't moved on, or 2) Something along the lines of what my dad had suggested – something like: Fuck you, you're indifferent, shove the €540 up your ass.

I didn't want to hide behind a text message. Option #1 would only give him satisfaction, but wouldn't lead to us getting back together. Option #2 would start a war and I'd end up regretting it. After way too much thought, I went with:

Me: *I'll mail the money to you this week. Thanks for a great trip!*

I felt empty after sending it and figured he wouldn't respond. I went about drying my hair and thought up a million other things I wish I had texted instead. When I turned off the hairdryer, I heard a text message alert. It was Aidan again. I read the message slowly:

Aidan: *I can't believe it's only been 2 weeks and you're already with someone new. Clearly I didn't mean that much to you. Then to rub it in my face was a really low move. I thought we could at least have some respect for each other. Good luck with this one, Jessica.*

I didn't have respect for *him*?! At that point, I wanted to smash the phone with a hammer to really make sure it was destroyed. Who the hell was *he* to lecture *me* on respect? As much as his decision to break up with me broke my heart, I didn't make him feel bad about it. I didn't try to change his mind or convince him to stay. I didn't cry on the phone. I didn't contact him afterward. I wanted to do all those things, but I didn't. As far as breakups go, I thought that was respect.

I set the phone on the kitchen counter, stepping back as if it were an explosive. After a few minutes, I picked it up and read the message again. And then again.

"Clearly I didn't mean that much to you…. Good luck with *this* one." I repeated the lines out loud. I put the phone back down and walked away to make my bed – I never make my bed. Then, I went through my dresser drawers refolding each article of clothing – anything to keep me away from the phone.

After my bed was made, the dresser was organized and I had a load of laundry going, I went back to my phone. I began typing a response, but as I was typing, I received another message from him:

Aidan: *Don't you EVER contact me about ANYTHING ever again! Just send me my money and that's the last I ever want to hear from you!!!*

I was trying to process the message when another one popped up:

Aidan: *I wish I never met you. I regret ever getting involved. I don't even want to LOOK at you ever again!!!*

Merrick was right… he certainly wasn't indifferent after all.

I erased the message that I had started to write before I received Aidan's last two messages.

I read his messages several more times. Once they were tattooed in my brain, I deleted them. Then, I deleted our entire text history and his contact details. I didn't want any of it in my phone for me to keep reading.

I took the Zara bag full of his belongings from my closet and threw it in the trash bin on the side of my building. I returned inside and wrote a check for €540 and set it on the table next to the front door so I'd remember to mail it to him next time I left the house. It felt as if someone had died.

I thought more about the comparison between the burgundy boots and myself. Admittedly, I was jealous of the woman who bought them. I wish she were my friend so I could borrow them from her, but I still didn't wish I had bought them. Similarly, Aidan didn't like seeing me with someone else, but it wasn't enough for him to regret breaking up with me and to try to get me back. The Slow Show was over.

THIRTY-FOUR
November 2013 – January 2014

The following week, I toggled between ending my contract early to move home and riding out the rest of the one year extension. If I ended it early, I'd be home in time for Christmas and I'd avoid a cold, rainy Irish winter… and the chance of running into Aidan with a new girlfriend. I missed home, but I wasn't sure if I was ready to leave Dublin. I felt like there were still things I needed to do. I hadn't seen Europe except for the trip to London with Simon. I was also really enjoying my role in the Dublin office. I had succeeded in the task I was brought over to do – to implement our digital media optimization products in Dublin. The plan was for us to grow the Irish market's use of social media marketing and break into Europe. The office had landed several huge accounts that week – large companies that weren't using social media at all. Under the assumption I was staying another year, they offered to put me in charge of managing them. The role was above my pay grade, but it was a huge opportunity to prove to my home office that I was ready for the next step. Orla had put in her notice so that she could move back to Galway to be with Gearoid. After five years of dating, they were going to move in together. Actually, they were going to house share, so they'd be moving in with another couple. Nonetheless, it was a big step for them. Orla leaving also probably drove the company's decision to ask me to be the lead on the new accounts.

Ultimately, I decided to stay in Dublin the full additional year, through to the summer of 2014. I wanted to spend more time with my friends in the city I had fallen in love with. I wanted to stay for myself.

Although Lindsay was very supportive of my decision to stay, no one was more excited than Simon. He declared that we'd go to Spain and he started researching travel logistics straight away.

It was a Sunday night, exactly two weeks after I had deleted Aidan from my phone. I had just crawled into bed when my phone buzzed and I saw it was a message from him, his number in place of where his name should have been. My heart sped as I read the preview sentence several times: *Hi Jessica. I've been doing a lot of thinking and I wanted to say...*

I thought it'd be an apology message. Or maybe it'd be something that would hurt me all over again? I wouldn't be able to sleep if I didn't read it, so I took a deep breath and opened it.

Aidan: *Hi Jessica. I've been doing a lot of thinking and I wanted to say that even though I was really disappointed and* *hurt, I've decided to let it go. You are a lovely girl and I will cherish our time together. We don't need to be friends but hopefully we can say hi if our paths cross. If you ever want to talk to me about anything, just let me know. I heard this loud American couple yell out 'Have a nice day!' in the coffee shop the other day and I had a good laugh. Thanks for sending the money and for all the good stuff too. Take good care of yourself Jessica.*

My initial reaction was that it was really sweet and maybe it was his way of saying he wanted to talk things out. Then I read it a few more times and noticed the message didn't actually contain the words 'I'm sorry'. *He's* been thinking, *he's* the hurt one, *he's* deciding to let it go, *he* wants to make nice so that it's not awkward if we run into each other. Maybe I'm jaded, but that message wasn't for me – it was for him. It was to make him feel better about his outburst that I never responded to. Nonetheless, I was glad he sent the message to clear the air.

My response came easily as I typed it out and sent it with only one read-over:

Me: *Thank you Aidan, that means a lot. After our phone call, I did have a lot of things I wanted to talk to you about in person. But now that some time has passed, it all seems moot ;) I will always think fondly of our time together as well. I will take care and I hope you do the same. Thanks again for the message – Jess.*

Although I felt sad that our relationship had come to that, I felt better about things for the first time since he had called to break up with me. Just as I reached to turn off the lamp on my bedside table, I received a response:

Aidan: *Can you let me know when you leave Dublin? Don't go without saying goodbye.*

I thought about responding with: *Cross my heart.* Instead, I sent:

Me: *Sure.*

* * * * *

Since I decided to stay in Dublin, I went home for two weeks over Thanksgiving. I was able to enjoy the holiday (and the Black Friday shopping), and attend Lindsay and Jason's engagement party as well as my parents' 40th wedding anniversary. I was also able to meet the two new babies that friends had had during the year and a half that I was away. The visit home was just what I needed.

The engagement party was at the Palma Ceia Country Club where Jason was a member. They were happy, genuinely happy. Lindz didn't look uncomfortable around Cody at all. I wasn't sure if that was due to the excitement of the event or if it was real progress between them. Cody called her Lee-Lee and I could tell she liked the nickname. I hung out with him most of the night so Jason and Lindsay could butterfly around with their guests. While we were playing dinosaurs with the centerpieces and cutlery, he said, "Lee-Lee looks like a princess!"

"Yes, yes she does! Which princess is she?" I asked.

"Cinderelly!" he shouted. "You can be Beauty and the Beast," he said, accidentally pushing a fork off the table.

"You mean Belle? She's the princess from *Beauty and the Beast*," I said, hoping to clarify that I wasn't the Beast. He just laughed and repeated, "Beauty and the Beast!" before completely losing interest in the conversation – ugh, men!

Cody was really cool and I could tell Lindsay knew it too. I hoped that she truly was bonding with him. Maybe she *did* just need time – maybe being a step-mom was a concept that was 'stretching out' and would eventually fit her just fine?

She came over to see what we were up to and scolded me under her breath for encouraging him to play with the silverware because it was dangerous. I explained that I had taken the sharp knives away, but she just rolled her eyes. It wouldn't have been noticeable to anyone else, but to me, she becoming a protective step-mom.

"Lee-Lee, is she your sister?" Cody asked while still sitting on my lap.

"Yes, yes she is," Lindsay said with a smile.

"Oh, okay." He kept his eyes on the table where he was playing with the silverware and a few Lego pieces they had brought for him. "I wanted to make sure because I think I want her to come over and play with my trucks. But she can't play with the red truck, Lee-Lee, because that's your favorite."

It was touching watching them talk about the trucks. Lindsay explained to me that he was very protective of his toy trucks and only lets her and his mommy play with them – oh and Raleigh, his five-year-old crush who lives down the street. Jason couldn't even play with them – Cody is clearly a ladies' man!

* * * * *

The day after the engagement party, Lindsay and I went out for a nice dinner and dirty martinis at Ruth's Chris Steakhouse. She wore the Laurence lace-ups which she swore didn't hurt anymore because she had finally broken them in. I knew that was bullshit because every time she stood still, she'd adjust in a way I knew was to relieve some of the pain. They were gorgeous shoes, but there's no way it could be worth the discomfort she was feeling.

As we toasted our second martinis, she told me how she and Jason had 'the talk' about Cody and her being a step-mom. It was the conversation that she had planned on having during their trip to Kinsale, but she squashed that plan when he proposed. She said she told him she was sorry that it was taking a long time to warm up to the idea of being a step-mom and that it was a big adjustment for her. She said he was very understanding and reassured her that he wasn't expecting her to be Cody's mother – he had a mother. He told her not to put any pressure on trying to rush a relationship with Cody because it would develop naturally in due time. Our shrimp appetizer arrived and interrupted Lindsay.

"It's true, Lindz, you don't need to be his mother. Keep doing what you're doing and it will all work out." I smiled after the generic comment, but it was true... after seeing her with him at the engagement party, I was convinced it'd all work out.

"Yeah, I do feel a connection growing with Cody. I can be like an aunt... Aunt Lindsay," she said in a posh voice.

She talked more about the conversation she had with Jason before moving onto the wedding planning. Somewhere between open bar options and table runners, I noticed she had slipped her feet halfway out of the shoes. She must have done it when I went to the bathroom because I would have noticed the struggle with all those laces. Why did she continue to wear them if they were so uncomfortable? And why was she lying to me about them being broken in? I hoped that wasn't the case with Cody too.

I knew she was lying to herself, but had it gone too far? Both her fabulous shoes and fabulous relationship looked perfect from the outside, but were definitely causing her pain on the inside.

After a few days of catching up with everyone in Tampa, I went to the east coast of Florida to see my family. My parents had moved into a smaller house just a few miles away from the one I grew up in. It was weird being there – a house that wasn't home. So much had changed in one year. My parents had taken up tennis, Dad had gotten into running and Mom got a new car. They looked older, but they looked good.

We went to Carrabba's Italian Grill to celebrate their anniversary. It was just our immediate family and two couples who had been family friends since I could remember. I had missed the dependable consistency of a chain restaurant. My Fettuccine Wessie dish tasted exactly as I remembered from when I was a teenager, before I started turning my nose up at chain restaurants.

Throughout dinner, I kept looking at my parents. I was trying to determine when it was that I had stopped seeing them as annoying, over-protective authoritarians and began to see them as the first people I wanted to call when anything happened – good or bad. When did I realize that they were my wellies? Their love was unconditional like how my wellies were dependable in all types of weather. I wished I had realized it sooner.

* * * * *

When I returned to Dublin, the entire month of December was a whirlwind thanks to crazy hours working on the new work project, mixed with countless holiday parties and 12 pubs of Christmas crawls. It seemed like the whole city of Dublin wore their ugly Christmas sweaters (or jumpers as they're called in Ireland) every day in December.

Merrick, Simon, two other expat friends and I took the trip to Spain over the Christmas and New Year's break. I was able to finally cross Spain off my bucket list – the number one country I wanted to visit before leaving Ireland. We flew into Madrid and took the train through the northern countryside. We ended the trip in Barcelona for three days. The New Year's celebration was nuts – Barcelona lived up to its reputation as a party city that loved to dance into the wee hours of the morning. I gained 10 pounds that trip thanks to non-stop pitchers of sangria and amazing tapas. During the days, we tried our best to visit the main historical sights, although it was impossible to see them all, especially when we were consistently hung over. Spain was everything I imagined it to be and more, and the trip was the way a trip should be – fun, carefree, full of laughter and funny bloopers. Not once did I cry myself to sleep.

January brought on that feeling of turning a new leaf, as it always tends to do. Although the days were short and the work hours were long, it was nice to have a routine again. I noticed Cleopatra the cat was lurking around a lot more. She would always emerge at the top of my street and walk next to me all the way to my building. I asked one of my neighbors about her and he explained that the couple who had been taking care of her had moved away. They didn't own her, just fed her and let her sleep on their front stoop (they were one of the cool people with a bright red Georgian door). As far as he knew, Cleopatra was an orphan. I felt sorry for her and since she had stopped being so creepy, I decided to take over and feed her.

It was a cold and rainy winter that year. Although I had acclimated and knew how to prepare for the weather (double layer of socks and wellies!), it broke my heart to see Cleopatra out in it. I had always hated cats and at one time, I thought she was a spawn of Satan, but I had slowly grown to have a bond with her. I decided I was going to adopt her and bring her inside, at least through the winter. I took her to the vet to get whatever shots and vaccines she needed. The vet told me all the things I needed to get for her and he also told me that Cleopatra was a boy! I was too invested in the name Cleopatra, so I simply called him Cleo.

I firmly told Cleo that the first time he clawed up any of my shit, he'd be out on the streets again. He must have understood my warning because he was a perfect gentleman and never ruined anything. He also ate the spiders because I never saw one again after he moved in. I really liked having him around. I didn't even mind the smell of the litter box, his shedding fur or the occasional hairball. Cleo became the man in my life – my fella.

THIRTY-FIVE
May 2014

I had seen Aidan a few times during the remainder of my time in Dublin. It was while out and about in town, but I'm pretty sure he didn't see me.

In May, I had gone down to Enniskerry with some friends. We could see Sugar Loaf and Little Sugar Loaf in full view. Enough time had passed that I felt I could send a friendly text to Aidan, so I sent him a picture of the infamous Dublin hills with the message:

Me: *I still think it looks like baking soda! Hope you're doing well – Jess*

He never responded.

It justified my hypothesis that his 'apology' message was bullshit and only sent to make himself feel better. His message had said that I could reach out to him about anything and he hoped we could still say 'hi' to each other –

it was obviously another careless promise he never intended to keep.

During one of the springtime social events at work, Claire voluntarily told me how Aidan had gone out with a few girls after me, but they were all 'nothing special' and he was currently single. I knew she had received her information from Emma. Although I wondered if it was Emma or Aidan that thought the girls weren't special, I didn't want to know any more details. I asked her not to bring him up anymore, which she understood. I did, however, want to know how Kate was doing. I wanted to know what books she had read and what recipes she had mastered at culinary school. I wanted so badly to meet her for lunch, but I thought it'd be inappropriate and potentially hurtful to see her.

Hearing about Aidan dating more girls he felt indifferent about had reminded me of the burgundy boots. Since the day I had decided not to buy them, I had come across several other pairs of riding boots that lured me into the stores to try them on. They were all nice, but even with the discounted, off-season prices, none of them made me want to twirl around in front of the mirror like I had done with the burgundy boots. They were 'nothing special' and I was still without THE ultimate pair of riding boots. I wondered if I'd ever find a pair that made me as excited from the moment I put them on as the burgundy boots had, or if I'd ever find a man that could give me butterflies the way Aidan had.

Simon was still head over (my mustard ankle boot) heels in love with Merrick. They were planning to move to

London together before the end of the year. Selfishly, I was glad that I would be leaving Dublin before him so that I wouldn't have to be in Dublin without my buddy.

I had decided to move back to America in August 2014 – just three months before Lindsay and Jason's wedding. I was looking forward to the wedding mainly because it'd mean Lindsay would no longer call me freaking out over things like whether or not there should be chargers on the tables. I told her they weren't necessary – simple, understated elegance was the way to go when it came to tables at weddings. She agreed and thanked me for helping her with such an *important* wedding decision. I still have no clue what a charger is.

* * * * *

It has always amazed me how vividly I can recall the smallest details that lead up to a significant moment. Like how I'll always remember walking down the hallway my sophomore year of high school (with my crimped hair and white eyeliner) heading to Mrs. Lawson's English class just before hearing about the attacks on the World Trade Center. The same is true about the moments right before Lindsay called to tell me the horrible news.

It was a Sunday. I was just back from the grocery store and making space in the cupboard, when I spilled a bag of brown sugar that wasn't closed properly. I can remember exactly how the mess looked – even which few groceries were on the counter top. I was cursing and looking for the dustpan when Lindsay rang.

I answered but only heard silence. I assumed we had a bad connection so I repeated, "Hello? Hello?"

She finally spit out, "Something horrible has happened..." She choked. My heart sank as I assumed the worst – that an accident had happened while Cody was in her care.

"Lindsay, what is it?" Silence. "Come on, Lindz... talk to me. Is it Cody?"

"No, he's fine," she managed.

I exhaled, feeling relieved before asking about Jason.

"He's fine too," she sputtered. "It's... it's... Hilary."

She had never referred to Jason's ex-wife as anything other than *her* or *she*, but I knew immediately that's who Hilary was.

"She... she has cancer. Apparently, she had been getting treatments for a while and it got better, but it came back. Doctors say she has a couple of months." I put my hand over my mouth and squeezed my eyes shut.

"She's a good mom, Jess. No, she's a great mom... and a great person. She's never caused any drama; she and Jason get along and respect each other. Why her? It's not fair, it's just so not fair!" she cried. I remembered Cody sitting on my lap at the engagement party. The thought of him being robbed of his mother broke my heart. I could remember, when I was about his age, my mom would walk me to school and pick me up every day. Later, she chaperoned for all the school field trips. I thought about how she'd sleep with me when I was sick, and as I got older, she became my best friend. Cody would never get that – unless Lindsay was to provide it to him. I couldn't hold back the tears.

"I'm so sorry," I whispered, not knowing what else to say. "Did Jason know anything was going on?" I asked.

"No. She had him over last night and filled him in on everything. She didn't tell him sooner because things were going well with her treatments and… she has a new husband so she wasn't alone. They told Jason they didn't want to burden him – BURDEN HIM?!" she screamed. "Jessica, the woman has cancer and SHE didn't want to BURDEN anyone?! Meanwhile, I'm prancing around like an idiot planning a stupid wedding, stressing over what kind of chair covers I want."

I let her cry.

She muttered, "She's a saint; how can I ever be half the mother she was – I mean – *is*?"

"Oh Lindz, don't talk like that. You don't have to be a replacement; do you hear me? Does Cody know?" I asked.

"No. She only told Jason yesterday. When she said she needed to talk to Jason, we thought for sure the news would be that she wanted to move to Atlanta, where her family is. We never expected this."

"Well, you couldn't have; she's so young," I said, still not knowing anything else to say.

She sighed and explained how Jason would go back over the following weekend, and they'd tell Cody together. The plan was to take him out of pre-school so they could spend precious time together. Hilary, her husband and Cody would spend her last months up in Atlanta with her family. They would stop at Disney World and Epcot on the drive up.

Lindsay had been relying on the fact that Hilary would always be in the picture. Hilary was the reason that Lindsay would never have to be a full-time mom. Jason was relying on it too – they had talked about it and although no one would admit it, it was what kept Lindsay on board with the whole situation. She had grown comfortable and accepting of being a step-mom and even looked forward to getting Cody every other weekend. Without Hilary, she'd have him all day, every day. Her life was flipped upside down. I offered my sincerest condolences and reassured Lindsay that I was there for her and would be home for good in two months. As much as I wanted to be there for her in person, that was when leaving Dublin became a reality. I didn't want to leave in a couple of months, but I knew it was time.

THIRTY-SIX
July 2014

So there I was. Back to that rainy July day when I was taking a break from sorting through my huge shoebox. I was leaning against my stove, peering out the window in a blurred wine daze, reminiscing on my two years in Dublin… and all the lessons I had learned through shoes.

Cleo rubbed the side of his face against my cankles. He often reminded me of Aidan. Not just because Aidan had named him (*her* at the time), but also because Cleo and I had gone through phases – like Aidan said all relationships go through. I had thought Cleo was a bad luck sign when I first moved to Dublin. But things changed. I got to know Cleo and discovered that he was a sweet *boy* and just wanted some attention. I never would have imagined that I would wind up adopting Cleo, but he became my dark, handsome Irish fella who I was bringing back to America with me.

Time had escaped me; it was 2:00 pm. I was dreading the call to Aidan to invite him to the going away drinks that Simon, Orla and a few other friends had organized. I didn't think he'd actually show up, but I had promised that I wouldn't leave without letting him know. I didn't know whether or not I actually wanted to see him, but it was important to me to, at least, extend the invite.

I called him. My heart raced – thank God for the wine. The last time I heard his voice was when he was telling me to have a nice life because he felt indifferent. It rang and rang until finally, I got his voicemail. I hung up in a panic. There was something about leaving my voice out there for him to play, or delete, as he pleased that made me feel uneasy. I had done as I said I would, so it was up to him to call back.

I went back to sorting my shoes – to the rack hanging on the back of my closet door. It was a flimsy thing, perfect for holding the light flip-flops and sandals. Some of the slots had two pairs, even three pairs shoved in them. I found it funny that I brought all of them over to Dublin where there was rarely a need for flip-flops and open-toed sun shoes. I'd throw on a pair to take the trash out and there was the pair that came with me to Morocco, but I certainly didn't need to bring all 20+ pairs to Ireland. However, having them wasn't an inconvenience, as they didn't take up much space and it was nice to have them when we did have the few months of warm weather. None of the sandals went into the 'Throw away' pile because you can never have too many pairs of them – never know when you'll need them, but you're glad to have them, when you do. Plus, they were inexpensive, so if I didn't end up liking them, then it wouldn't be a big deal to toss them.

The day of sorting and packing flew and suddenly, it was 7:00 pm. Orla and Simon told me to meet them at Café

En Seine at 8:00 pm for dinner. A few co-workers would join us for drinks after dinner. I threw my hair up in a messy bun and put on my going out makeup. I got dressed, gave myself a quick check in the full-length mirror and headed out the door. Before I did, I traded the brown jazz flats I had on for the blue suede heels on top of the 'Keep' pile. I had just made a mental note earlier that day to start wearing them more often… no better time than the present!

I said: *Faiche Stiabhna… Is é seo an stad deireanach* even before the recording on the Luas did. Even though it had been a year, I *still* thought about the screw-up in front of Aidan's family at the dinner table. When I stepped off, I helped a lost couple find their way to their hotel and jotted down some restaurant recommendations. A lot had changed from when I was staring at the Luas door, wondering why it wouldn't open.

It was 8:05 pm when I arrived outside Café En Seine. Simon had texted that he and Orla had a table in the back and a drink waiting for me. I walked passed a huge group of people having a party that stretched all the way into the back of the place. I kept walking.

I noticed in the middle of the group was… Simon? It took me a while to realize what was going on. They had thrown me a surprise party – it wasn't just a handful of us having a few drinks like I had thought. Good thing I put on the blue suede shoes and makeup!

"Dahling!" Simon exclaimed, throwing his arms up, careful not to spill his drink.

I scanned the room. Sitting next to Orla was Gearoid and her two roommates, whom I'd gone out with a few times. Next to them were Merrick and their friend, Sebastian, who bartends at Mother, the gay bar they'd drag me to. Orla and Simon had managed to round up my fellow American expat friends and their significant others. From work, I saw Declan, Claire, and my immediate boss, Steve, along with my entire department of about 20 people. Drinks covered all the tables, balloons floated everywhere and a 'Good-bye Sunshine!' poster hung on the back wall.

I was overwhelmed. It wasn't until then that I appreciated just how many friends I had made during my time in Dublin. I was so glad I didn't give up after those first few crappy months.

I made my rounds to everyone, thanking them, laughing, drinking, having a great time. Some of the people I had gotten very close to, and some were simply good acquaintances. I realized the friends and positive acquaintances you surround yourself with are a lot like that rack of flip-flops and sandals. It doesn't matter how many you have – you can never have too many. You never know when you'll need them, but you're glad to have them when you do and, as I found out those first few months in Dublin, it really sucks when you don't. I'd accumulated these friends over time and did so with minimal upfront investment – usually just the cost of a pint at the pub.

A few drinks in, Claire walked over to me. "Jess! Who's going to help me plan all the social events – and encourage people to actually show up?" she asked, putting her hands on her face.

"Girl, as long as there's an open bar tab, people will come," I said, sipping the Jack Daniels and Coke Simon handed to me. Claire looked over my shoulder, toward the entrance.

"Umm… Jessica? I hope you don't mind, but I invited…" She bit her lip as she trailed off. My heart stopped.

Before she could finish the sentence, I turned around and saw Aidan's sister, Kate, walking nervously toward us. She looked adorably out of place at Café En Seine. I was so glad to see her, my eyes watered. On the other hand, there was a tiny part of me that was disappointed that Aidan wasn't with her.

"Kate!" I shrieked. I ran to her and gave her a tight bear hug. "Gosh, I've missed you; I'm so glad you came! Thank you, thank you!" I pulled back with my hands still on her shoulders.

"Of course I would. I know it's been a long time, but I wanted to say goodbye and… to give you this." She handed me a blue gift bag. There was nothing inside except for a book. My eyes watered even more as I pulled it out. It was a scuffed up, used copy of *The Lion, the Witch and the Wardrobe*.

"It's silly… and I'm sure you've already read it when you were a child," she said, clasping her hands in front of her.

"No, I haven't – I know the gist of the story, but I never read it," I replied.

"I want you to have it. The author is Irish and it's the first book I ever fell in love with." I was touched by the thoughtfulness of her gift. "I didn't have a lot of friends when I was younger – well, I still don't have a lot." She laughed awkwardly. "I read *The Chronicles of Narnia* over and over – my parents thought it was odd. I'd pretend that I was Lucy, Emma was Susan, Philip was Edmund and Aidan was Peter... the four siblings on an adventure together."

"Oh, Kate, I can't take your copy – I know what it's like to have *your* copy of a book. You love it too much... no." I tried to hand it back to her, but she insisted, so I accepted it and hugged her again.

"Jess? Umm... Aidan..." Her head dropped. "He wanted me to tell you that he..."

"Kate," I cut her off and grabbed her shoulders again. "I am so glad you came, really. I wanted to stay in touch, but... well, it doesn't matter. But can you please not tell me what Aidan said? I... I don't want to know." I shook my head and looked away. The thought of hearing that he said something along the lines of, 'Best of luck with everything,' was something I couldn't bear.

"Jess, I'm sorry. I love my brother, but I don't know what goes through his head. He never told any of us anything. When we'd ask what happened, he just said that it didn't work out and you guys both agreed to end it."

"Oh, did he?!" I raised an eyebrow. "Funny, that's not how I remember it. But it doesn't matter anymore," I said, looking away again.

She sighed before saying, "I don't know what happened, but I know for a fact that he really cared for you because he was a mess when he thought you were seeing someone. For months he'd always ask Emma if she knew what you were up to and..."

"Kate, please! STOP IT!" I tried not to let my watery eyes turn into a full-fledged cry. I put the bag on the table and took a few deep breaths.

There was a long pause.

"I'm sorry. And I'm sorry for how much he hurt you." She put her hand on my shoulder. "Will you promise to read the book one day soon? All of it – cover to cover, please?"

It sounded like an odd request – cover to cover? But I figured she wanted me to love the book as much as she did. I smiled and said, "Of course I will. Now, come on... let's get you a drink!"

The party was a blast. Declan was kicking back the Middleton while revealing a funny side that none of us had seen before. When he told us about the time he and his wife ended up dancing with Thai lady-boys in Bangkok, it was Simon's cue to come out of the closet.

It wasn't *as* awkward as we had imagined. Declan hesitated before saying, "I don't care that you're gay... in fact, my wife and I love to watch *Glee!*"

That wasn't nearly as bad as Donal from the IT department, who shouted, "High five!" and put his hand in the air. The look on Simon's face was a mix of endearment and confusion as he high-fived to his gayness.

My fellow American expat girlfriends and I sang the entire lyrics of Sir Mix-a-Lot's "I Like Big Butts" – we really went all out with the charades when we sang the 'itty bitty waist and a round thang in your face' part. It was a great night, and it ended perfectly... with my first trip to Coppers! 'Coppers' was the fun night club that Orla told me about the first time we went to lunch together. I was *finally* a true Dubliner.

THIRTY-SEVEN

August 2014

The weeks before I left Dublin were really hard for Lindsay. Hilary's condition had been deteriorating quickly and Lindsay was trying to hold it together. They decided to postpone the wedding, so she spent all her energy on the administrative burden of trying to call off such an affair – begging for refunds from the vendors and non-stop explaining and apologizing. The day Lindsay had dreamed about since she could walk had become a nightmare. She remained supportive and encouraged Jason to go to Atlanta. She didn't know what the protocol was in their situation. I assured her that there wasn't one.

Suddenly, it was moving day and Simon was driving me to the airport. It was windy and overcast with just a five-minute shower as if to send me off with a touch of Ireland. Cleo was in a little travel cage and drifting in and out of sleep thanks to the kitty tranquilizer the vet gave me.

"Ugh, J. D. – I can't do this… this goodbye nonsense," Simon said, fidgeting outside the security line of Terminal 2. "You're family to me; I bloody love you." He gave me a lingering hug.

"I love you too, Simon. I'm not sure what I would have done without you these last two years. I probably would have had a lot less hangovers, but hey… details!" I forced a laugh. "Thank you, Simon. I know you know… and you know I know… so let's not say it, okay? I'll be over to visit the first chance I get."

"You'd better. Let me know when you've landed."

"I will." I hugged him again.

"You're my girl, J. D." He squeezed harder while I sniffled like a baby.

I grabbed the handle of my carry-on, put my bag over my shoulder and headed to the security line. It reminded me of the walk through security at Tampa International the day I left for Dublin, but I was just sad – not sad and scared and excited.

I handed the attendant my boarding pass and passport. As she handed it back to me, I turned to look at Simon one last time. He was waving and jumping like my parents had done when they sent me off to Ireland.

As the plane took off, I thought about Aidan. Was he trying to open his law firm, or maybe he already had? Did he ever think about me? Did he know how hurt I had been? Ahhhhh! Why was I still thinking about him?! I knew it was toxic and the answers to those questions didn't matter. I was leaving Dublin, going home where we'd never have a chance run-in. He was just a memory.

After the Aer Lingus stewardess cleared away dinner, I pulled out *The Lion, the Witch and the Wardrobe* from my carry-on bag. I could hear Kate's voice, 'Will you promise to read the book one day soon? All of it – cover to cover, please?'

I opened to the first page, the title page, and rubbed my hand over it. I flipped past the copyright page and on to the dedication page, my favorite page in any book. The author had dedicated it to his goddaughter, Lucy, whom the main character is named after:

To Lucy Barfield

My dear Lucy,

> I wrote this story for you, but when I began it
> I had not realized that girls grow quicker than
> books. As a result you are already too old for
> fairy tales, and by the time it is printed and
> bound you will be older still. But some day
> you will be old enough to start reading fairy
> tales again. You can then take it down from
> some upper shelf, dust it, and tell me what
> you think of it. I shall probably be too deaf to
> hear, and too old to understand a word you
> say, but I shall still be.

> Your affectionate Godfather,
> C.S. Lewis

It was so personal. I felt a connection to the author and to Kate, knowing she had read those exact words. Maybe that's why Kate said to read it cover to cover, so I didn't miss something like that? I pulled the book to my face to smell it... when I did, something fell out and onto my lap.

It was a yellow envelope with 'Jessica' written on the front. I had only seen Aidan's handwriting when he wrote out the itinerary for Lindsay and Jason's visit and when he filled out the forms in Morocco, but I knew without a doubt it was his. It was the way he dotted the 'i' – not a dot at all but a diagonal line like an accent mark. Also, his 's' looked more like three straight lines as opposed to a fluid, curvy symbol.

That's what Kate meant when she said she wanted me to read the whole book, including the note from Aidan. I thought about what could be inside the envelope. Would it be a letter that explained what happened, what caused the sudden change, why he ended things the way he did? Would it be a proper apology that would give me the closure I thought I'd never get? Maybe it wasn't a note at all but some stupid store bought 'Good Luck' card with nothing more than his name signed.

It was almost ten months since he had broken up with me – twice as long as we had dated. I hadn't moved apartments, I hadn't changed jobs, I hadn't changed my phone number and he had both my email addresses. He never contacted me. Why did he wait till I was leaving to say something?

I wasn't ready to read it. I wasn't sure when, or if, I'd ever want to open it, but it wasn't going to be there on the plane. I put the envelope in my bag. I would later put it into a shoebox in my closet with other old pictures and notes I had saved – just like C.S. Lewis instructed Lucy to do. The shoebox would be my proverbial shelf and I'd pull it out when I was ready.

* * * * *

The tram that takes passengers from the terminal to the main airport in Tampa reminded me of the Luas, but there was no funny Irish pronunciation. Also unlike the Luas, the airport tram opened automatically – no buttons needed. I had just landed and was already missing Dublin.

In the airport, my parents, Lindsay and Jason were waiting for me. Lindsay must have raided her events supply room because she made a huge 'Welcome home Jessie!' poster with all sorts of fancy bedazzlements, lace and ribbon. Jason had flowers in his hand and my dad – he had a stuffed animal pig with little red socks on its feet. He and my mom had made me a little Clive the Pig.

My parents had brought my Jeep over from their house. They had been holding it for my one –turned two – year absence. Cleo and I stayed with Lindsay and Jason for a couple of weeks while I looked for an apartment in Tampa. I felt bad because Jason was allergic to cats, but he insisted (through the sneezing) that he was fine and happy to have us.

It was strange settling back into my home office. There were loads of new faces, new processes and a stupid new copy machine that I swear had it out for me. But, as I had done before, I eventually settled back into the swing of things. My bosses in Dublin were very pleased with my work, especially during the last year, and it was fed back to my home office. After a month of being back, my boss, Melissa, called me into her office to discuss the opportunity in Chicago – the one I had wanted. The position wouldn't require me to move until springtime, so I had time to decide.

THIRTY-EIGHT
November 2014

It was the first Tuesday in November when Hilary passed.

Jason left the following Thursday to fly to Atlanta for the wake, the funeral and to bring Cody back. I went over the night he left and stayed with Lindsay through the weekend. I had only ever cheered her up after breakups or a bad day at work. For those, I'd do silly things to make her laugh such as imitate a kernel of popcorn popping or run around our apartment on my hands and knees pretending to be a dinosaur. Such tactics weren't appropriate. I didn't know what to do, so I just listened to her and kept her company.

We passed the weekend doing the things we used to do when we lived together. We painted our toenails and drank jalapeno infused dirty martinis while watching *Love Actually*, went to our favorite brunch spot, Datz, and took Tucker for a walk along Bayshore Boulevard. I stayed most of the day on Sunday, with our final activity being to fold a mountain of laundry. Something about all the clothes reminded me of the Laurence lace-ups.

"Hey Lindz, have you worn your Louboutins lately?" I asked, strategically picking around Jason's boxers and grabbing one of her shirts instead.

"No. One of the straps busted," she replied toneless. "They were too small. I don't know why I even kidded myself." She folded the pair of boxers I had dodged. "Jessie?" she said in a pre-cry voice. "I'm going to be a mom when they get back in a week. This wasn't supposed to happen." She began crying hysterically into the boxers.

"How do you know what's supposed to happen?" I said, immediately thinking how dumb that sounded, but I couldn't think of anything better.

"I don't – I don't know anything. Why does it have to be like this? Why can't it just be easy?" She was sobbing hysterically.

"Lindz, listen to me... I know this isn't fair and I don't know why it happened, but it has and now you need to decide if you really want it... all of it. Being with Jason means being with Cody full-time. There's no faking it anymore – either they fit into your life or..."

"Or I'm going to break them like I did my shoes?" She looked at me blankly, her face red and wet.

I didn't say anything. She was right. I wasn't going to say it, but it was the truth.

I got up from the floor and joined her on the sofa, holding her while she cried and repeated, "I can't do this, I can't do this," over and over until she eventually fell asleep.

We had planned that I'd come back the next day after work, so after all the laundry was folded, I left. When I kissed her head, she whispered, "Love you, Jessie," half asleep.

* * * * *

It was the hour before the sun set, my favorite time in Florida. Instead of stopping at the grocery store like I needed to, I decided to drive. It was the perfect weather to have the top down on the Jeep. I could hardly hear my music through the wind as I drove across the Courtney Campbell Causeway, heading toward Clearwater Beach. The traffic was coming from the other direction with people heading home after a day at the beach. I, on the other hand, was able to cruise quickly into the horizon.

I parked a ways down from the lingering crowds at Pier 60. I reached into my glove compartment box and grabbed the letter which I'd recently taken out of the shoebox in my closet. I figured there was no better place to read it than on the beach.

At the top of the wooden deck leading to the beach, I inhaled the salty sea air. I carefully stepped down the splinter-laden stairs and onto the sand. I took off my shoes and rolled up my torn jeans to walk along the shoreline.

There were no waves; just the gentle to and fro of the water meeting the white sand. After about a mile, I sat and admired the sun sinking into the sea. The wind blew through my hair while I thought peacefully.

I had been playing in the sand – sifting the sand through my hands and watching it fall, being carried away by the wind. I had created a shallow hole from grabbing so many handfuls.

I reached in my pocket and pulled out the envelope from Aidan. I rubbed my hand over the handwritten 'Jessica' before flipping it over and pushing my thumb into the loose corner.

My heart pounded. Emotions were making their way back in. I took a deep breath, wondering what it was that Aidan had to say to me... that he couldn't actually say to me.

With one side fully torn open, I stopped.

My attention was stolen by a squawking seagull flying above. The colors of the horizon were unbelievable. I tore further into the envelope but stopped.

I already had the most closure I was going to get – anything in that letter would either uncover old wounds, or leave me feeling empty, and I wasn't sure which would be worse.

I pushed the open flap into the envelope and placed it in the hole I had dug beside me and covered it up.

Dad was right... some things are better left buried in the sand.

With my finger, I drew an 'X' over the buried envelope and whispered, "Cross my heart".

I stood and walked along the shore, barefoot.

No sandals or flip-flops, no boots, no fancy heels, no casual sneakers, no wellies.

Shoes are important and serve many different purposes, but there's nothing like walking along the beach... barefoot.

I didn't move to Dublin for my job. I didn't move to find a man and wasn't *really* expecting to find THE ultimate pair of riding boots while I was there. I didn't know it at the time, but I moved to Dublin to find myself.

And that's exactly what I did.

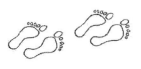

ACKNOWLEDGEMENTS

First, I'd like to thank the people of Dublin for welcoming me into their beautiful city and allowing me to truly experience Irish culture. Everyone I've met during my past three years in Dublin is woven throughout this book. From the baristas at my favorite coffee shops and the owners of my favorite Chippers to the children I'd watch cross the street under the lollypop lady's watchful eye. From the characters on the Luas, to the talkative taxi drivers, to my unorthodox landlord and everyone in between – Thank you, Dubliners, for helping me create a second home.

Thank you to my wonderful co-workers at PricewaterhouseCoopers both in the Dublin and Florida offices. I'd especially like to thank the partners I've worked for and with who have been so supportive of all my goals. Special shout out to my team on the RAC audit – both the A-team and the B-team. Sharing my weekly (sometimes daily) book updates was such great motivation and kept me from ever taking more than a couple of days off of writing and editing. You all made me feel like a best-selling author and I don't even care if it was just to get a better appraisal from me. I'm very proud to work with such an awesome, fun group of people at a company that has really taken care of me.

Thank you to all my Irish friends and colleagues for helping me make sure the Irish parts were accurate and realistic. Without you, my Irish characters would be saying funny things like, "let's *hang out* and watch *movies*".

I can't thank enough the people who read and critiqued the various versions of my manuscript. Special thank you to my initial critique group who read the earliest and most gruesomely raw and embarrassing versions: Mama-dukes, Lauren Brennan, Erica Dunhour Harrison (thanks for the name too), Matthew Garnett, Lauren Solomon, Cassie Mahar, Jolie Niland, Brittany David, Mike Waterhouse, Steve Rose, Jill Worden, Simon Parmar, Niamh Penrose, Aisling Duignan, Sarah Hargaden, Sarah Coffey and Eadaoin Ni Fhearghail. From each person's encouragement and constructive criticism, progressively better versions were created – thank you all so much!

I worked with several talented editors from all different backgrounds which allowed me to learn so much more during the editing process than I ever could have imagined. Krystal Boots, you were the first editor to see my baby and you provided some of the most insightful and encouraging comments throughout which allowed me to really go back and develop the story more before worrying too much about the grammar. Tracey Watts ("T1"), thank you for helping me to not *over-think* the word *overthink* or the words *over* and *think*. Your advice to pick one and apply it *consistently* helped me keep my sanity. Thank you for checking in on me and for discussing my book with your husband over breakfast. Emily Heill, thank you for all your motivation before publishing – and I'm so grateful for your "extreme attention to detail" ;) Each one of you was so knowledgeable and protected my writing style. I'm sorry for any edits that seem unapplied – I either missed them on accident or I'm just stubborn. Either way, I take full responsibility for any errors. Thank you so much to each of you!

Thank you to my friends who have always been so incredibly supportive of everything I set out to do – my "Veg" friend, Desiree Cyrgalis, Julianne Wolbers ("Soft lips"), Vimar Gutierrez, Danielle Jones, Jill Worden, Steve Rose, Yadira Navarro and Anastasia Myachina. Big thanks to all my Book/Wine Club ladies in Dublin that I've grown so close to (stupid ugly bows and all).

I share the week I published this book with a very special birthday girl... Happy 1st Birthday to sweet Ella Cyrgalis – your "Uncle" TT loves you!

Matt – thank you for reminding me to write in a way that I stayed true to both my present and future selves. Dane – I'm so glad you were there when the Nile was created ;) Thank you for not batting an eyelash when my visions led us to the beach with suitcases full of weird shit. Keep being your bold and fabulous self! Damian "T" – thank you for staying so supportive during the most "dramatic" months of this book. I promise to share all indecent fan mail I receive with you. Fact! Brittany – thank you for always believing in me before I believe in myself, especially with this book. You really are my SMF!

And finally, thank you Mom and Dad. The unconditional love and support you have given me has been the fuel that kept me going when I wanted to quit – quit Dublin, quit my career, quit dating, quit writing, quit trying to stay positive. You guys wouldn't let me quit anything without making sure I had given it one more chance. It's uncomprehendable to think of what I would have missed out on if I had given up on any of the aforementioned. I promise to put you two in the best possible nursing home I can find ;) Don't worry, I'll come to visit all the time and remind you that:

> I'll love you forever,
> I'll like you for always,
> as long as I'm living,
> my wellies you'll be.*

*From the children's book *Love You Forever* by Robert Munsch (although I've replaced 'baby' with 'wellies').

And Mom, you were right… everything happens for a reason.

The Shoebox

Playlist

1. Far Too Young To Die – Panic! At The Disco
2. You've Really Got a Hold on Me – Smokey Robinson
3. How D'ya Like Your Eggs In The Morning – Dean Martin and Helen O'Connell
4. I Want You So Bad – James Brown
5. Try Me – James Brown
6. Drop The Game – Chet Faker Ft. Flume
7. Dreaming Of You – The Coral
8. She's Everything – Brad Paisley
9. Slow Show – The National
10. Bitter Poem – Cold War Kids
11. Amourland – Everything Everything

About the Author

Tracy was born and raised in central Florida and graduated from the University of South Florida with a degree in Accounting. *The Shoebox* is her first novel. She is currently living in Dublin, Ireland.

Kickstarter Backers

Thank you so much to the people listed below for their generosity in helping to fund my Kickstarter project. With your help, I was able to ensure my book looked professional. I really appreciate your interest in this project!

Ted Ploch Jr.
Linda Ploch
Elizabeth and Phil Smith
Barbara and Mike McCormick
Paul O'Connor
Damian and Suzanne Byrne
Enda McDonagh
Tim O'Hara
Steve Rose
Nadine Watters
Dane Martin Hickey
Shannon and Corey Holthaus
Siobhain Vickers
Paul Barrie
Ciaran Collins
Jill Marie Worden
The Kadechkas
Ciaran Quinn
Roisin Flanagan
Michael and Jennifer Johnson
Simon Parmar
Cassie Mahar
Drew and Lauren Solomon
Lauren Brennan
Nicole Kogler
Rosemarie Yagoda-Oelrich
Colleen Cummins
Heather Nicole
Lauren Kates
Sarah Baldwin
Delvin DEE Kariuki
Joe Diskin
"John"

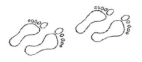